RADIANT FIERCE

BRIGHT WICKED 2

EVERLY FROST

DISCOVER THE EVER REALMS

Seven series set in the same world.

Suggested Reading Order:

Bright Wicked
Storm Princess
Assassin's Magic
Soul Bitten Shifter
Supernatural Legacy
Dark Magic Shifters
Kingdom of Betrayal

For everyone who battles through the darkness to reach the light.

CHAPTER 1

I try to exhale the sour air, but there's no escaping it.

The cold mist envelops me on every side. Visibility is reduced so severely that I can't make out any shapes around us as we run through the foggy marsh.

Nathaniel's hand anchors me in space and time, my only connection with the living. He tugs me to the left and then the right, as if he knows the path by heart.

Neither of us has spoken since we entered the mist.

Now the silence feels fragile. The trust between us is like the first layer of ice on the Spinning Lake. Breakable. Unstable. Thin.

In two days, one of us will kill the other. We don't have any choice. I unwittingly invoked the Law of Champions, not knowing that it would tie my fate to Nathaniel's.

The Law was sealed by the Vanem Dragon himself. The old magic now demands that we fight to the death by the end of the third day.

Our first day is over. The second day has just begun.

Mist drips down my face and neck as my arms and legs pump, the fog so heavy that it mingles with my sweat.

The black full-body armor I'm wearing was designed for stealth, not prolonged exertion. I would peel the top half of the armor down to my waist, but my underwear is far too skimpy and I need to remain protected from whatever dangers lurk in this marsh. Animals. Humans. Even the environment here is a treacherous unknown to me.

In the last twelve hours, the foundations of my world fell apart. The Queen I trusted—the woman I would have given my life for—threatened the people I love.

She revealed that she will crush anyone who dares to question her. She will allow the vulnerable fae in our society to die. All to maintain her power.

The Queen I served has become my adversary.

To escape her, I've run into enemy territory—Fell country. A place of dark magic and old law. Human law. I've chosen to flee into darkness, leaving Bright behind.

We've only run for a quarter of a mile, but I already sense the different lifeforms within the misty marsh—creatures I've only heard about and never encountered before. They wriggle beneath my feet in the muddy sludge, glide in the air beyond my sight, and crawl across the stones at the base of the trees we pass.

The trees themselves are fleeting silhouettes, set far apart from each other, each one leafless and bony, struggling to survive without sunlight.

Nathaniel's presence is the strongest of all, filling my senses with overwhelming strength. He's taller than me, his broad chest clothed in the tight black shirt I chose for him to wear to the Ball last night.

The sleeves hug his biceps in a way that makes his muscles look even larger as he runs. The dew clings to his jaw, strands of his walnut brown hair plastered against his cheeks, while the dark flecks in his brown eyes are somehow more forbidding in our new environment.

If I allow myself to focus fully on him, his presence would fill my senses entirely.

I am never far from his attention, his hand gripping mine, his quick glances telling me he's making sure I'm still with him.

"Stay with me, Aura."

His command as we left the border echoes in my ears. He hasn't let go of me since.

His true nature is a mystery to me—who he is. Who his father was. Why Nathaniel came to Bright for me—

Movement in the far distance forces my attention away from him. My already heightened senses pick up the movement as if I can see it with my eyes.

Creatures are racing toward us from afar. There are at least ten of them, canine in nature but larger than any dog I've ever sensed. They're far enough away that they aren't an immediate threat. But they soon will be.

My senses explode with the violence pulsing from their oncoming bodies. Their growls are a faint whisper in my heightened hearing, their actions telling me they're darting around the trees—and they're gaining on us.

Nathaniel won't hear them with his human ears. Not yet. Not like I can.

I try to keep my voice low, but it's difficult while I'm running. "Nathaniel! Wolves!"

He doesn't miss a beat, appearing completely unsurprised. It's almost as if he'd been expecting them.

His response is clipped. "How far away?"

"Less than a minute."

He doesn't waste time, his focus shifting from me to our

surroundings—a quick assessing glance—before his speed increases and he urges me to run faster.

The muscles in my legs burn and scream, but I refuse to slow Nathaniel down. I'm counting on fear and adrenaline to power my movements when my muscles are finally pushed beyond endurance.

The wolves are running toward us at a pace that astounds me.

I still can't see them, but I sense the shape of their bodies, sleek and large, picture their heads and necks kept low to streamline their forms as they leap lightly through the mud and over rocks, the breath rasping past their sharp teeth.

Nathaniel's quick glance in their direction tells me that he finally hears them, his human ears picking up the sound of their movements sooner than I thought he would.

He darts right, driving us in a straight line in that direction as if he knows exactly what's there.

"Tree!" he shouts.

A second later, the largest tree I've seen in the marsh so far materializes in the mist. Its craggy branches spear outward before they angle sharply upward in shapes that resemble immobilized swings that sit high above the ground.

I'm sure Nathaniel wants me to climb it, but the wolves' heavy breathing is amplified in my hearing now, sending fear shrieking through me.

I'm not about to run from a fight with them, not when I can use my power to take them down.

Starlight gathers inside my chest, shooting through my shoulder and arm toward my free hand—the one Nathaniel isn't holding. I'm ready to let my power loose the moment I see the beasts—sooner if I sense them clearly enough to take a clean shot.

Just one more second...

The mist shifts beyond us, violently swirling as the creatures disturb it, multiple unstoppable forces.

Just as I prepare to release my rage, Nathaniel shouts.

"Aura! Up!"

My focus snaps back to him at the same moment he plows into me. He knocks the air out of my lungs as his arm clamps around my ribs, his other arm slipping beneath my backside.

I gasp for breath as he swings me right off my feet and into the air, throwing me with astonishing strength and speed toward one of the highest branches.

All the times I've leaped onto Treble's back has given me the muscle memory I need to react swiftly.

Soaring upward, I twist my body to reduce my velocity and guide my flight. Planting my outstretched hand against the tree's trunk, I swing my legs across the branch Nathaniel threw me toward, finding myself sitting neatly along it.

It wasn't a graceful maneuver, but I don't care.

All I care about now is the *thud* below me.

To hoist me in the right direction, Nathaniel plowed himself into the tree. The shuddering wood tells me he hit it hard. His shout indicates he hurt himself, but he's already rising to meet the oncoming threat.

A scream forms in my throat and my power shrieks into my hands again as the first animal bounds out of the mist, its jaws open wide, its teeth slashing the air.

I wobble violently on the branch as I reach outward, ready to release my power, but the wolf is already too close to Nathaniel for a clean shot. I can't risk hurting him.

To my shock, Nathaniel doesn't try to get out of the animal's way.

At the last possible moment, he drops, dives forward onto one knee, and presses his palms upward. With split-second precision, he plants his hands under the wolf's torso—one on the leaping animal's belly and the other beneath its shoulder.

In one powerful move, he launches himself upward, using his rising strength to thrust the beast away from himself.

The creature yelps. Its body arcs at an awkward angle as it flies through the air and lands in a scrambling heap in the mud, still alive and apparently unhurt.

The whole move is over within the blink of an eye, leaving me breathless and gasping, but Nathaniel's focus is unbreakable.

The next wolf leaps at him, but Nathaniel darts out of its path, spinning on his heel to face it as it skids to a stop so it doesn't bang against the base of the tree.

Nathaniel goes on the attack, lunging at the animal with a threatening roar that sends a shiver down my spine. In an instant, he becomes the predator instead of the prey.

For nearly the entire day he spent in Bright, he was dominated by fae. He defended himself but never struck back. He couldn't. The Law of Champions prevents him from hurting a fae until the final fight is over.

But now I catch a glimpse of a wild nature I've never sensed in him before—a fury and abandon that makes me shiver in anticipation. Of what, I'm not sure, but my heart is pounding in my chest.

He leaps at the wolf before it can turn to face him again, scooping one arm under its belly and smacking its cheek with the flat of his free hand to push its gnashing mouth in the other direction.

He keeps its jaw at bay for the split second it takes him to fling it after the first wolf. The second beast rolls over the first, which is just getting to its feet, knocking them both into the base of the neighboring tree.

Their yelps echo around the clearing as the remaining

eight wolves emerge from the fog, slower now, heads hanging low and teeth bared as they circle around Nathaniel.

He grabs his shoulder, but not in a way that indicates he's hurt. It's as if he's reaching for something that should be there.

His hand comes away empty.

He curses, low and soft.

Whatever's wrong, he shakes it off quickly, hunches his shoulders, balls his fists, and roars at the wolves again.

"I acknowledge your right for revenge!" he shouts. "Take my life if you can. But whatever you do, I will not dishonor you."

For a moment, I wonder if the wolves can understand him like my thunderbird can understand me. But I don't think so. It felt like Nathaniel was shouting at himself as much as at them.

I don't know what he means by revenge, but there's an edge of regret in his voice that I wasn't expecting.

One of the wolves prowls closer than the others. It's hard to tell, but I sense a distinctly female nature. She is the largest, her charcoal fur tinged blue while her nose is inky black.

Nathaniel stares her down, his shoulders relaxing, and his expression softening, but it seems deliberate, as if he's preparing himself. He hasn't tried to escape or climb the tree. In fact, he seems resigned to face each and every one of the beasts.

I'm not inclined to wait and watch this fight play out. Every instinct in my body tells me to jump to the ground and fight beside him.

It cost him a lot to throw me onto the branch and I don't want to squander the safety he gave me, but that won't stop me from blasting the wolves apart with my power from above.

Starlight pools in my palm as I aim at the leader of the pack, ready to kill her the moment she makes a move.

The female wolf growls deep in her throat, her teeth bared as her gaze flickers upward in my direction, but she hangs back.

Too late, I realize she's a diversion.

Without warning, a wolf with fur the color of coal leaps from the side. Once again, it's upon Nathaniel too fast for me to help him.

Nathaniel reacts like water, flowing away from the attack, avoiding the wolf's claws and teeth before he lashes out, his open palm following the wolf's path, his flat-fisted punch cracking across its ribs as it flies past.

My eyes widen when he pulls the hit.

I'm sure he could have broken its bones, but he didn't...

Even so, the impact is like a trigger. All of the creatures bound at him at once.

He reacts as swiftly as he responded to the Border Guards' attacks yesterday morning, evading every attempt to bite and maul him before he fights back, sending each wolf sprawling through the mud.

The breath catches in my throat as I watch him move. He is impossibly agile, every muscle in his body primed to deflect, his palms flattening against a wolf's shoulder, another's jaw, a third's hide, pushing each away before he strikes back—but only enough to send each animal to the ground, not to hurt them.

He is even stronger here, surrounded by the gloom of this place, than he was in Bright.

It strikes me with frightening clarity that he's at home in this murky darkness.

How many times did he narrow his eyes in the glare of Bright's sunlight? How much slower were his reflexes compared to now?

As if, like me, sunlight is his weakness.

I've barely had time to take a breath when three wolves run at him from the side.

As fast as he is, he won't be able to avoid all of them.

My power shrieks from my hand, hitting the ground in front of them, forcing them to split up. They scatter around him, racing wide of his position.

Damn. I'd meant to end at least one of them.

I suddenly find myself the focus of Nathaniel's attention, his dark eyes flashing at me. "Don't kill them!" he shouts.

Fear floods me as I realize that distracting Nathaniel was the worst thing I could have done.

The female springs from his other side, her body a dark blur.

She knocks him to the dirty ground.

Nathaniel twists as he falls, his hands flying upward—just in time—to plant under her jaw and keep her slashing teeth at bay, inches from his face.

Her claws press against his chest. Her snarling mouth lurches toward his neck.

He isn't wearing armor like me.

He has less than two seconds before she mauls him to death.

CHAPTER 2

I don't think or even scream. I don't have time to consider what I'm doing.

Launching myself from the tree, I throw myself across the space between Nathaniel and me

Fear controls my movements and with it comes power.

Starlight pours from my hands, chest, legs—every part of me glowing with a force fueled by panic as I drop and run, light streaking around me as my feet pound the earth.

The surrounding wolves yelp and scatter as starlight bursts from my body and fills the clearing. Bright, white light floods across Nathaniel and the wolf, but I rein it in with a desperate scream.

I refuse to hurt him.

Struggling with the wolf, Nathaniel's shout echoes in my ears—a sustained roar—his teeth gritted as he pushes against her savage attempts to sink her teeth into his neck.

I recognize the quick shift in his grip. He's preparing to break her neck, but he wouldn't have told me not to kill her unless he meant it.

I reach them in the next moment.

Throwing myself at the beast, I collide with her side, starlight pouring off me as I shove her as hard as I can.

I dig in my heels at the last moment, dropping to my knees beside Nathaniel, my hands outstretched, extended protectively across his body.

The wolf yelps in shock as she flies backward, my power sizzling through her spine and ribcage, lighting up her bones. It's not enough to kill or hurt her. Just enough to give her a frightening zap.

She hits the mud, scrambles to her feet, and twists toward me.

Despite the power flooding the space around me, she doesn't give up, snarling as she bounds toward us again.

"Stop!" I scream.

My power hums at the same frequency as my shout—a sound it never made before—as it pulses across the clearing.

Starlight brightens to blinding levels around my fingertips, a force growing in the air between me and the wolf like a shield.

Still, she fights it. As powerful as my starlight is, I sense her determination and rage, her instincts fueled by a terrible animalistic loss, the most basic motivation to keep fighting even when the danger to herself is high.

Revenge, Nathaniel had said. *What did he do to cause this fierce creature so much pain?*

I vaguely register his voice. He's lying very still beneath me, my power curving around him without touching him, but I can't hear what he's saying above the hum of starlight. The shield around us extends the length and width of his body.

All that matters to me right now is that I'm not hurting him and the wolf can't get to him.

Snarling, she pushes through my glow, her movements slowing as my starlight increases until she's forced to stop only inches away from my fingertips.

She lowers her head, her forehead pressing valiantly against my light while her cerulean blue eyes pierce mine.

I recognize the fight in her eyes. She's willing to die right now if it means she can follow her instincts.

I could easily extend my left hand, strike with starlight so powerful, it would melt her insides, but how can I destroy her?

As I return her desperate glare, I take a deep breath, calming myself.

Warmth flows from my chest down my arms and across my hands, changing the nature of my power from sharp and prickly to soothing and calming.

It's the same warmth I used to calm the sick girl yesterday morning—the same element of my power that I used to ease my brother, Evander's, pain after Nathaniel fought him.

"Be calm," I whisper.

The hum of my power changes, washing outward like flowing water over the wolf's body.

She jolts. Freezes. Her legs suddenly wobble.

I lean farther forward as her legs buckle and she drops to her stomach in the mud, her limbs limp, but her head lifted, her eyes now revealing sudden panic. She won't understand why her body isn't obeying her, why she can't keep fighting.

I stare right back at her, increasing the flow of my power, filling it with the sort of warmth that would send her into a peaceful sleep. If she would let me.

This time, I don't speak aloud. *Stop fighting.*

She whimpers in response to my silent command.

Leaning as far across Nathaniel as I dare, I stretch out to press my forefinger against the wolf's forehead.

She trembles. Hard.

"You will obey me," I say.

Growls tell me that the other wolves are recovering from the shock of my attack. I sense them pacing around the clearing, staying away from the starlight spilling around me. They're smart enough not to try to breach the circle of light.

The female wolf doesn't seem to hear their growls. Her nose moves as she inhales, lifting to briefly touch my palm.

Her fur is unexpectedly soft against my hand before she jolts backward, scrabbling through the sludge with all her might.

Despite the threat she poses, I admire her spirit. She would prefer to give up on revenge than give in to my commands.

Making it to the edge of my glow, she finally rises to her feet, tips her head back, and howls into the foggy sky, her low keening filling the sudden silence.

The other wolves become still, listening to her cry.

Moments later, they tip their heads back, their howls wailing around us in a strange and unsettling song. I don't know what it means, but a beat later, the female wolf bounds to the edge of the clearing, gathering up the other wolves before she races away.

Within seconds, they disappear into the mist again.

I exhale into the stillness, my power humming quietly as I expand my senses to reassure myself that the wolves are really gone.

I count out the seconds while I struggle to pull back my power, the shield around us still glowing brightly. My heart is pounding. I can't lower my hands—can't retract the shield —until I'm certain the threat is over.

But more than that, I'm suddenly afraid to look down because all I thought about was protecting Nathaniel.

I don't know if he's hurt. He could be dying and I won't be able to do anything about it. I'm not a healer and I don't—

"Aura?" Nathaniel's warm hand wraps around my outstretched arm.

His touch is like a catalyst. I drop the shield and lower my hands to his chest, searching for signs of injury.

His features are calm—far calmer than I expected.

Despite my anxiety, I don't see a drop of blood on his face or neck. I check his hands, turning them over in mine before I search his arms and chest for cuts or claw marks.

He lies patiently beneath me while I carry out my search.

His clothing is intact. There isn't a single scratch on his arms.

"Aura." He finally grips my hands and forces me to stop searching for damage. "I'm okay."

The space between us glows from the skin-on-skin contact between our bodies. Every time we touch, he makes me glow and we still don't know why, but right now, that's the least of my concerns.

Now that my hands are trapped, I search his face and chest with my eyes. There must be something wrong. He would have gotten back to his feet by now if he were okay.

"Then why are you still lying there?" I demand to know.

His mouth twitches upward into a smile as his fingers lace slowly with mine in the space above his chest. "Maybe I like you fussing over me."

I glare at him. "I don't fuss."

"Worry, then."

My scowl deepens.

He sighs. "Okay, you got me. I like wallowing in mud."

To prove his point, he disentangles one of his hands and buries his fingers in the patch of sludge beside where I kneel.

He arches an eyebrow at me, as if challenging me to contradict his claim.

His humor only worries me more. He's deflecting, but I'm not sure from what.

If I search his eyes hard enough, there's a hint of pain behind his smile, but I don't know its source—physical or emotional. Either could be bad.

Only half a day ago, I justified my fears about him dying by telling myself I want to kill him myself—that I can't let him die by anyone else's hand. Since then, he fought beside me, defended me against my own people, and breathed life into me when I couldn't breathe for myself.

This morning, I chose to fall from the sky with him.

Our fates are intertwined and all I know for sure is that I'll fight to keep him alive until the final moment when I'm forced to kill him.

CHAPTER 3

*N*athaniel's expression softens as I continue to glare at him.

He doesn't make a move to stand, his gaze passing across my eyes to rest on my lips.

My cheeks heat as I remember the way he kissed me last night, my body's intense reaction to the contact between us.

"Well," he says, "since neither one of us seems inclined to get up…"

He pulls our laced fingers closer to his chest, drawing me toward him, gripping me lightly.

The tension drains out of me as I relax into his arms. He doesn't make a move beyond pulling me closer, even though his gaze burns across my face.

There's a stillness about him, the reason for which I can't place, but I take advantage of it in a way I never would have before we fell from the sky together.

Impulsively, I lean forward and brush my lips across his. Just like last night, even a light touch sparks embers inside me, strong enough to make me want more than I can have.

My cheeks heat again as I quickly make myself draw back, already regretting whatever compulsion made me think it was okay to kiss him right after we were attacked by wolves and despite the fact that we're headed for death.

A slow smile grows on his face as he watches me withdraw, one corner of his lips hitching higher than the other, the darkness in his eyes lifting.

Before I know what he's doing, the thumb of his free hand—the one he buried in the mud—grazes across my left cheek in a slow movement.

It's covered in mud.

My eyes fly wide at the ticklish, sandpapery sensation before a laugh bursts out of me. "If you're trying to prove you love mud—"

"Shh. This is important." His smile continues to play around his lips, but he suppresses it with a stern order while his eyes twinkle at me. "Stay still."

My forehead creases as he dips his forefinger into the mud and draws another line across my face, this time at an angle from beneath my cheekbone to my earlobe. He follows it with a third short line up my forehead at an angle above my left eyebrow.

Finally, his hand sweeps to the other side of my face and his forefinger curves from the corner of my right eye all the way to my jawline, leaving a fourth trail of mud behind.

He smiles as he surveys his handiwork. He seems very pleased about it. "There."

My scowl morphs from disgruntled to confused and finally to curious. His movements were deliberate, concentrated, as if he were tracing the outline of something important. "What did you draw on my face?"

He hovers his hand across my left cheek without smudging the lines. "These are the rays of the sun." His hand travels past my nose to my other cheek. "This is the curve of the moon."

My confusion clears. I can't see what he drew, but I recognize the pattern from what he described. "That's the symbol on your weapon."

He fought me with a gleaming halberd yesterday—a weapon with a curved blade on one side and a wicked spike on the other. It was his father's weapon. He left it behind in Bright when we fled, along with his pelt and human clothing.

I understand now why he chose to wear only long pants when he first emerged out of the mist to fight me yesterday morning. Despite the winter weather in Bright, it's much warmer in Fell country. Humid and dank. Not a breath of wind.

"This symbol is important to me," he says. "Not just because it was my father's, but because it represents my true name."

Queen Imatra said that humans take their second name from their occupation. Nathaniel's second name is Shield because he is King Cyrian's bodyguard—his Champion. Until now, Nathaniel has refused to talk about his real name.

I hold my breath as I ask, "Will you tell me about it?"

"No." He shakes his head, but his expression is gentle, not angry. "Not because I don't want to, Aura. King Cyrian bound my true name in dark magic and now nobody can speak it aloud."

My lips part in surprise. "So... yesterday when Queen Imatra tried to make you talk about your name... and later you said your true name was taken from you... you meant it literally."

"I promised I would always tell you the truth."

He has. At every turn. Even when I didn't want to hear it.

I disentangle my fingers from his and press my hand over

his heart. "You also said there are some things you *can't* tell me."

"Again, literally," he says, his eyes searching mine.

Not knowing who he is... It scares me for reasons I don't understand.

Lying here in the mud with him suddenly feels... familiar in a way that I can't pinpoint. I'm transported back to the moment I woke up in the ash when I was seven years old, with no memories of my life before that moment.

According to Imatra, I was placed under a spell after I was born because my parents were afraid of my power. They wanted me to grow old enough to control it before they woke me up.

They were right to be afraid. I woke up before the intended time and decimated the entire human army with my waking power. Somehow Imatra survived.

But I don't know where Nathaniel's father was at that time. Imatra was the only one I saw when I regained consciousness.

"What about the wolves?" I ask, needing to distract myself from my fears. "Why did you stop me killing them?"

A gusty sigh leaves his lips. "Because it was my fault they attacked."

I tilt my head in confusion. "You didn't do anything to provoke them."

"I did," he says with a single, sure nod. "You already know that the old law rules Fell country. It doesn't only govern humans, but the environment as well. It's part of everything here. Every creature, every change of season, every human heartbeat... The animals obey it instinctively. It's part of their nature."

His lips press together in a line of regret. "The wolves wouldn't have attacked if I'd been wearing my pelt."

I press my hand against his shoulder—the place that he touched before he fought the wolves. "That's what you reached for?"

"The old law is harsh and unbending, but it maintains balance in our environment," he says. "This part of the marsh belongs to the wolves. Humans only come here with *bare* shoulders if they intend to kill a wolf. If I was wearing my pelt like I should have been, the wolves would have smelled it and accepted that I wasn't here to hurt them."

"But your pelt... you must have gotten it somehow."

"I did come here to kill once." His voice becomes low. Soft. "A few years ago, I killed the alpha male."

My eyes widen as I remember the she-wolf's pain, her instinctive compulsion to kill Nathaniel. "You killed their leader's mate? That's what you meant by revenge. That's why she hates you?"

He nods. "I dishonored her by stepping foot here without her mate's pelt. She read it as a message that I was here to kill again. One kill is within the law. Another is dishonorable. She had every right to rip out my heart."

"That's why you didn't want to hurt them. It was a matter of honor."

Nathaniel has proven to me time and time again that he operates within a code. I don't always understand it, but I know he won't betray his sense of honor.

I worry at my lip. "What about me? I'm not wearing a pelt."

He grimaces. "I had a plan for that, but I've been gone a whole day, so it fell apart..." He shakes his head, suddenly unwilling to explain himself. "I was hoping the wolves would be confused because you don't smell like a human."

I raise an eyebrow at him, not sure what to read into his statement. "Are you saying that I... smell?"

The corner of his mouth twitches upward. A soft smile. "You have a presence, Aura. Like a summer breeze right before the night falls."

His arm slides around my waist, drawing me closer. I wasn't aware of my own scent, but I'm acutely aware of his. Burned caramel. Both calming and stirring, emotions I try to fight as I picture myself kissing him again.

His hand circles my lower back and I'm suddenly far too aware of how close our bodies are situated. My armor stops me feeling the full impact of his touch, but the way he rubs my back fills me with warmth all the same.

"Aura," he says softly, drawing me closer. "I need you to do something for me."

"What is it?" I whisper.

His gaze flickers past me, focused for a second on something beyond me. "I need you to lie down here with me. Very slowly. No sudden movements."

Again, his gaze shifts past me.

A breath of air stirs at my back.

Oh, dear stars.

Here I was thinking warm thoughts and now I realize his intentions are purely about survival.

"There's something behind me, isn't there?" I ask, swallowing.

His head moves in a single, careful nod. "I'm afraid there is."

CHAPTER 4

"Come here," Nathaniel says. "Slowly now."

I sink into the crook of his arm, slipping my arm around his waist and angling myself slightly backward so I can see upward.

A flying form hovers above us.

A large, brown moth.

Nothing scary.

Not scary at all, in fact, except that it's the size of a crow, its body the width of my arm, and its wingspan so wide, I have to swivel my eyes to see from one side to the other.

Dear stars. I've heard about giant moths, but I never imagined they would look like this.

It languidly descends toward us so quietly that my breath stops.

I didn't even sense it. Even now as it approaches, I get nothing from it. No spirit at all. It's as if there's a blank spot in my senses where it flies. It continues to sail toward us as if it thinks it's welcome to do whatever it wants.

I tell myself it's just a moth. It's just a... *damn...* moth.

Nothing to be afraid of, but my instinctive response to its darkness makes me uncertain.

Nathaniel's strong arms slide around me, firm, holding me in place. "Easy, Aura," he whispers against the top of my hair. "Don't hurt it."

The glow at the corner of my eyes tells me that my starlight power has been triggered. I suppress it with all my might as the moth continues on its alarming path.

It lands right on top of Nathaniel's chest, but it's facing me, its antennae turned in my direction while its giant wings beat across his face and chest.

Nathaniel is turned toward me, but he closes his eyes when the moth's wing brushes his cheek.

Up close, I can see that the creature is covered in short fur the color of the muddy ground, its legs are like crooked twigs, and it smells... *dear stars...* it reeks as badly as the bottom of a still well.

I squeeze my eyes shut as the moth's antennae brush against my neck and across my cheeks as if it's looking for something, quietly seeking...

It feels like it's sucking away a tiny part of me...

Panic shoots through me as its feelers pass across my eyes.

Surely, killing a moth won't break the law?

As if he senses my growing unease, Nathaniel tightens his grip around me, refusing to let me go.

"Easy," he whispers again, drawing out the command. "Stay very still."

A second later, the tickling antennae leave my face. My eyes fly open again to see the creature move on to my hand, where I rest it against Nathaniel's chest.

Tiny smudges of ash rest in the crevices between my fingertips. I'd stopped breathing when Nathaniel and I stayed too long at the burn site where my parents were killed. Where *I* killed them.

Ash had formed across my skin, coming both from inside me and from my surroundings—some sort of catastrophic reaction to the events of the past when my power had exploded across the border and killed thousands of humans. The entire human army...

I shudder as the moth's antennae brush across my fingers, pressing firmly before moving on.

The breeze caused by the moth's wings fades. It lifts from Nathaniel's chest and flies upward, flitting through the air and quickly disappearing into the mist.

I try to calm my breathing, intense embarrassment washing through me at the fear I felt. Along with a thick sense of shame.

I could have easily killed it. I was afraid of it because I didn't understand it. If it had been a Bright butterfly instead of a moth, having it land on me would have been a gift, not a trauma.

Nathaniel's arms soften around me, a relenting cage. His left hand slips between us and quickly presses against my rapidly beating heart.

He doesn't speak, but I welcome the firm pressure of his hand like a lifeline, the sensation reminding me that I'm strong, that the cold emptiness of panic isn't going to suck me down into a void.

"What was that creature?" I ask.

"A mold moth," he answers, his tone calm, moderated, as if he's also taking a moment to breathe. "Don't ever kill one. We need them."

I cast a quizzical glance skyward. Now that I'm not looking down at him, I can see the branches of the tree next to the one Nathaniel threw me into.

This one has sprawling limbs that resemble crooked spires that zigzag across the space above us as if it once chased sunlight from side to side in an effort to grow.

"Why do you need moths?"

His voice softens. "Look up."

I hold my tongue before I growl at him that I already am facing upward. Squinting harder at the tree's branches for a long moment, I don't see anything other than its mottled bark.

I startle as something shifts on its surface. Nathaniel's hold tightens around me again. Just as well, since I'm as on edge as a jittery humblebee right now.

Another moth unfolds from around the branch above me. When the creature drops away from the branch's surface, the branch looks somehow cleaner and brighter compared to other parts of it.

I crane my head upward for a moment without leaving Nathaniel's arms. The parts of the tree the moth wasn't touching are covered with intermittent patches of some sort of gray substance. "What is that stuff?"

"Mold," Nathaniel says. "Sunlight doesn't reach the ground in Fell country. Even beyond the marsh, a haze covers our country. That makes mold a real problem for us. It attacks plant growth as well as homes. The moths help us by eating it."

My eyebrows rise in surprise. "They clean your environment?"

My gaze flickers to my hand—where the ash dusted my fingertips. It's gone. Clean now.

"They do," Nathaniel says, "but unfortunately, there aren't enough of them. So we like to keep them alive. Also…" His smile fades. "Their bodies are full of the toxins they ingest.

You don't want them to explode on you if you value your health."

I exhale carefully as another moth sails toward the tree, wraps its wings around the trunk, and buries its antennae in a patch of gray mold.

I don't know anything about the challenges that humans face. I have no idea what their lives are like, what they have to battle through. My life in Bright is already looking overly spoiled.

Easing upward within the circle of his arms, I position myself so I can see him again. His hand slips away from my heart, sliding around my waist to rest against the small of my back.

In my heart, I know that my fear is about more than the moth.

I am afraid because of what the creature represents for me: *uncertainty*.

My situation right now is more precarious, more dangerous than anything I've ever experienced.

I don't understand human laws. I know nothing about their world. I would have struck all of the wolves down and turned that moth into dust without a single thought.

It would be easier to admit my uncertainty without looking Nathaniel in the eye, but he promised he would always tell me the truth. I want to give him the same respect.

"I suspect that what I know about your land and your people is all wrong," I say. "I don't know what you face living here. I don't know your laws. I'm going to make mistakes. I'm going to… need your help."

"You have it, Aura."

His statement is so sure, so immediate, that it takes my breath away.

His eyes darken as he takes a deep breath, as if he's

weighed down by the importance of what he needs to say. "You left your world behind with no guarantees that I'm going to help you survive. You followed me into the dark despite knowing that in another two days... it's in my best interests for you to die. That takes courage."

I bite my lip so hard, it hurts. My instinct is to brush off what he said because acknowledging it feels far heavier. "You did it first. You left your world behind when you came to Bright."

He shakes his head, a careful movement while his body remains completely still beneath me. "It wasn't the same. I went with a plan and a purpose. Sure, it all went wrong, but it's easier to make choices out of hatred than out of trust. Hatred means you can fight whatever threatens you, no matter what. Trust means you have to weigh the consequences before you act."

He stops speaking and the silence between us suddenly feels jagged.

There's too much truth in his statement. I could have allowed the Queen's Day Guard to kill him in Bright. Moments before we crossed the border, I could have chosen to leap onto the back of another thunderbird and let the Solstice fae use their power over sunlight to burn him to death.

I could have let go of his hand as we ran through the deadly glitter field and allowed the field to cut his body to shreds.

I had a million chances to end all of this. If I had taken those chances, I would be alive and victorious right now. Instead, I chose a path with no certain outcomes.

By the same token, he had no reason to defend me during the fight.

He'd fought at my back, protecting me from attacks.

Then, when Imatra announced that I was the one who'd killed the human army and murdered my own parents fifteen years ago, Nathaniel spoke up in my defense, questioning her claims.

He has everything to gain from my death—just as I have everything to gain from his—yet neither of us has chosen to act without thinking first, without weighing the consequences, just like he said.

He breaks the brittle silence. "I think I can get up now."

He finally rises beneath me, pulling me up with him. He is an immense figure of a man, surprising me at the way he seems to gain in strength with every inch as he resumes his full height.

He suddenly winces. His right arm is half-raised, having just brushed his waist. We're both covered in mud, but the dark sludge is barely visible against the backdrop of our black clothing.

He slowly lowers his arm as if nothing happened and turns to walk away, but his shirt is tight enough that I can see the catch in his breathing as he moves.

I smother an unhappy murmur.

I was right: He's hurt. There's no other reason he would have lain still for so long. Now he's attempting to hide whatever pain he's feeling by turning away from me.

I press my lips together. I'm not having any of that. "Where are you hurt?" I demand to know. "Was it the wolves? Or your crash into the tree?"

He stops walking with a quiet, *"Damn."*

I guess he thought he could get away with it.

"Show me," I order him, zeroing in on his back since that's where he was wiping off the mud when he winced.

His chest rises and falls, catching again on the inhale.

Without turning, he tugs the bottom of his shirt up. "Bottom right ribs."

I carefully peel his shirt further upward.

An angry bruise is already growing across his middle three ribs on the right-hand side of his spine. It's the side on which he crashed into the tree. It's also the side I was lying on when the moth flew down on us.

I can't believe he lay there for so long with my weight on him.

Stubborn man.

Lightly running my fingertips across his skin, I check for breaks, relieved when I don't sense any.

"Your ribs are intact, but you're already developing an almighty bruise."

He starts to pull away. "I'll be fine—"

"Hush. Let me help you." I'm not a healer like my adoptive father Crispin, who is a Dawn fae, but my power has calming properties, the same kind I used on the wolf just before.

I hover my palm over the site of Nathaniel's wound and draw on a glimmer of starlight, allowing my power to trickle between my fingertips until it fills the space between my hand and his back with a soft, white glow.

His breathing eases immediately.

"That feels much better." He sounds surprised. "What are you doing?"

"Using my power to ease your pain."

He is suddenly still. "Your power has many facets, Aura. It has the capacity to destroy as well as the power to heal."

Yesterday morning, I healed a fae girl infected with an illness that Nathaniel calls the Ebon Rot. He told me it affects humans when they age—that they come to the border for a quick death because of its debilitating effects. They dress themselves in furs and cover their faces with animal skins to hide the disfiguring effect of the Rot on their bodies.

I killed many of them, never seeing their true human forms beneath their coverings.

Neither one of us has spoken about that since Nathaniel said that fate couldn't be so cruel that *I* would have the power to heal the illness.

If I can heal his people... and yet he's destined to kill me and take the cure away from them...

He turns back to me sooner than I expected, and the starlight I was administering to his bruise spills into the air between us, trailing like a broken thread.

"What now, Aura?" he asks.

The misty marsh is quiet around us. Only the moths disturb the air.

Until now we were either running or lying still. Two extremes. Now I have to choose a path.

I try to bring moisture to my suddenly dry lips. "You told me that you came to Bright for me," I say. "If everything had gone to plan, where would you have taken me?"

All Nathaniel told me before we started running was that he came to Bright to take me into Fell country. He said he did it because he promised his dying father that he would, but he didn't explain why.

He says, "Fell country is set out in a mirror of Bright. Your cities and villages are circled by mountains. Ours are circled by this marsh. We call this place the Misty Gallows because it rings our land like a noose. The northern part of the Gallows—where we are now—is wolf territory. The southern part of the Gallows belongs to the bears. The east is King Cyrian's hunting ground. And the west belongs to Mathilda. She's the witch I told you about."

I nod to show him that I understand. He told me that a

witch had created the spells he used to subdue the Border Guards yesterday morning.

She's the same woman who made the careful cuts across each of his shoulders—one cut for each person he lost. He told me that her magic is as powerful as Queen Imatra's.

An edge of tension enters his shoulders. He watches me carefully as he speaks. "There's a small village near the western Gallows. It's a place of no consequence to anyone. Ignored by the King. Tolerated by Mathilda. It's so insignificant that it's called Null. I want to take you there."

"Why?" It's such a small question, but I'm not sure if I want the answer.

He chews his lip for a moment. "I want to tell you, but just like King Cyrian used dark magic to stop anyone speaking my name, I asked Mathilda to cast a spell so I can't talk about Null. Saying anything is dangerous and would threaten..."

He swallows, clearing his throat. Then he shakes his head as if he's attempting to bat away a mental block. "I can't tell you why. I'm sorry."

He takes a deep breath, as if he's centering himself before he holds out his hand to me. "Will you come with me and let me show you?"

CHAPTER 5

*N*athaniel's asking me to trust him.

A massive leap of faith when all I've known over the last few hours is betrayal.

He could be taking me anywhere. He could be taking me to a place where my power will be limited somehow and I won't be able to fight back...

I mentally stomp on my spiraling fears. Sunlight is my only weakness and there is very little of it here. I just subdued a pack of wolves, survived an encounter with hungry moths, and eased Nathaniel's pain.

To answer him, I place my hand in his, allowing his fingers to close over mine. His grip is firm. I have a feeling that now that he's holding my hand again, he won't let go of it easily.

"This way," he says.

He urges me in a generally westerly direction, but this time at a brisk walk instead of a run.

"You seem to know the Misty Gallows by heart," I say as he steers me left and right despite the visibility issues.

He pauses for a beat. "I've been through this part of it many times. I've trained myself to read the environment here. The trees make it easy. They all have distinct shapes."

He tugs me to a stop beside another jagged tree. This one's branches stretch directly upward like prongs.

Nathaniel presses his free hand against the trunk, a crease settling across his forehead as he surveys the mist. "I was hoping he'd be here..."

"Who?" I ask.

Nathaniel places his fingers to his lips. He gives two quick, soft whistles. They sound like bird calls as they waft away into the mist. They're similar to the calls I use to summon Treble, except not as sharp.

My heart fills with worry at the thought of Treble. He was struck with fire in our fight to escape. Evander healed him, but that doesn't mean Treble is safe.

He was *my* thunderbird, and I am now a traitor to the throne. I don't know what Queen Imatra will do to Treble now and my worry is a heavy weight in my stomach.

I jolt as a soft drumming sound meets my ears and my senses expand again.

What now?

Unlike the moths, this creature has an intense presence—it's large and approaches swiftly from our left. It's big enough that its footfalls thud against the earth, increasingly loud as it draws nearer at speed.

Nathaniel's hand squeezes mine as he studies my face. "You hear something? Animal or human?"

"Animal. Large. Four legs."

He relaxes and it makes me wonder how tense he would have been if I'd said I heard humans.

"The environment here is neither bright nor beautiful, Aura," he says. "Everything you face will appear dangerous to you. Just like the moth. If you see an animal you don't understand, please don't fear it. Chances are it's peaceful. Okay?"

I take a deep breath as the thudding creature continues to approach. I give Nathaniel a firm nod. "Okay."

"Good." His smile broadens. "Because I'd hate for you to kill my horse."

The stallion bursts into view, a black-as-coal beast with a wild mane that billows around his head as he rears up in the mist.

His powerful forelegs pummel the air before his silver hooves pound down into the earth, crushing the stones beneath him with a single stab.

The stallion's eyes are solid white and the steam puffing from his nostrils is like smoke from a fire. My eyes widen when I see that his shoulders and belly glow amber with every indrawn breath, fiery light inside his torso making his ribs visible.

I've seen sketches of horses, but I never imagined they would look like this, let alone breathe magic the way this horse does.

He's wearing a bridle as well as a harness that consists of soft-looking straps wrapped around his shoulders and stomach. A satchel is attached to one side of the harness and a pelt attached to the other, both sitting precariously across the horse's shoulders.

I guess the pelt was Nathaniel's intended method to get me past the wolves.

I lower my voice to a whisper. "What is he?"

Nathaniel smiles. "His name is Flare. He's a firehorse. A creature of dark magic. One of the few left."

Nathaniel tugs me along as he approaches the horse. "Easy, Flare."

The horse paws the earth, snorting angrily and bouncing

his head at Nathaniel. He reminds me so clearly of Treble when he's mad at me that I miss a step. Nathaniel pauses too.

"Can he understand you?" I ask.

Nathaniel gives me a quick nod. "Like your thunderbird. But he can't speak back."

He quickly turns back to Flare, his tone placating as he tries to calm the stallion. "I know, I know," he says. "I was gone a long time. I didn't mean to be."

Nathaniel reaches out to stroke Flare's nose, but the fire-horse jerks away from him. Flare snorts again, jabbing at the ground with his right foreleg, an increasingly irritated movement.

"C'mon, buddy. You have to—"

Flare doesn't let him finish. With a sharply indrawn breath, the horse exhales a wash of smoke all over Nathaniel.

I close my eyes and hold my breath as the acidic substance fills the air around me. *Ugh.* It burns the inside of my mouth and nose, although the scent isn't too bad—like a campfire.

Nathaniel coughs and wheezes, his eyes streaming as he bats at the smoke. "You have to forgive me."

Flare shakes his head with a 'fat chance' snort that covers Nathaniel so completely in smoke that he has to step back into the clear, taking me with him.

"No?" Nathaniel's forehead crinkles in dismay as he looks at Flare. "Really?"

Ignoring Nathaniel, Flare swings his head in my direction, fixing me with his white-eyed gaze. Despite the fact that he doesn't have pupils or irises, he somehow manages to look accusing.

Since he can understand me the same way that Treble can, I plant my free hand on my hip and look him squarely in the eyes. "Yes. It was my fault."

Flare's eyelids lower until his eyes are narrow, white slits, his eyelashes a surprising shade of amber despite his thick coat of black hair.

He extends his neck toward me, stomping his hooves and shaking his mane aggressively enough that Nathaniel steps between us protectively.

Nathaniel doesn't know what I went through to tame my thunderbird and that this animal's aggression scares me far less than the wolves. Flare may be fueled by flames, but his power is no more frightening to me than the crackling lightning I'm used to dealing with.

When I chose Treble, I climbed the northern mountains alone and hiked for days until my feet were bloody and my water ran out. I passed twenty other birds, but it only took a glance for my heart to tell me they were wrong for me.

I found Treble on the highest peak and that was when the real challenge began. I had to earn his respect—just as he had to earn mine.

It's time for me to make an equally aggressive move.

"Don't expect an apology," I snap at the horse, dropping Nathaniel's hand to circle toward Flare.

My power rushes through my arms, snapping and crackling around my fingertips as I advance. "You think it's hard to spend a day alone. Try seven years surrounded by people only to discover that you were alone the whole time."

Flare's eyes fly wide at my approach. He rapidly backs up, a quick *thud-thud* of his hooves as my power flickers dangerously in the air around me, sizzling and sharp, leaping like lightning between us.

A tendril snaps close to his forehead, making him jolt.

Flare darts a look at Nathaniel, who watches us carefully but doesn't make a move to get between us.

With a quick snort, Flare digs in his hooves, stomping his

foot at me again, trying to reassert his dominance with a clear warning to keep my distance.

I ignore the message, drawing to a halt a mere few inches from his smoking nostrils.

Leaning forward, I look him in his white eyes and whisper, "You don't scare me."

He returns my gaze for a second. He's quiet, but it's a ploy —and I know it. Heat gathers around his belly, racing along his neck as he prepares to smother me in acidic smoke.

In a great gust, he exhales all over me, but I'm already holding my breath. I refuse to close my streaming eyes.

I raise a single glowing finger through the haze and tap Flare's nose.

A spark of starlight shoots through his soft nose, streaking up his forehead, lighting up the outline of a surprising diamond shape before it sizzles past his right ear and away into his mane.

He jolts and blinks back at me, suddenly becoming very still.

"Do we understand each other?" I ask.

I wait another moment, my fingertip hovering above his nose, ready to tap again if I have to.

His eyes glow, an eerie brighter white for a second before they fade again.

His answer is to lower his head and stretch out his front right leg to lower his shoulder.

He'll only give me a second to accept his gesture, so I don't hesitate, taking a step for momentum before I leap upward. Planting my hands on his withers, I swing myself over his back, landing neatly in place behind the satchel and pelt.

Flare doesn't stand nearly as far off the ground as Treble does, so it's not that daunting sitting on his back. I don't anticipate that he can gallop faster than Treble can fly, so his speed shouldn't be a problem for me, either.

I smile down at Nathaniel. "He forgives you."

Nathaniel grins up at me, his arms folded across his chest. His gaze passes from my face all the way to my thighs, where I grip Flare's back. "It certainly looks like it."

I arch my eyebrow at him. "I'm not sure how you're going to get up here, though. Since I've taken up the prime position."

"I guess I'll have to take the easy approach," he says, striding toward us.

This time, Flare doesn't react to Nathaniel's presence with a cloud of smoke.

Reaching out without pausing in his stride, Nathaniel lightly taps Flare's right shoulder in front of my thigh.

Flare immediately lurches forward, kneeling so far down that I have to compensate by leaning backward so that I don't fall right over his head.

I bump downward as he rapidly folds his hind legs too. He ends up lying on the ground and I end up with my knees pulled up around my ears to avoid my feet getting caught beneath him.

Nathaniel slips onto the stallion's back behind me and Flare rises to his feet again. The whole maneuver takes place so quickly, I'm still catching my breath as Nathaniel settles in behind me, the front of his thighs pressing against the backs of mine.

Wrapping his left arm around my waist, he reaches past me to take hold of the reins.

He pauses, his cheek brushing mine. "Have you ever ridden a horse before?"

I give a small shake of my head. "It can't be more difficult than riding a thunderbird."

A soft chuckle escapes his lips, his dark eyes lighting up as he considers me. "You might be surprised. Let's take it slow. Once you're ready, I'll let him run."

His body presses against mine as he leans farther forward. "Flare, take us to Null, but go easy. Aura doesn't need another fall today."

CHAPTER 6

*F*lare sets off at a gentle walk, but I sense his restraint.

I'm sure he isn't used to having a leash put on his fiery inner nature. Just like Treble, he would rather be traveling at full speed than this stately pace.

Still, it's an unfamiliar motion. I didn't think it would be harder than riding a thunderbird, but—*dear stars*—it is. Unlike when I'm flying on Treble, our path is uneven and Flare's unfamiliar gait requires my uninterrupted concentration.

Nathaniel's grip around my waist tightens as he leans forward. "Flare will take us southwest to the edge of the Gallows, but we'll travel within the cover of the mist for as long as we can. Most of the land just beyond the Gallows is worked by farmers. They don't come too close to the Gallows if they can help it, but there's still a chance we'll be seen."

Seeming satisfied that I'm not going to lose my seat, Nathaniel leans back again, but not far. On his way, he drops a kiss against the back of my exposed neck, a light and unexpected touch.

The contact makes me shiver hard enough for him to feel it.

"Cold?" he asks, reaching past me again to pull the pelt from Flare's harness.

He passes me the reins and I grip them tightly, nervous about being in charge.

The air wafts through the sudden gap between our bodies as he leans back to slide the pelt over my shoulders and rest it down between us.

I tug the pelt closer around my shoulders. Now that we're not running, the cold is starting to seep in.

The thermal properties of my armor will keep me warm enough to stave off any sickness, but the pelt will ensure I stay warm. My people never wear animal skins. We don't eat meat or kill animals for any reason, so I should probably feel disgusted wearing this fur. Instead, it's oddly comforting.

"The pelt will help you blend in," Nathaniel says.

Yesterday, I attempted to pass Nathaniel off as a fae by dressing him in a fleece coat like the Harvest Fae wear. Now I guess he's trying to make me look more human by placing the pelt around my shoulders.

I've never seen a human woman, but since Nathaniel looks very much like a fae, I imagine that, at a distance, I might look human. My eyes are a dull green, not bright like most fae, and my skin is pale. The rings beneath my eyes are dark, my lips are colorless, and my hair looks like an old fae's.

I don't imagine that the pelt will confuse anyone who sees me up close. Even if my whiter-than-white hair doesn't give me away, my armor will.

"Is it really worth pretending I'm human?" I ask.

"It's essential. Any human who thinks you're fae will attack you without mercy. The same way your people would have attacked me if you hadn't protected me."

I sigh. "I protected you by treating you like my prisoner. You could do the same to me?"

He shakes his head at the corner of my vision. "That won't work here because it would mean I'd have to take you to the King. That's the last place you should go."

Despite the warning in his voice, Nathaniel presses his cheek to mine for a brief moment before he drops another startlingly light kiss against my jaw. "This pelt isn't only for camouflage. You faced the wolves. You deserve this fur. Consider it yours."

I brush the edge of the fur, finding it softer than I expected. "You said that two kills is dishonorable, so I'm assuming this pelt isn't yours."

He gives me a quick nod. "It was my mother's. She wanted you to have it."

"But she didn't know me—"

He's already reaching past me and the question I want to ask is brushed away as he flips open the satchel and rummages around inside it.

First he pulls out a flask of water, which he hands to me. Then a strange-looking yellow fruit that resembles an apple. It tastes pulpy and not as sweet as the fruit in Bright. I'm too hungry to worry about the taste.

Finally, he reaches into the satchel again, saying, "This will confuse any humans who see you from a distance."

He pulls a black scarf from the satchel. The material makes a whispering sound as he runs it through his hands that tells me it's spun from a substance as fine as silk. "For your hair."

He presses the scarf into my hand, his fingers closing

around mine before he releases the scarf into my possession. It's softer than I thought Fell material would be and has a light stretch.

He continues. "Before we get to Null, we will pass through a place called the Bitter Patch. There are plants there filled with a sap that you can use to dye your hair black. I tried harvesting some of the sap to see whether I could bring it with me, but it dries out, so this will have to do until we get there."

Careful not to bump Nathaniel with my elbows, I quickly retie my braid, wrapping it into a bun before I secure the scarf around my head with a firm knot at the base of my neck. It fits securely around my face while I run my fingers around the edge to make sure there are no visible strands of hair.

"Now you'll pass as human," Nathaniel says, a smile in his voice. "The only one you won't fool is Mathilda, but that's only because she knows you're fae. Other than my mother, she's the only one who knows what my father said before he died."

"What about my armor?" I ask.

"What about it?"

I tilt my head toward him. "It's fae."

He steers Flare around a gnarled tree that is more stump than anything else. "Humans were designing armor long before the fae. We didn't have magic to protect us, so we had to use what we could. What you're wearing is a copy of a human design."

I can't hide my disbelief. "My armor looks like human armor?"

"The human army wore armor very close in design to what you're wearing now," he says. "Most of our armor was destroyed in the last battle, but some of it still remains in the royal armory and many families have suits of armor that have been handed down through the generations. Those pieces of armor are treated like relics, but they're still functional."

"But... I'm female. I thought your army was all male."

He laughs, a deep rumble, as he adjusts his arm around my waist. "My father may have led the army, but my mother trained the soldiers."

"Your mother did?"

His tone remains casual. "She trained me. And many others." He quickly clears his throat, as if he feels the need to explain. "After my father died, King Cyrian asked her to continue training a new generation. But only boys this time. She did what he asked." Nathaniel's tone hardens. "Then he turned them all into his hunters."

Nathaniel falls silent and I consider the way his arm has clamped around me, the heavy silence, and the sudden absence of kisses—just when I was getting used to them.

"The hunters don't only hunt animals," I say. "Do they?"

"They don't. They use the skills my mother taught them to punish anyone who speaks out against the King. They're extremely dangerous."

Nathaniel inhales a deep, calming breath. "As the King's Shield, I rank above them, but that only means they stay away from me. I don't control them. We should avoid encountering them at all costs."

I remember the way he hurried me along at the border yesterday morning before we took to the air on Treble. He told me that others were coming and we didn't want to be around when they arrived. "Are they the same ones you wanted to avoid yesterday morning?"

"They are."

I lean into him. "Did your mother train anyone else after that?"

The smile returns to his voice. He drops another kiss against my cheek at the edge of the scarf. "There's a story among my people that my mother—she was called Luciana—trained a new generation of warriors in secret. Nobody knew the location of her training ground or who was trained. There are whispers that one day, Luciana's warriors will rise up against Cyrian and his hunters and overthrow him."

"Is there any truth in the rumors?"

His lips whisper across my ear. "Whether or not there is, you now wear her pelt, my family symbol on your face, and armor that passes as human. As long as they don't see your hair, they will believe you're one of hers."

I suck in a sharp breath, twisting to him before I discover that moving so suddenly was a really bad idea. Turning around on a horse is *not* the same as twisting around on Treble.

Nathaniel catches me before I bounce right off Flare's back, carefully tightening Flare's reins at the same time so the firehorse comes to a stop.

"Is this your plan?" I ask. "To turn myth into reality?"

He purses his lips. "I can't tell you, remember?"

"But you just told me—"

"A story. Nothing more." He exhales softly. "If I can use a long-held spark of hope among my people to keep you safe on the way to Null, then I'll do it. I'll use everything at my disposal to make sure you aren't threatened."

I find myself gripping his torso. "I can't walk around dressed in a lie. Not when they should fear me."

"They shouldn't fear you." Carefully easing out of the reins, he slips his hands under the pelt and wraps his fingers around my waist and hip. "I've seen into your heart. You don't strike unless you have no other choice."

His gaze pierces mine, but there's a hint of unexplained pain behind it. "When you kill, it's as clean and as quick as you can make it."

He firmly maneuvers me around on the horse so I'm facing forward again. Then he reasserts the position of his arm around my waist and urges Flare to resume walking.

"If humans have armor, why didn't you wear yours when you came for me?" I ask. "You would have been much safer in it."

I sense the shrug of his shoulders against my back. "There isn't a suit of armor that fits me. My father's was damaged and I refuse to wear it."

His father was stabbed in the back three times before his horse dragged him home again. Somehow, he survived the blast of my starlight before that.

I have a sudden thought. "Was Flare your father's horse?"

"No. Cyrian killed that horse long ago—"

"*Killed*! Why?"

"He harvested the dark magic inside it." Nathaniel's response is unemotional, but it feels forced.

"I'm sorry," I say.

"It was a long time ago." Again, he shrugs. "When I became the King's shield, I bargained for Flare's life. I keep him away from the castle as much as possible."

Flare's ears twitch and I sense his need to run. I need to move also, need the wind in my face to battle the uncertainties I'm facing.

"I think I have the hang of riding now," I say.

"Then you might want to hold on," Nathaniel whispers to me, making me shiver in anticipation before he says to Flare, "Take us to Null, Flare. And go as fast as you like."

I don't ignore Nathaniel's warning. I already sense the energy building inside Flare's body. Despite the visible flames, his body isn't hot beneath my calves when he draws a deep breath. When he moves, it's going to be as wild as when Treble takes to the air.

I lean low and brace, comfortable now with the proximity of my body to Nathaniel's. His arm is a firm anchor around my waist, and his chest is a shield at my back.

As soon as I settle my weight, Flare's back legs bunch and he leaps forward, breaking into a gallop so fast, it snatches the breath from my chest.

CHAPTER 7

*F*lare darts between the trees, navigating the environment as if he knows it as well as Nathaniel does.

I spend the next ten minutes relaxing into this new experience of riding a galloping horse, but the more at home I feel on Flare's back, the more conscious I become of Nathaniel's body pressed against mine.

Every small movement Nathaniel makes helps me lean in the right direction to counteract Flare's turns and to balance my weight to accommodate Flare's gait, keeping us connected like a single unit on Flare's back.

When we finally reach the edge of the Gallows, I expect the sky to open up ahead of us and let the sunlight through, but Nathaniel wasn't exaggerating about the haze.

The light is murky and impure, and the sky is gray. I can't even tell what time it is because the light is the same everywhere I look. All I see are varying shades of darkness. At a pinch, we could be approaching the sixth hour of the morning, but I can't be sure.

A field of crops fills the space in front of us as far as I can see. It looks like a form of wheat, waist height with slim stems, but it's a muddy brown color, not honey-colored like the wheat in Bright.

Sunlight is my weakness—sometimes I actively hate it—but I respect its power to help the environment grow and flourish. I'm not sure how humans survive without it.

Just as Nathaniel promised, Flare keeps to the edge of the Gallows, remaining within the cover of the mist. Above the rhythmic thud of Flare's hooves, I sense slithering animals moving through the nearby fields, along with small, panicky furred creatures—maybe rabbits or whatever version of them the Fell have.

An hour later, the crop fields give way to a thick wilderness of bushes and vines. The bushes are as tall as trees and the color of a crow's wings—stems and leaves inky black—but the vines are crimson, thorny and twisted, strangling the bushes so savagely that black sap trickles and drips from them onto the dusty ground.

This must be the plant Nathaniel wants me to use to dye my hair.

The vines and bushes form a wall penning us in on our right-hand side while the Misty Gallows continues to curve at our left, leaving a path for us that is only ten paces wide.

Nathaniel's arm tightens around my waist. "We call this place the Bitter Patch. It's a warning to all humans who dare to pass into Mathilda's land."

"I take it that's us," I say.

He nods. "Don't worry. She won't hurt us."

"You," I say, trying to make light of the darkness around us. The way Nathaniel spoke about the witch yesterday, she sounded almost like his friend. At the very least, not like an enemy. I'm not sure how she'll feel about me. "She won't hurt *you*."

"Us," he corrects me firmly. "You have my protection."

I'm not sure what he means by that, but my response sticks in my throat. A hush has fallen over this place and it feels like the environment has eyes. Even whispering sounds too loud.

My inner tension increases when Nathaniel steers Flare away from the Gallows toward a particularly prickly-looking patch of thorns and bushes.

Drawing Flare to a halt in front of it, he slips from the horse's back. "Wait here for a moment."

He strides toward the nearest bush, reaches carefully into the thick mess, and draws back a wash of vines.

My eyes widen when he reveals a tunnel of sorts through the wall of vegetation. It stretches far into the distance, carving its way through to form a dusty path trickling with black sap.

Nathaniel catches hold of one of the vines and uses it to tie the rest of the covering back, leaving an opening wide enough for Flare to walk through.

Returning to me, he stops at my thigh. "We need to travel along the tunnel to reach Null, but the Bitter Patch grows quickly. I'll need to cut parts of it along the way so we can pass through. I left my weapon behind in Bright. Can I use your sword?"

"Of course." Reaching for the liquid weapon attached to my left shoulder, I detach it so that it takes solid form again.

The moment it solidifies, the air shifts around me.

A cold breeze scrapes across my cheeks like fingernails.

I jolt away from the sensation, suddenly on edge.

Flare jostles to the side as if he sensed it too. His sudden movement forces me to grip with my thighs so I don't fall off while I lurch for his reins with my free hand.

Nathaniel quickly sidesteps Flare's big body so he doesn't get crushed. "Aura? What's wrong?"

"Did you feel that?" Gripping Flare's reins, I cast a worried look back along the path between the Bitter Patch and the Misty Gallows. I'm not sure which direction the strange wind came from, but Flare snorts in the direction of the Gallows.

Nathaniel shakes his head but swings in that direction too, suddenly tense. "What did you feel?"

I struggle to describe it. "Pain. Anger."

If there's a threat, I need to face it. Sliding quickly from Flare's back, I step clear of the nervous horse, gripping my sword as I turn to face the Gallows.

Nathaniel doesn't have a weapon, but he urges Flare back toward the Bitter Patch, quickly slinging his reins around a vine to keep him out of the way.

"It's okay, buddy," he says, speaking calmly. "We'll take care of it."

Returning to stand beside me, he studies the mist as tension grows around his mouth. "It could be Mathilda, but I don't know why she'd make her presence known like this unless she's angry about something."

The silence is heavy. It's like waiting for the mist to exhale.

Inwardly, I sigh.

It feels like everything wants to come at me out of the fog today. Wolves, moths, horses, and now what? I guess I'll find out soon enough.

Flare nickers and backs into the Bitter Patch behind us. The fact that he'd rather prick his hide on thorns than face the oncoming threat tells me that whatever's coming is far worse.

I can't sense anything now. It's all too quiet.

I start counting heartbeats, inhaling calming breaths. Whether it's the dark witch herself or not, I tell myself I can handle it.

In preparation, my starlight power simmers within my chest, ready to release if I need it.

A sudden *crack* splits my hearing.

The trees at the edge of the Gallows directly in front of us shudder and sway as a woman appears out of nothing. A branch behind her crumbles into dust as if she annihilated it with her magic.

Her hair is long, wild, and as black as a crow's feathers, the same color as the vines behind me, while her eyes are a piercing green, large and luminescent, her lashes darkened to jet black.

A fire-colored pelt, possibly from a tawny fox, rests across her shoulders while beneath it she wears a ragged, charcoal dress that hugs her voluptuous curves. The dress plunges in a low V at her neck with a high slit up her right leg that splits apart as she storms toward us.

"Nathaniel Shield," she screams, her voice so sharp that I wince. "How dare you bring this violence to my home!"

"Mathilda?" He stands his ground despite the fact that he's weaponless. "What in the dark stars—?"

"Fae weapon!" she screams, pointing at me. She continues to storm toward me. "That weapon bears the blood of innocents. I heard the echoes of their screams..." She gasps for breath, her hand pressed to her heart. "All the screams..."

Nathaniel's focus flashes to my sword. The blade must have upset her.

The sword isn't mine. It came with the armor I'm wearing, which belongs to a fae named Serena—the Queen's former Champion. She tried to kill Nathaniel last night. I stole her armor after I defeated her.

My stomach turns because I don't know what Serena did with this sword, whom she might have hurt—humans *and* fae probably.

If she killed humans, then I can understand why Mathilda is so upset that I raised the sword here.

I have to get rid of it, but my options are slim. As much as I hate what crimes might have been committed with it, we need this blade.

Opting for the easiest solution, I slap the sword to my shoulder so that it liquifies and disappears against my armor again.

I quickly hold out my hands, palms up and empty.

"It's gone!" I say. "I won't reach for it again."

Mathilda's wild eyes rise to mine. "I'm not talking about the sword!"

I stare at her in confusion.

If not the sword, then... what?

Her lips twist as she inhales to cry out again. "I'm talking about you!"

CHAPTER 8

*M*athilda spins to Nathaniel, who has frozen beside me.

"This fae is a weapon," she says. "She has killed a thousand humans. I sense their deaths on her like blood." She squeezes her eyes shut, tears leaking from them. "Damn you for bringing her here."

Nathaniel's expression hardens in the same way it did when he faced Imatra this morning. "You deal in darkness, Mathilda. Darkness and death. You are not innocent—"

"But I always calculate my actions. Weigh them against the consequences. What she did—"

Nathaniel's roar cuts her off. "Was not her fault!"

Mathilda jolts. "How can you be sure?"

"Because she was a child when it happened. She doesn't remember it."

I'm rocked to my core by Nathaniel's defense of me. The sincerity and genuine belief in his statements shock me. He's acting like my shield, my defender, *my* champion.

I don't remember anything about the night I killed the army. Not the deaths, only the pain in my chest when I gained consciousness, forming my first thoughts as I escaped the vast, cold place my mind was trapped in.

Mathilda glares back at Nathaniel, stepping right up to him. "You're wrong."

He shakes his head. "I'm not."

Mathilda's voice softens, becoming quiet in a way that feels dangerous. "You were wrong all along. You misinterpreted what your father said. The white-haired girl needs to die."

Her silhouette flickers.

Behind her, another tree branch cracks and crumbles to dust.

She reappears right in front of me.

Her clawed fingers reach for my throat. Her eyes are glowing emerald orbs, dark magic flickering and swirling inside them, a power itself drawn from death.

The vines and bushes at the edges of my vision curl and shrink as if the life is being sucked from them to power her spell.

Her voice whispers inside my mind...

...blood of innocent humans...

...from blood to blood...

...they will be avenged...

My starlight power cracks inside me, a powerful bright surge as I raise my arms to defend myself.

Mathilda's hand closes around my neck, but my power blasts outward, an explosion so violent that it throws her back onto the path. Dark light washes out from her body as she tumbles through the mud.

Mathilda skids to a stop at the edge of the path, carving a

groove in the mud, her pelt askew and her hair even more wild around her head. Her mouth gapes open as she stares at me in astonishment.

I only now realize how dangerous my actions might have been.

Under the Law of Champions, I'm not allowed to hurt a human in any way. The punishment is my death. I'm lucky Mathilda is a witch.

Mathilda's surprise quickly shifts into anger, her eyebrows drawn down and her face draining pale.

She rises to her feet, lifting from the ground with a power I can't see or feel.

Her magic isn't like Imatra's or the power of the Frost fae over wind—it sucks at the air as if she's draining the natural environment to make herself stronger.

Vines wither and curl on the other side of me, crumbling like the tree branches.

Every time she uses her power, some part of the natural environment dies. I've never seen dark magic in action, but the death of nature appears to be the consequence.

She stares at her hands as if she's trying to work something out. "I sensed darkness and light. A binding. A challenge…"

I didn't think she could get any paler, but she wobbles before she regains her balance. "You invoked the Law of Champions."

She strides toward me again, but Nathaniel reaches for me this time, his hand closing around my arm. He murmurs, "Stay calm. Mathilda and I have to work this out."

Mathilda grinds to a stop in front of me.

Her sharp eyes follow the curve of my cheeks from one side to the other. The line of her sight as it flickers from one part of my face to the other traces the symbol that Nathaniel drew on my skin.

"She invoked the Law of Champions, killed your people, and still you gave her your family name. Why?"

"I'm doing what I promised my father."

"He never told you to mark her."

Nathaniel's eyes narrow to dangerous slits. "Aura has my trust. You need to accept that."

"She will kill you, Nathaniel!"

Pain suddenly stabs my heart. Mathilda is volatile and powerful, but her worry is genuine. She may not be human, but she acts like Nathaniel's protector.

"You have betrayed your name," she cries. "You have spat on your father's grave. You have destroyed his memory—"

Nathaniel's fierce roar cuts her off. "No!"

She blinks at him in surprise, taking a step back like she did when he yelled at her the first time. She seems genuinely shocked by his anger.

I don't understand the nature of their relationship, but her expression makes me wonder if he's ever acted against her wishes before.

"My father taught me to follow my heart," he says, lowering his voice. "He taught me honor. He taught me to trust my instincts. He taught me *everything* that compels me to—"

He stops so suddenly that the silence is like a weight descending around us.

Mathilda narrows her eyes at him. "Compels you to what, Nathaniel? And *for* what? A faded fae who will never return what you give?" She spins from him to me. "Why don't we see what motivates *her* heart?"

I freeze as she dares to hover her hand above my chest

without my permission. At least she doesn't touch me this time.

The gap between us fills with dark light and a look of concentration crosses her face. In the distance, another tree branch cracks and disappears into dust. At this rate, she'll strip all of its branches.

"Stop," I order her, but not because she's hurting me. I grew up with a deep respect for nature. My people harness the power of our environment but never to its detriment.

Our magic works in harmony with nature, unlike this dark magic. It hurts me every time she sucks the life from a branch or a vine. I sense the pain she's causing the environment, even if she doesn't.

"I'll tell you whatever you want to know," I say. "Ask me anything and I'll speak the truth."

My offer has no effect on her, her gaze fixed on the location of my heart. Her forehead suddenly creases deeply as if she's very confused. Then her eyes fly wide.

She gasps.

Nathaniel's fist snaps out, wrapping around Mathilda's wrist.

"That's enough," he says, but Mathilda is already pulling away from me.

She stares at me as she backs away, stopping three paces from us. "Darkest of stars," she whispers. She looks at me as if she's seeing me for the first time, her eyes searching my face, her gaze running across my hair.

Her speech is disjointed, like parts of complete sentences that she's refusing to speak aloud. "White-haired girl... faded now... but she glows when you touch her..."

A deep sense of unease spreads through me. I suddenly feel the need to press the heel of my hand against my heart to remind myself that my heart is beating. That she hasn't taken anything from me or hurt me in any way.

A glance at Nathaniel tells me he's just as unsettled by her reaction.

"Speak, Mathilda," he orders her. "Explain what you saw."

She casts a glance at me before she shakes her head. "No."

But her expression is softer now as she turns to him with a sigh. "You've made a complicated choice, Nathaniel. You were already walking an impossible path. Every step you take now will come at a cost."

He says, "There's no price too high."

I don't fully understand what's going on right now, but I recognize the determination in Nathaniel's declaration.

He's planning something that involves me—that he seems determined to carry out despite the Law of Champions—and he's willing to risk everything along the way.

Before I can speak, Mathilda says to me, "You carry Nathaniel's family name. It's written on your body in the most fundamental bond of loyalty. It will give you hope, but also pain. What remains of your heart will be torn apart before the beginning of the third day. I pray you survive it."

She spins to Nathaniel. "I sense a shift in the east. Cyrian has been drawing massive amounts of energy from his environment in the last day, but I don't know why. As for Aura... you will hurt her more than I ever could."

I shiver as her silhouette flickers.

In the distance, the remainder of the tree crumbles as she disappears.

Nathaniel stares at the empty space she left behind. We're both frozen where we stand.

"Please explain to me what just happened," I say, needing answers.

"After my father died, I told Mathilda about his last words. She always questioned my interpretation. She disagrees with me bringing you here. She thinks I was supposed to kill you."

I suck in a sharp breath, but Nathaniel quickly continues. "That's why she said I was wrong all along."

"Does she have Sight?" I ask, trying to shake off her predictions.

"She can't see the future—she can't see details or events—but she can sense pain and suffering, both future and past. That's how she sensed your past just now. She warned my father about the final battle, too, but he didn't listen. Now she thinks I'm not listening to her, either."

"She's worried about you." I stare at the empty space she left behind, knowing that Mathilda's fears are well founded.

Nathaniel clears his throat as he turns to settle Flare. The firehorse shakes his head vehemently while Nathaniel unwinds his reins from around the thorny vines.

"She's not wrong about me," I say quietly. "I have the blood of innocent humans on my hands."

In less than two days, I may have Nathaniel's blood on my hands too. Although… Mathilda's prediction places my greatest pain earlier than that. Less than a day away, in fact.

I try, and fail, to suppress the shudder raging down my spine.

Nathaniel pauses in the process of straightening Flare's harness. "When I look at you, I see a woman, not a killer with blood on her hands. I need you to remember that."

I swallow against the emotions rising inside me, my fear of what lies ahead of us battling with my desire to believe what he says.

He inclines his head toward the tunnel and holds out his hand for the second time today. "I've known what I had to do since the day my father died. We're almost there. Are you willing to come with me?"

Nearly everything I've encountered today has come at me with ferocity, taking me by surprise. It's time for me to start confronting my environment head on.

I take his outstretched hand, but only to wrap my fingers around his for a brief moment before I step into the tunnel.

I catch his breaking smile as he watches me stride ahead of him into the dark.

CHAPTER 9

*T*he air inside the tunnel is surprisingly fresh and crisp.

The scent of the sap isn't heavy, but instead lightly sweet.

When I accidently brush up against the crimson thorns, I discover that they're soft and malleable to the touch.

Nathaniel asks for my sword to cut the first set of vines that block the way. I would prefer not to destroy them, but I can see how Flare's hooves could get tangled in them and put him in danger, so I hand over my weapon.

I'm surprised when I don't sense any pain from the plants.

"How are these formed?"

"Mathilda created them from dark magic," Nathaniel says. "They're only partially living. But they serve an important purpose—hiding Null from the King's eyes. Even with all of his dark magic, all he sees here is a wilderness of Mathilda's making."

Halfway along, he stops Flare, ties his reins to a new set of vines, and passes me the water flask to take a drink.

"We need to dye your hair before we go any farther. I'll get the sap."

"How do you know this will work?" I ask, looking for a place to sit down before I give up and simply kneel on the ground.

He grins at me. "Many women travel out here to the edge of the Bitter Patch to dye their hair with this sap. Even my mother did. It makes their hair glossy. I suspect Mathilda might have added some extra color to the plants once she saw what they were being used for."

"She cares about your people."

He nods. "She's not what you expected."

"Not what I imagined a witch would be like."

"Mathilda is never predictable." He takes a vial from his satchel, borrows one of my daggers to pierce a vine, and then squeezes the sap into the bottle until it's full. "That should do it."

Returning to me, he kneels behind me and gently eases the scarf off my head, loosening my hair before he pours some sap onto the scarf and uses it to work the liquid through my hair.

The sap is surprisingly light, not goopy, and the sweet smell fills my senses.

I close my eyes as he takes care around my face, making sure he covers every strand of white all the way to the ends. Luckily, my armor is black, so any drips won't matter.

The movement of his fingers through my hair is soothing in the extreme, so much that my shoulders relax, my thoughts drift, and I find myself falling asleep.

Dark stars, how does he do that?

I normally can't sleep unless I'm lying in complete darkness surrounded by an empty space—or as empty as I can make it.

I give myself a shake and open my eyes to find him kneeling in front of me.

His palm brushes my cheek, the contact making me glow across his hand.

His thumb grazes my jaw as if he's coaxing me back to wakefulness. "Aura? Just a little farther and you can get some sleep, okay?"

"My hair's finished?" *Damn. I did* fall asleep.

With a crooked smile, he hooks his hand through my locks and draws them over my shoulder so I can see the color—as black as my armor and shinier than my hair has ever been.

"It's already dry," he says. "I'm sorry I had to wake you."

I cautiously run my fingers through my tresses, wary of getting sap all over my fingers, but it's smooth and waterless. If it dries that fast, it's not a surprise he couldn't bring a bottle of the sap to the border.

His serious eyes meet mine as his arm descends to wind around my waist and pull me upward. "You seemed surprised yesterday when I told you that I knew who you are. But I need to warn you that every human knows your name."

Surprise makes me jolt, but he seems ready for that, his arms closing more tightly around me. "The only identifying feature they would recognize is your hair. The other sign would be your glow. I wasn't prepared for that, so I'll need to find gloves for you somehow. Until then, we need to avoid touching each other in public once we enter Null."

My peaceful moments of sleep are suddenly long gone. "How do they know so much about me?"

Nathaniel rubs my arms. "Do you remember how I said that sometimes family members follow their loved ones to the border?"

"You're talking about the humans sick with the Ebon Rot who come to the border to die."

Nathaniel nods. "Family members often watch from the safety of the mist. The Border Guards who were with you would call you by name. Sometimes, afterward, you would sit with the human's body."

I gasp. "I took off my mask afterward."

"You did."

"I wasn't supposed to..."

It was against the rules to remove my mask at the border, but the air is so dank there and I always struggled to breathe after I killed a Fell. I would wait until the Border Guards finished burying the body, and then I would sit by the grave, alone.

At the time, I put my emotions down to my overwhelming anger. All my life, I blamed the humans for killing my parents.

Nathaniel reaches for my hair, wrapping his fingers around the strands, which are no longer white. "It's hard to miss your hair in the dark."

I've tried to apologize to him before, but now it feels even more important. "I can't even begin to ask for your forgiveness—"

"Stop." His determined gaze rakes over me. "You're here. You're not the only one who has sins to atone for. Let's take it one step at a time."

"What will your people do if they find out who I am?"

"They won't stop until they kill you," he says. "From now on, you are a Warrior of Luciana. That's all anyone can know."

I worry at my lip. "I don't know anything about your mother. What if they ask questions—"

He gives me a small smile, his expression softening. "My

mother was an intensely private person, dedicated to her duty. They won't expect you to talk about her."

He drops another surprisingly gentle kiss against my cheek, this time on the corner of my mouth, his lips hovering for a fleeting moment across mine before he withdraws.

"Okay," I whisper, my lips tingling from the contact.

His arms slide away from my waist, but I lightly clasp his arm, trying to work some moisture into my mouth to ask for the answers I need. "Nathaniel?"

"Hmm?"

I'm suddenly acutely aware of every sensation across my skin—the pull of my armor, the slightly too-long sleeves, the pinch of my toes in my boots, the cool air across my exposed neck.

I whisper, "What is this between us?"

His arms return to my waist, but slowly this time, one hand stroking up my back to rest between my shoulder blades.

Once again, my armor stops me from feeling the full impact of his touch, and I fight the urge to press against his hand so I can sense the contours of his fingers and how they fit to the space beneath my shoulder blade.

Giving me every opportunity to pull away or tell him to stop, he slowly lowers his lips to mine, but his kiss is a mere whisper of sensation, a tiny breath of air, before he breaks the contact.

"What does it feel like to you?" he asks, a quiet rumble.

I open my eyes. "Like the Law of Champions doesn't exist. Like we aren't enemies."

"We *aren't* enemies." His quiet declaration sounds so sure. His gaze shifts across my face, tracing the symbol and following the curve of my cheeks before his focus lowers to my lips. "We could be much more to each other." He pauses. "If you want."

"I..." His hands stroke my back, soothing, irritating strokes, because they don't come close to easing the tumult of heat and emotion building inside me.

My mind tells me to be logical. The Law stands. One of us will die.

But my heart is expanding, opening to the possibility that Nathaniel and I can be more than Fell and fae. And my body... dark stars... my body remembers what a single kiss did to me last night.

"Yes," I say.

"Yes?" The small crease in his forehead eases, the slight tension around his mouth fades, and the dark flecks in his chestnut brown eyes seem lighter despite our scarlet and black surroundings.

The weight of uncertainty seems to lift off him, but it only settles down on me.

My smile slips, but his arms tighten around me, as if he reads all of the doubts suddenly crowding into my mind.

"Don't rethink it, Aura," he murmurs. "Don't second-guess what this is."

"The Law—"

"We have two days to defeat it. To find a way for us both to survive. We will reach the end of this alive. Both of us."

"You really believe that?" I ask, searching his eyes for any doubt, any lie.

"I do."

Sudden shivers strike through me. He's like the rock that supports a waterfall, standing despite the torrent raging around him. So certain. So sure. While I feel like a ragged reed of grass caught up in the downpour, twisting and turn-ing. Bound to crash.

He bends his head to kiss the top curve of my lip. Then the other corner. Each touch fleeting. His hand slips to mine as he gives me a mysterious smile. "Come and meet my people."

Taking Flare's reins, he leads him along behind us.

Flare nudges my lower back with his soft nose, demanding attention. I rub his nose for a moment before I allow Nathaniel to lead me onward.

The tunnel slowly bends to the left until we reach another wash of vines and charcoal leaves. This blockage appears so thick that it looks impossible to cut through.

"Null is through here," Nathaniel says.

Knowing we can't touch skin on skin from here on out, I draw my hand from his. He will be able to touch my arms, which are covered with armor, but his arms are bare, so I'll have to be careful I don't reach for him.

He adjusts the pelt around my shoulders while I hesitate in front of the wall of vines. Expanding my senses, I try to detect what lies behind it, but my instincts are frustratingly silent. I can't sense any movement beyond the leaves, not any sound or hint of any living creature.

All I feel is Nathaniel's presence, stronger than ever.

"I can't sense anything," I say.

"Mathilda's magic protects everything behind this veil," he says. "Many lives would be at stake if Cyrian ever found this place." His expression is open, hiding nothing. "Come and see for yourself."

Swallowing, I nod my agreement.

Nathaniel reaches into the wash of greenery to pull back the vines. I catch sight of a green field and many moving shapes beyond us before he pauses, turning to me again.

He casts me a smile that lights up his eyes with rare

humor. "You should know before we go in—they're going to think we're married."

"What? Why?" My shrill questions are drowned in the rush of sound as he curls his hand around my lower bicep and draws me through the opening.

I quickly discover that the real barrier is not the foliage, but rather a magical shield that hums as I step through it.

The magic feels like air across my face, a soft breeze. As soon as I pass beyond it, I'm assailed with sound so sudden that my senses spin.

A large, green courtyard fills the space in front of us, its nearest edge as far as fifty paces away.

Humans stand in neat rows around the courtyard— maybe forty of them. They're all dressed in beige pants and shirts, and they're practicing a series of combat exercises.

I recognize the maneuvers from my own training—a series of defensive moves that build strength and stamina and can be practiced without an opponent.

The humans yell in unison at the end of each quick segment of the exercise, their unified shouts punching the air like a drum.

A village spreads out behind them with more green fields visible beyond that. The Bitter Patch extends all around the perimeter as far as I can see.

Despite the gray sky, the scenery is more alive, more vibrant than any part of Fell country that I've observed so far.

"Nathaniel... What is this place?"

He takes a deep breath, his chest expanding, as if he's testing his ability to speak. He exhales a sound of relief. "I can finally tell you everything."

His smile becomes serious and his hand tightens on my arm.

He spreads his free arm out at the men and women gathered on the grassy courtyard. "This is where I'm building an army to overthrow the King."

CHAPTER 10

*T*he warriors shout in unison as my mind churns.

A human army to kill the King.

There hasn't been a human army since the last battle. Since I annihilated it, to be precise.

Nathaniel told me that King Cyrian uses his hunters to keep the people under control. If Cyrian had tried to build another army, Imatra would have raged across Fell country to cut him—and his soldiers—down. I would have led the charge.

But here... this place... the spells cast around it protect it from detection—from both Cyrian and Imatra.

The humans don't seem to have spotted us yet. They're far enough away that our black clothing will allow us to blend in to the thorny backdrop, but I'm not sure what sort of reception we'll receive once they become aware of our presence.

At the head of the rows of warriors, a tall, blonde woman stands with her back to us. She's also dressed in beige clothing that fits to her curves as she strides along the first row, stopping to speak directly with a dark-haired woman in the first row, guiding the brunette's movements until she perfects the maneuver.

"Where do I fit into this?" I ask Nathaniel.

"You're a Warrior of Luciana," he says. "I went to find you and bring you out of hiding so you would help us."

"That's your story." I give him a pointed look. "But where do I *really* fit into all of this?"

He's quiet as he observes the humans in the distance. "We need your light, Aura. King Cyrian's dark magic is a thousand times stronger than Mathilda's and his malice is worse still. My people have been searching for a light in the darkness for a long time."

Pain crosses his features, but he rolls his shoulders as if he's trying to shake it off. "We need you."

He just finished warning me that if I reveal my true identity, the humans will hunt me down and kill me. Using my power will definitely give me away. "Assuming I'm willing to join your fight, how do I use my power when revealing it will get me killed?"

The corner of his mouth hitches up into a brief smile. "Because we can call it dark magic." He arches his eyebrows at me. "Who knows what Luciana taught you before she died?"

I feel a bit in awe of this woman I never met. "Your mother seems to have a legendary reputation."

"In life and in death," he says. "My people loved her."

A shout rises up in the distance. One of the trainees—the brunette whose technique was being corrected—points in our direction.

"Nathaniel!" She breaks away from the others and runs toward us, causing the blonde to spin in our direction too.

Nathaniel's worried expression disappears. He breaks

into a grin as the brunette sprints across the distance, her brown hair flying out behind her. Her hair tie flies off, but she doesn't seem to care. "Nathaniel's back!"

Behind her, Nathaniel's name is shouted over and over and the formation breaks up in a chaotic ripple. All of the trainees peel away from their rows and run toward us.

I stand my ground as they approach, taking slow, calming breaths. I tell myself I'm a Warrior of Luciana. Supposedly. I just have to remember the new rules: Don't touch Nathaniel, don't use my power, forget my real name.

Damn! I didn't ask Nathaniel what name I should use—and it's too late now.

The brunette hits us first, colliding with Nathaniel so fast that she nearly knocks him over.

I'm not surprised when he merely scoops her up, a deep laugh bursting from him.

She hugs him tightly, her hair flying around her. From a distance, she looked older but up close, I realize she can't be more than fourteen. She's so familiar with him that I wonder if she's family.

The others reach us, crowding around Nathaniel, grinning wildly.

The brunette releases him so the other women can hug him while the men clap him on the back.

My eyes grow wide at the affection they show each other, greeting Nathaniel like a brother while he responds as if they're all family, hugging them back. It's a far warmer reception than fae show each other. Even my brother, Evander, rarely hugs me.

A sudden sharp pain pricks my chest right where my scar is.

Moving slowly so I don't attract attention, I press my hand to the location of my heart, easing the heel of my palm against it. It's the second time in the space of an hour that my heart has hurt. The first was when Mathilda used her power to try to see into my thoughts.

"Dark stars, Nathaniel," the brunette says, her eyes glistening. "You were gone so long. We thought something had happened to you."

He drags her into another hug. "Emily," he says in an admonishing tone. "It would take more than a few mold moths and a couple of wolves to kill me."

I've never heard Nathaniel lie, but he sidesteps the truth far more easily than I expected him to.

Nathaniel sets Emily back on the ground when the crowd separates to allow the blonde woman through.

Up close, she's older than Nathaniel—but maybe only by a few years—and startlingly beautiful. Her golden hair flows past her shoulders all the way to her narrow waist and her eyes are cornflower blue. Combined with high cheekbones and a delicate chin, she is as graceful as a fae, but she wears an expression that reminds me of the most determined fae warrior.

Her smile grows wider as she leans in to kiss Nathaniel on the cheek. "I'm glad you're back. We were worried."

Yesterday, Nathaniel told me that some human women are more beautiful than Bright Ones. Even this woman's voice is like honey.

"Esther," he says, his tone slightly more reserved than it was with the others. "There were some complications, but we're fine."

He glances past Esther, searching the faces of the people around him. "Where's Christiana?"

"She went looking for you," Esther replies. "She's not with you?"

The first hint of worry crosses Nathaniel's expression. "When did she leave?"

"At dawn this morning." Esther places her hand on Nathaniel's arm, her tone soothing. "Don't worry. Your sister knows how to look after herself. She'll be back soon. I'm sure of it."

Nathaniel gives her a nod, but I don't think he agrees with her. I've become attuned to Nathaniel's moods over the last day. The tension in his shoulders tells me he's worried.

By the time Nathaniel turns to me, I've lowered my hand from my heart and composed myself.

As Esther, Emily, and the other humans follow Nathaniel's line of sight to me, I draw myself upright, assuming the posture I've cultivated for years—a Queen's Champion. Untouchable. At the same time, I relax my arms and hands so I don't appear threatening.

The gap between Nathaniel and I grew with the people crowding around him, but now he closes it. "This is one of Luciana's Warriors. The one I told you about. She has agreed to join us."

Silence falls around us as everyone finally focuses on me. I sense the hush extend far back to the village as they study me—starting with my face, then my pelt and armor. Their reactions run the full spectrum from excited to reserved.

Esther pauses in the act of stepping forward, her quick gaze following the lines of mud drawn on my face.

Her posture stiffens for a moment and a shot of surprise breaks her serene expression. She buries it quickly, extending her hand.

"Welcome," she says. "We've been waiting for this day for seven years."

I take her hand briefly. Despite her graceful movements,

her palms are calloused at all the points that indicate she handles weapons on a daily basis.

She squeezes my hand, sizing me up, no doubt discovering that my hand is more calloused than hers.

I give her a reserved smile, wary of reacting to her now-hidden emotions. "It's a pleasure to meet you, Esther."

She clears her throat, staring at my muddy cheeks. "I see you've accepted Nathaniel's name. You're bonded. That's... unexpected."

So that's why Nathaniel said they'd think we're married. It's this damn mark on my face. When he drew it on me, he seemed far too pleased about it.

I hold Esther's gaze, fighting the instinct to cast a glare at Nathaniel. Seven years as the Queen's Champion has taught me how to hide my emotions completely. Nathaniel is the only one who seems to draw them out of me against my will.

"Some of the strongest bonds form quickly," I say, keeping my calm and hoping she'll leave it at that.

"Indeed," she replies, a challenging light entering her eyes. "But quick bonds break just as fast."

My hackles rise, even though I probably shouldn't react. I'm accustomed to hearing what people don't say, reading between the lines of their polite declarations to discover their true motivations.

When we first arrived, Esther was training the others. Whatever the hierarchy is here, she's high up in it, possibly only second to Nathaniel.

Now that I've arrived, I'll displace her and threaten her position—even if I don't intend to.

I maintain eye contact with her as I step forward, conscious of the pelt swishing around my shoulders and the way my armor gleams. "The only things I break are people who threaten me or anyone I care about."

She blinks at me for a moment, and I can see her reassessing her assumptions about me. "Then we're lucky you care about Nathaniel."

She takes a step back. "There will be plenty of time to find out everything else there is to know about you in due course."

She spins on her heel, clapping her hands twice. "Everyone, back to practice! Let's give Luciana Elect some space to settle in and get her bearings. Emily—not you! You will take Flare to the stables and brush him down."

My forehead creases at the name Esther called me— *Luciana Elect*—and I make a mental note to ask Nathaniel about it.

Now that the tension has broken, I'm surprised to find most of the trainees are grinning at me, glancing between Esther and me.

I was worried I might have come across too aggressively, but Emily veers toward me on her way to Flare. She speaks in a not-so-quiet whisper. "It's nice to see someone take Esther on. I can't wait to see you in action." She pauses. "You'll be training us, won't you?"

I give her a nod, making a quick assumption that it's the response I'm supposed to give, even though it twinges my conscience. I won't be here long enough to train anybody.

"Great. Okay, then. I'd better get a wriggle on." She casts a worried glance at Esther, who's impaling her with a dagger-filled glare.

"Get a *what* on?" I ask, confused by her human speech.

She laughs. "I forgot you've been secluded most of your life. I mean I'd better hurry before Esther whips my backside." She dashes toward Flare, who waited patiently during the whole interaction.

"I'm taking care of Flare now," she calls back to Esther, who folds her arms across her chest.

Taking hold of Flare's reins, Emily prepares to lead him away, but I quickly join her, reaching out to rub Flare's nose and press my cheek to his. "Thank you for bringing us here safely."

He bounces his head at me, nickering softly in my ear before I let him go. Emily casts me a final smile before she leads him away.

Nathaniel snags Esther's attention. "Luciana Elect and I need to get some sleep, but I want you to let me know the minute Christiana returns."

She gives him a business-like nod. "I sent scouts out at the same time as she left this morning. They're due back soon. I'll make sure they come straight to you. In the meantime, I'll have food brought to your hut. Perhaps some comfortable clothing for Luciana Elect as well."

"I'd appreciate that," Nathaniel says.

She strides away without a backward glance.

I exhale what feels like a long-held breath.

Nathaniel smiles at me, his eyes crinkled at the corners. "I'll explain everything once we get inside," he says.

I make an unhappy sound in the back of my throat. "Don't expect me to hold all of my questions until we get there."

Walking with him toward the courtyard where the group has resumed training, I ask, "Where did you find all of these people?"

"I've been building Null since I was eighteen." Nathaniel's jaw clenches again and I sense an irrepressible rage growing inside him. "Every person here is someone Cyrian hurt and left for dead. Emily's family was killed by hunters. I pulled her from beneath her mother's body when she was only nine years old."

He points to an older man standing at the edge of the row. "That's Geordie—his wife and baby were killed in front of him and he was strung up in a tree to die. He stayed alive for another minute by resting his foot on a broken branch. I got there just in time to save him."

My heart hurts, a new ache. "This is a village of ghosts. That's why Cyrian doesn't come looking for them?"

"As far as he knows, they're all dead," Nathaniel says, darkness growing in his expression. "I couldn't save everyone."

I reach out to touch his shoulder where his scars are hidden behind his shirt. He told me he asked Mathilda to make a cut—to carve a scar—for every person he lost. "You marked them on your body and carry them with you now."

"Yes."

We've reached the courtyard and the trainees are back at work on their maneuvers.

Despite the affection they showed Nathaniel when he first arrived, they demonstrate their discipline by remaining focused on their tasks, even though Esther isn't here to instruct them. She's disappeared ahead of us into the village.

"What about Esther?" I ask.

"Esther was once part of Cyrian's Court, but she was betrayed by her sister. She doesn't trust anyone easily—and she's very protective of everyone here. Don't worry; she likes you."

I choke at his last statement. "I don't think so."

"She respects your strength." The darkness leaves his expression as he adds, "*Luciana Elect.*"

"Is that who I am now?" I screw up my face with dislike. "It's your mother's name."

He laughs. "Luciana means 'leader.' It's a title. My mother's actual name was Paloma."

"Then what does 'Luciana Elect' mean?"

"'Future leader,'" he says.

I miss a step. "Nathaniel." I shake my head at him. "That's not... I can't..."

I suddenly realize that I'm too close to the trainees to speak plainly, so I quickly swallow my objection.

The trainee Nathaniel pointed out before—Geordie—stops the maneuver he's practicing and gives me a polite smile. "Luciana Elect," he says. "Will you teach us something?"

"Oh... uh..."

The other trainees also turn in my direction, pausing in their practice. I'm suddenly the focus of attention again.

I lean close to Nathaniel and keep my voice down. "I don't want to hurt them."

Geordie's smile widens. "You won't hurt us." He has a mop of blond hair that he flicks out of his eyes, a challenge growing on his face. "We can hold our own."

Nathaniel understands what I mean. I can't lay hands on any of the humans if it chances hurting them and breaking the Law. But of course... that rule doesn't apply to him...

"Why don't we give you a demonstration?" he says to them, his grin growing wide.

His relaxed smile is catching, even though I'm not sure how I feel about engaging him in mock battle right now.

"Sure," I say. "Why not?"

CHAPTER 11

$\mathcal{N}$athaniel catches my arm, careful not to touch my bare skin as he leads me forward.

The trainees back away from the center of the courtyard, creating a wide circle around us. The ground is well-cushioned with soft grass. I quickly gauge how springy the surface is and the extent of the space I will have to move within it.

Nathaniel draws me close with a hurried whisper. "They'll expect us to take a knee and bow. It was my mother's way. No matter how much you hate your opponent, you always show respect." His dark eyes glitter at me. "Just like the respect you showed Calida yesterday."

I draw away from him so that we can take a knee at the same time.

Gliding back to my feet, I quietly remove my pelt, folding it up and laying it on the ground behind me.

My senses expand as my focus narrows.

Nathaniel tilts his head, a quick, challenging movement as I stalk toward him, but a playful smile tugs at his lips.

So that's how it's going to be.

I give him a sweet smile before my fist darts out, testing his reflexes.

He sidesteps the blow—just like he should. He turns his body in a defensive move and catches my covered wrist along its forward trajectory, tugging me so that I would lose my balance if I wasn't ready.

My other palm plants on his chest—my real target. Knocking him onto his back foot, I spin and kick high.

My foot stops a scant inch from his face. It was never my intention to make contact, but he's already caught my ankle, pushing upward.

I happily backflip and somersault away from him.

He strides after me and this time, I know that play is over. Around us, I sense the trainees holding their breath. I guess they also sense that we were just getting warmed up.

Jumping to my feet, I avoid the series of rapid hits he throws my way, retaliating with my own sequence of flat-handed moves and rapid kicks, enjoying testing my strength against an equal partner.

It's been a long time since I've practiced against someone who can hold their own—in a situation where we aren't trying to kill each other.

For the next minute, we trade near hits and careful misses in a sequence that begins to feel a lot like a careful dance between us.

Nathaniel never lands a blow and neither do I, even though we both work up a sweat, our bodies moving at rapid speed—every attack defended and every defense tested.

Finally, Nathaniel leans just a little too far forward and I see an opening that I can't resist.

Stepping into him instead of avoiding the blow, I take his

flat-handed hit across my left shoulder, turning and at the same time hooking my right leg behind his foot.

He wobbles, his eyes widening a split second before I sweep him off his feet.

He lands on his backside while I innocently arch an eyebrow at him.

Grinning up at me, he takes a breath before he bounces back to his feet. "That's enough for now, I think. Back to drills, everyone!"

The trainees audibly exhale, casting smiles at both of us as they rearrange themselves to continue their own practice.

A shout precedes Emily as she runs up to the side of the courtyard, puffing.

"Did I miss it?" Her face falls. "I missed it, didn't I?"

Nathaniel picks up my pelt and hands it to me, inclining his head toward the village.

He squeezes Emily's shoulder as we pass her. "Next time."

"Darn," she says.

As much as I enjoyed the fight, Nathaniel is right to get us moving. There's a whole mountain of questions to which I need answers and I have no doubt he won't speak openly out here.

Esther appears ahead of us on the path as we reach the edge of the village. "I've left food and clothing on your porch," she says to Nathaniel. "Emily took care of Flare. And Maggie is baking a cake to celebrate your bond." She rolls her eyes as she strides away. "I nearly broke a tooth on the last 'cake' she made."

"Maggie is our oldest resident," Nathaniel explains. "She's thirty-five."

Yesterday, Nathaniel told me that the Ebon Rot slowly kills humans once they reach forty years of age. Maggie is only five years away from that.

He leads me past several rows of neat-looking huts, some larger than others. "Maggie doesn't train with the others. But they all help out with cooking and tending to the fields and animals."

He points out the food hall, the kitchen, and the stables as we keep walking.

In the distance on the left of the village, I make out the shapes of cattle and horses. On the right are fields filled with crops, far more vibrant than the fields outside of Null.

Farther back from all of the other buildings sits another hut, larger than the others, which Nathaniel leads me toward.

I shiver as we approach it. It has a porch around the front and is solidly built, but there's a force around it that makes my skin prickle.

Nathaniel brushes my arm. "Do you sense the dark magic? There's an extra layer of protection over my quarters in case Null is ever breached. You can enter only by my invitation. Once inside, we can speak openly. Nobody will hear us."

I take the porch steps slowly one at a time, inhaling the scent of cedar. Nathaniel scoops up the basket at the top of the steps and opens the door with a quiet murmur. "Come inside, Aura Lucidia."

The veil of magic whispers across my skin like it did when I first stepped into Null. It's quiet inside, the outside noises canceled out as soon as Nathaniel closes the door.

The building has a simple layout consisting of a living area with a table, chairs, and a fireplace on the left and a bedroom on the right. There's another smallish room at the back on the right that I assume must be a bathroom.

A wide window on the opposite wall reveals the other side of Null—fields ringed by the Bitter Patch. The crimson-

and-black wilderness is a monstrous sight compared to the earthy tones and simplicity of Nathaniel's home.

"How is it so green here?" I ask.

While I fold my pelt across one of the kitchen chairs, Nathaniel unpacks the contents of the hamper onto the table.

He finishes with a cloth bag that I assume contains fresh clothing. "Cyrian is constantly draining our environment, but his dark magic can't reach inside Null."

Now that we're alone, I rub my eyes. It must be mid-morning. I already had a quick nap in the tunnel through the Bitter Patch on the way here—but fatigue is catching up with me.

"You're Cyrian's Shield. How do you spend time here without him noticing your absence?"

Nathaniel's jaw clenches. "I can come and go—the same way you fly out on Treble when you need to check the border. But I have to be careful. If Cyrian wants something and I'm not at the castle, he sends out a hunter to find me. That's why our scouts are so important. They alert me if a hunter's tracking me. I can't be here as often as I want to be."

He pushes a bowl across the table. It's filled with warm vegetable stew with fresh buttered bread on the side.

He pours water from a flask into the cup beside my bowl while I try not to eat too fast as I fill my empty stomach. I need strength for the conversation ahead of me.

Carefully mopping up the final smudges of stew from my bowl, I try to swallow despite my suddenly dry mouth. "I need to know what your father said that made you come for me."

I meet his eyes, demanding that he answer me. "I'm fae. I need to know what he said to make you believe I would help you."

Nathaniel pauses in the act of breaking his last piece of bread. He stares into his bowl for so long that I don't think he's going to answer me. Then he puts his bread down and silently rises from his seat.

Walking to the mantelpiece over the fireplace, he takes a small box from the top of it and returns to the kitchen table beside me. The tiny case nearly disappears inside his fist.

"My father was holding the contents of this box when he died," Nathaniel says, placing the box on the table.

The container is wooden and circular except for the flat base.

My hand suddenly shakes as I reach to open it. I sense a chasm inside it, as if this tiny box contains a whole universe. A shock of electricity shoots through my chest the moment I hover my fingers over the case. My ears hum and my palm tingles.

At the same time, an empty space opens up inside my chest, a cold, vast expanse spreading at a rapid pace. Shivers run up and down my spine and my breath is suddenly rapid.

My power runs cold inside me, nearly freezing me to the spot.

"Aura?" Nathaniel drops to his knees beside me, searching my face.

I fight my sudden, unexplainable fear as I take off the lid.

The box is lined in black silk just like the scarf I wore to hide my hair before we reached Null.

Nestled inside the silk lining is a tiny, glittering fragment of stone. It's very small, the slightest sliver of rock.

Crescent-shaped, just like the scar across my heart.

CHAPTER 12

*M*y power sizzles through my hand, glowing brightly as I reach for the stone.

It's so thin that I could press my finger against it and it would fit against the curve of my fingertip.

I stop an inch away from connecting with it.

"I've carried that stone with me every day of my life since my father died," Nathaniel says. "I left it behind for the first time yesterday morning so I would be sure it was safe."

He clasps my arm, still searching my face—for what, I'm not sure, but he's looking at me the same way he did before I stopped breathing at the burn site.

"What did your father say?" I ask, my forefinger hovering over the stone.

The energy within the box is too much. I don't know what this stone has to do with me, or why it's the same shape and size as the scar on my chest, but my heart is thumping hard and I can't control my breathing.

Panic threatens to overwhelm me, panic like I've never experienced before.

"He said you don't belong to them."

I focus on Nathaniel, on the flecks in his eyes and the scent of caramel. I suck his scent into my lungs like a lifeline, filling my senses with it in an attempt to drown out the magnetic pull of the stone.

I'm suddenly aware of the smudges of dirt across his shirt and the way his sleeves pull across his biceps as he slides his arms around my waist and pulls me up and away from the box.

My head clears the farther he draws me from the stone.

"Belong... to whom?" I ask.

"The fae," he says. "He made me promise to tell you: You don't belong to them."

"Wh-Why would he say something like that?"

Nathaniel strokes my hair, pulling me closer while I glow with every stroke, my heartbeat slowing and my breathing less irregular as his touch calms me.

"I don't know, Aura. I've searched for answers but never found them." His voice is a deep rumble resonating through me. He's finally giving me answers, but they only bring more questions. "My father told me I had to find the girl with hair whiter than bone."

"But... why?"

"Because you have the power to turn the war."

I shake hard in Nathaniel's arms, my heart resuming its unnaturally fast rhythm.

I don't understand what Nathaniel said about not belonging to the fae, but I do understand my power and its capacity to kill. It explains why Mathilda thought Nathaniel was supposed to end me.

"Your father survived the blast," I say. "He saw what I did to your people. Despite that, he told you to come for me—to find me—but not to kill me? How could he want me to live after all that?"

I search Nathaniel's eyes for answers—as keenly as he was searching mine before—following the fall of his hair across his cheeks.

"I don't have the answers you need, Aura," he says. "I've grappled with my father's final words my whole life, thought about them nearly every waking moment, trying to understand what he meant. All I knew for sure was that I had to come for you. That you have the power to help us. My father didn't see you as an enemy, and I have to trust that he was right about that."

"But I *was* your enemy!" I push against Nathaniel's chest, pressing my palms hard up against his muscles, trying to make him acknowledge that we're on different sides, that we will hurt each other. "For years! I blamed your people for killing my parents. I hated the Fell!"

He refuses to let me go, his gaze burning me with an intensity I can't push away. "Not anymore. You don't hate me anymore."

Anger and confusion swirl inside me as his hand rises to curl around the base of my head, tangling in my hair. His thumb strokes my neck, making my heart beat faster, but not from fear.

"I have to tell you something," he says, the quietness of his voice making me stop still.

I drag in air as he continues to hold me tightly, waiting for him to speak.

"I hated you once too," he says. "The day you became the Queen's Champion was the day I lost everything. You were the catalyst—this constant catalyst in my life—that brought pain and loss. My father's death. Losing my name. Forced to become Cyrian's Shield. Losing my..."

He takes a deep breath. Despite what he said, the glow around his hand brightens and fades as he continues to drag his fingers through my hair and across my neck and shoulders, exploring my shape.

"I thought about killing you instead of honoring my father's dying wish," he says. "Yesterday morning, I didn't know what I was going to do. I hadn't decided. I told myself that I just wanted to see your face. That I would know when I looked into your eyes."

His expression softens, the tension around his eyes fading. "And I did."

"What did you know?" I whisper.

"That you are the center point of my life. Every ripple, every consequence, belongs to you. Without you, my world would be torn apart. And now..." He pulls his fingers across my cheek, the sandpapery mud catching and dragging, but it doesn't hurt, tingling instead. "Now our lives are bound together."

The stone is suddenly forgotten. Mathilda said that Nathaniel's family name is now written on my body in the most fundamental bond of loyalty. Esther also said we were bonded. And Nathaniel said everyone would think we were married.

But surely he doesn't mean we *actually* are.

"Did you bind me to you when you drew on my face?" I ask.

Nathaniel's lips curve up into a slow smile. "I danced with you, I wrote my family name on your face, and then you said *yes*."

"Wait..." The world suddenly spins around me. My heart lurches and my stomach drops. "We're really married."

"By human law—old law. Yes."

My power zaps through my hands as I shove him away from me.

He lets me go just in time before I turn his bones into dust. Stepping back with an unapologetic smile, he folds his big arms across his chest and watches me pace the room.

Back and forth, my power crackles around my torso, arms, and legs as I move, swirling around me.

I stop and point my fist at him. "We're... *really*... married?"

His grin grows broader. "Like I said... you said *yes*."

My eyes narrow to angry slits. "An answer doesn't mean anything if I don't understand the question."

He arches an eyebrow at me. "Then what were you saying *yes* to?"

Dark stars.

He slowly prowls toward me, keeping an eye on the sharp bolts of my light. "Why don't we start this again and see if we end up somewhere different?"

He stops in front of me, daring me to strike as he holds out his hand. "Will you dance with me?"

Clamping down on my power, I step right up to him, anger boiling inside me.

At least, I think it's anger.

From the moment he appeared out of the mist, Nathaniel has made me question everything—everything I knew about my world and my life. He even made me question my heart, to dive beneath the icy layers I carefully built to protect my thoughts.

Last night, I lay on the surface of the Spinning Lake with him and we watched the water dance far beneath us.

For the first time in years, I felt connected to something —*him*.

I fight my pride and my fears and slide my hand into his,

my palm rasping against his, my heart thudding a hard beat inside me.

He doesn't hesitate, catching me firmly around my waist before spinning me out and back again, pulling me so close that I press hard up against his thighs and chest.

Last night, his movements were cautious. Careful at first. But now they have an intensity, a certainty to them.

He moves me backward, his hands and arms guiding my movements before he spins me again, his movements short and sharp, snapping me right back to him.

I recognize the turns now—especially when he spins me out only to pull me back in—the way he creates gaps only to close them. It's as if he's telling me that no matter how far away I am, he will always be there when I come back.

I will always *want* to come back.

Last night, dancing with him made me feel light, recklessly happy, but now my steps are weighted. Every press and pull triggers my heart to thud and my breathing to increase. Every rhythmic movement reminds me of the brush of his lips on mine, the grip of his hands around my hips, and the warmth of his mouth.

He pulls me to a stop, his head tilted to mine, his gaze a constant burn.

Sliding his hand down the back of my thigh, he hooks my leg around his hips and bends me backward at the waist, gently swaying with me as my back arches. Last night, he drew me up again within moments, but this time, he bends with me, planting a lingering kiss between my breasts.

I barely feel it through my armor.

An excruciating absence of sensation.

He drags me upward, my leg still hooked around his hip, hard up against his chest so that my head tilts back and my now-black hair falls across his arms.

His burning gaze never leaves my face as he drops his weight, urging my knees to bend. I'm not sure what he's doing—this wasn't a move from the dance last night—until he rapidly hooks his free hand beneath my other thigh and hooks my other leg around his hip.

I gasp as he rises, discovering that his placement of my body against his was intensely deliberate, the pressure on the sensitive center between my legs increasing so much that even my armor doesn't stop me from enjoying his body's response to mine.

My fingers splay and curl against his back as every indrawn breath makes our bodies press and ease against each other.

His lips graze across my cheek right where the mud pulls at my skin.

"Let's wash this off so we can start over," he says, his voice a deep rumble.

CHAPTER 13

*L*ifting me higher around his waist, Nathaniel carries me into the smaller room I assumed was a bathroom.

Like the rest of the hut, this room is simply furnished. A wooden chair sits in the nearest corner on the left. A claw-foot bath rests in the center with a cast-iron water pump located at the back of it, its spout situated directly above the end of the bath. A small wooden table holds towels and bars of soap.

Nathaniel lowers me onto the chair, but his hands slide down my ribs to grip my hips on either side.

His lips nudge my cheek, then my jaw, trailing down my neck, planting kisses between my breasts and down my stomach. Too light for me to feel. *Damn armor.*

Stopping above my pelvis, his fingers drag from my hips along the tops of my thighs before he stands and prowls toward the bath.

He pauses in the middle of the room before he half-turns back to me. "The door is open, Aura. Remember that."

I glance at the opening. He's telling me that I can leave whenever I want. He's not trapping me here.

I stay right where I am.

He pumps the lever, his biceps tensing, and seconds later, water pours into the bath.

He tests it with a smile. "We source our bathing water from a natural hot spring. It's warm enough."

Continuing to pump the lever, he fills the bath full enough that the water level will rise to the top if someone gets into it. Then he dips a small cloth into the water, squeezes out the excess liquid, and carries it to me.

He kneels in front of me, turning the cloth over in his hands. I struggle to read his expression. Or maybe I don't want to because it suddenly hurts my heart.

"You'll have to wipe my name off yourself," he says, looking up at me. "I can't do it."

I take the cloth from him, my fingers sliding across his. The material is soft and warm. I'm grateful it's not cold.

Rising to my feet while he continues to kneel in front of me, I place the cloth onto the chair behind me before I reach for the clasps down the left side of my armor.

He gives me a questioning look, glancing at the abandoned cloth, but I remain quiet, my decisions falling heavily on my heart.

Underneath my armor, I'm only wearing the black underwear that I wore to the ball. There's nothing substantial about the skimpy lace. It doesn't hide a thing, but it won't be the first time he's seen me naked.

I peel the armor down my torso to my waist before slipping out of my boots and kicking them to the side. Dragging my armor down past my backside, I take care not to kick Nathaniel as I drop back to the chair to pull the black suit off my legs.

He watches every movement, his hands planted flat on the top of his kneeling thighs. There's no window here, just a small skylight in the ceiling, and the shadows play across his face. Whatever he's thinking, he's hiding it.

I desperately want to know his thoughts, but he's frustratingly silent. I guess I am too. Both of us pulling and pushing at the things we want but can't have.

Unclasping my bra at the back, I drop it to the floor, the scanty material barely making a sound as it floats downward.

I have no illusions of beauty. My body is a weapon. My hands are for holding daggers and swords. My legs are for running, leaping, and kicking. My torso is a shield and my mind is for strategizing, assessing my opponent's weaknesses, and planning my next move.

The only moment I felt truly beautiful was when Nathaniel turned me to face the mirror while he stroked my cheek. His touch lit me up, alive for the first time. Briefly. Until he stopped.

I stand up again and remove my underpants, now completely naked. Then I retrieve the cloth and walk to the bath, my bare feet slapping the wooden floor.

He doesn't reach for me or stop me, twisting only to watch me.

With my back to him, I pause at the side of the bath to ask a question. "Will the sap wash off my hair?"

His voice is a husky murmur. "Only if you wash it with soap many times. Water alone doesn't strip the color."

Now that I'm facing away from him, it's hard to turn around, but I make myself face him again before I step into the bath and lower myself into the water.

All the way in.

The warm liquid closes over my face.

Nathaniel and the world disappear.

It's been a long time since I indulged in a bath. Immersing myself and closing my eyes is the closest I can get to the *nothing* that I need around me so that I can fall asleep.

That is, unless Nathaniel is there to stroke my hair or simply stand under running water—both times at which I fell asleep unguarded and unexpectedly in his presence.

The cloth feels like a dagger in my hand, but the mud is already dissolving from my face.

A few rapid scrubs remove it completely.

His family name is gone.

I exhale under the water and open my eyes, still gripping the material. The bubbles of my expelled breath meander to the surface before they burst. Little dreams of unreachable *wants* self-destruct above me.

My eyes burn as I arch back up, breaking the surface to inhale a deep breath. He won't see my tears in the wash of water streaming down my cheeks, so I'm not afraid to let them fall.

He stands at the edge of the bath, a massive form blocking out the light, his expression unreadable as his gaze rakes across my bare face, ending at the corner of my right eye.

His flinty expression softens as he follows the trickle of water down my cheek and neck to the surface of the water.

The light shines around me again as he kneels at the side of the bath and reaches across to press his forefinger to curve of my cheekbone.

"Your tears follow the shape of the moon," he says, stroking a soft arc, as if he could draw his name with water.

I can't seem to hide anything from him. Somehow, my usual defenses don't work. He sees right through my barriers and boundaries. My facades.

His finger follows a careful trail down my neck, across

my shoulder, tracing a dangerous course lower still. His wrist and arm immerse as he follows the soft outer curve of my breast, brushing against my ribs to my waist, where his fingers splay out across my lower stomach and come to a rest at the top of my thigh.

A glowing spark of my power chases his touch, flickers of starlight burning across my skin under the water, my own body betraying me as I fight the desire to pull him into the bath with me.

With a slow smile, he reaches across with his other hand, tracing the curve of my other cheek, my neck, playing across the hair slicked across my shoulder.

He tugs my tresses gently across my breast as he dares to skim across them, stroking his entire palm down across my stomach until both of his arms are immersed and his palms rest across the tops of my legs.

Drawing them apart just the slightest, he strokes the inside of my thighs.

The whole time, he doesn't take his eyes off my face, tracing my body by feel alone. Or maybe by memory.

"Let me give you my family name," he says, refusing to release me from his gaze.

My breathing is erratic. Uneven. Out of control. Like the needy burn aching in my center.

I squeeze my eyes shut as he continues to explore every part of my inner thighs all the way from the underside, along the join at the top of my legs, to the curve at the bottom of my hips.

"Let me give you my name..." he repeats, leaning forward without putting pressure on my legs. His thumb brushes across my center, sending a shock like electricity through me. "Let me give you what you want."

"That's not fair," I whisper, trying to breathe. "Being married is about more than sex."

His thumb returns to my center, but this time, he doesn't move it back or forth.

It's up to me whether I take advantage of the position of his hand.

A challenge.

"You're right," he says, his voice rough. Suddenly emotional. His jaw clenches. "It's about trusting someone enough to fall off a thunderbird with them. Trusting them enough to run into an unknown wilderness with them. We've both shown trust, Aura. The kind of trust many people never find in an entire lifetime, but we built it in a day."

I fight my body, fight the temptation to rock against his hand, because if I do, it will give him permission to make me his. "But the Law of Ch—"

"Forget the Law! Forget everything else. If nothing else existed outside this hut—no fae, no Fell, no Queens or Kings, no duty. If it were just you and me, what would you choose?"

"Just you and me?" I ask. "No fae. No Fell."

He nods, his eyes searching mine, his full lips drawn into a vulnerable line. "I need to know."

Oh, dear stars, help me.

I rock against his hand, sensation exploding through me, so strong that I fight to breathe. Fight to speak. "I would ask you to write your name on every inch of my body."

CHAPTER 14

*N*athaniel wrenches his arms out of the water, splashing liquid around us as he arches back to rip off his shirt.

In another heartbeat, his arms plunge back into the water, sliding beneath my back, dragging me up and out of the bath and up against him.

Liquid sloshes across the floor, pouring down his legs and across his feet as he hooks one arm under my knees, the other behind my shoulders.

He doesn't pause for breath and he doesn't slow down, carrying me from the bathroom into the bedroom. Aside from the bed, it contains only a small chest of drawers and a closet, not unlike my room in Bright.

He slides me to my feet, the pressure between us setting my senses alight. His expression is intent, unwavering, and I shiver as I realize that whatever he intends right now, nothing will stop him from doing it.

"Trust me," he says, more a command than a request.

"I do."

As soon as I speak, he spins me so I'm facing away from him, but he releases my hips just as quickly, the gap between us filling with cold air as he steps to the side.

Reaching past me, he wrenches a blanket off the bed and wraps it around my shoulders to keep me warm. It's large enough that it reaches my feet and covers me completely.

Still standing behind me, he draws my wet hair across my back and positions it across my right shoulder, leaving it to drip down the front of the blanket.

Then he tugs the blanket down to expose my left shoulder.

I gasp as he drops a kiss against my bared shoulder blade. His touch is not light like before, but demanding, his lips tasting my skin before he draws back.

"Stay there."

I count my heartbeats as he steps to the drawers, opens the bottom one, and pulls out a small bottle. Inky gold liquid swirls inside it that reminds me of molten metal.

Striding back to me, he removes the lid and drops it onto the bed. Placing his finger over the small opening, he tips the liquid over the forefinger of his right hand.

Still intent on my shoulder, his finger sweeps across my skin. Three strokes on the right—the rays of the sun—and a strong curve on the left—the shape of the moon.

But then he surprises me by making another mark, one he didn't make before—a press of his finger in the center of the symbol.

I shiver as he blows across the ink to help it dry, his breath whispering back and forth across my skin.

Wrapping his free arm around my waist, he turns me back to face him. I meet the intensity in his eyes as he propels me back to the edge of the bed, moving me like he's dancing with me again.

When I bump against it, he eases me down so I'm sitting on its edge.

His movements now are determined and intent. With a challenging smile, he eases my left knee to the side, his hand slipping beneath the blanket to press firmly against the inside of my thigh so he can kneel between my legs.

Despite the brief stroke of his fingers, he removes his hand, remaining focused on my left shoulder, this time around the location of my heart.

Tugging the blanket lower so it barely conceals my breast, he kisses the scar that sits above my heart, his lips warm and soft, but just as demanding as when he kissed my back.

Drawing back, he paints his name across my heart—three rays on the right—before he sweeps slowly across the upper curve of my breast, his touch lingering in a way that makes my toes curl against the wooden floor.

He presses his finger above the curve of my scar, a nearly perfect circle in the middle of his family name.

"This is you," he says, meeting my eyes. "The center of my world."

Droplets of water cling to his chest. His jaw is damp from pressing against my hair. The bottle is still gripped firmly in his hand, so I know he's not finished marking me.

Even so, I edge forward, duck under his chin, and plant a kiss at the edge of his jaw, inhaling the intoxicating caramel scent of his skin as I graze my lips against his stubble. "You missed a spot."

A crease appears on his forehead at my declaration.

I pull back and tug the blanket down to my waist, pointing to the space beneath my right breast. "Here."

The crease in his forehead vanishes. In a single determined stroke, his left hand follows the curve of my breast down to rest across my ribs.

I gasp at the sensations that shoot through to my center. Every time he touches me, every stroke is like fanning flames, but nothing comes close to easing the ache growing inside me.

"Here too," I whisper, dragging the blanket away from my waist and pointing to the lower curve of my hip.

The corner of his mouth hitches up into a sudden half-smile, but he gives me a firm shake of his head. *No.*

Damn.

My body is beyond aching.

He tips the bottle one more time before he replaces the lid and reaches for my face.

I close my eyes as his finger sweeps across my cheeks in firm movements. No gentle strokes. His palm cups my jaw, my chin, and my neck in turns, branding my entire face, even though he's only drawing on parts of it.

He finally presses his fingertip against the space between my eyebrows, leaving what I imagine looks like a golden jewel on my forehead.

His head tilts to mine so he can blow across the ink, casting shivery sensations through me so intense that goosebumps form and my stomach tightens. I can't stop the moan that escapes from my mouth, needing release.

Dark stars. I fight the instinct to rock into him, to shift forward and demand the warmth of his body against mine.

His hands grip me firmly, compelling me to stay where I am.

"The ink isn't allowed to smudge," he says, releasing me to slide his hands through my hair, drawing the strands more firmly across my right shoulder. "That means we have to take care until it dries."

I now wear his name on both the back and front of my left shoulder, along with my face.

I'll smudge it if I lie down on either side.

I'll smudge it if my hair falls across it.

He could smudge it if he kisses me on either side of my mouth.

Tipping his head to the side, he very carefully fits a kiss to the central curve of my lips, nudging them apart to taste the soft dip of my upper lip. At the same time, he firmly grips my right shoulder so I can't lean into him.

I let out a frustrated groan that turns into a heated inhale when he drags his palm down my right side to rest across my breast, his fingers tangling half in my hair, half cupping my curves.

His lips hover above mine, but his breathing is not in control anymore.

"When I came for you, I had no idea I'd find a strong, complicated, beautiful woman who challenges everything I do and say," he says. "I've already chosen you, Aura. All that remains is for you to choose me."

He dips his head, tastes my upper lip again. His thumb grazes across my breast. I spiral beneath his touch, my back arching, reaching for his torso, needing to drag him up against me and close the gap, even though he stops me, holding me tightly and forcing me to remain where I am.

"Say *yes*," he whispers.

Saying *yes* means accepting the consequences of loving him. The consequences of loving him will kill me. He wants me to make a decision based only on us, but everything outside this place makes a difference too.

He wants me to forget about the Law of Champions and be with him, but I can't.

He wants me to fight for his people, but I can't.

He wants to claim me—has already claimed me—but I can't let him.

"All we have is now, Aura," he says, compelling me to listen to him. "Nothing else is certain. Tomorrow isn't certain. But I promise you, I will die before I let anything happen to you."

My eyes fly wide. The only way I won't die in the final fight is if I beat him... or if he *chooses* to let me kill him.

"No!" My power shrieks through me and I shove him away from me so hard that he loses his balance and lands on his backside.

Even leaning back on his hands, he somehow manages to appear in control, muscles tensed, eyes alight, lethally dangerous despite the fact that I knocked him on his ass.

The bright flash of starlight fades, leaving the room somehow darker as I stand over him.

My sudden movement upset the blanket and it slips from my waist, one side barely clinging to my hip, but I don't care that I'm fully naked again.

"You will not die for me, Nathaniel Shield," I say through gritted teeth, a hot mess of stormy rage rising inside me. "At the end of the third day, you will fight me with all of your strength. You will strike and cleave and hurt me. You *will* try to tear me apart. You will fight me as your enemy because that's what I'll be."

Yesterday, he told me that he and I would grapple against each other, fight our honor, fight our hearts, and struggle to do what we need to do, right up until the bloody end.

He jumps back to his feet, moving with stealth, his

powerful legs bringing him closer with each step, dangerously close despite the tingle of power in my fingertips, starlight swirling around my hands and threatening to strike again.

He speaks forcefully. "If I promise to fight you on the last day with every power within me, will you choose me?" he asks. "Even if I also promise to protect you against everyone else before then?"

My breathing is erratic. My heart pounds. He's offering to love me for what remains of the last two days we have left, to protect me from whatever threatens us. And then, on the final day, to fight me as he should.

I place all of the strength of my power into my voice. "You will promise me, Nathaniel. And you won't lie."

He watches me like a prowling wolf. "I promise you."

I shoot back. "Yes."

He halts. The friction between us increases as he registers my response. His gaze burns a line from my bare toes to my hair slung over my shoulder, to my eyes and lips, taking in every inch of me.

Two powerful strides bring him to me.

Sweeping the clinging blanket away from my side, he grips both of my hips, his calloused palms resting against the tops of my thighs, before he propels me back toward the edge of the bed, but this time, he turns us so that he's the one bumping the edge of it.

He lets me go, only to remove his clothing, discarding his boots and pants and kicking them to the side before he pulls me toward him again.

One hand on my hip. The other on my right shoulder.

"No smudges." He growls, sinking onto the edge of the bed and pulling me with him.

Lifting one leg after the other, I climb onto the bed as he

guides me forward, one knee on either side of his thighs while he continues to grip both my hip and my shoulder.

He stops me before I can sink downward, applying force to my hip that pins me above him, my legs apart, straddling him in a position that leaves me more vulnerable than I've ever been.

"Trust me," he whispers.

His breathing is frustratingly even again. One corner of his mouth hitches into a smile, his lips slightly parted as he shifts both of his hands. One to splay around my torso across my breast. The other stroking down to my center, easing across my sensitive folds before sliding a finger inside me.

I shiver and rock against his hand, moving on instinct as pleasure strikes through me. My back arches and I plant my hands against his shoulders, anchoring myself as moans escape my mouth.

My eyes fly open when he slips his finger from me, only to slide two fingers in. Intense sensation bursts through me and it feels like I'm going to tear apart as he gives me control, allowing me to slide slowly down onto his hand.

His grip tightens around my torso and his voice is gruff, suddenly questioning. "Aura... have you done this before?"

I attempt to form coherent speech as I move ever-so-slowly against him. "Once. I think. I don't remember it."

He looks thoughtful, maybe even concerned, and I know what he's thinking—how can I not remember? I can't explain that I passed out in the middle. I was drunk on bluebells at the Ball after I ascended to Champion. It was a willing encounter but I didn't know the fae's name, woke up alone, and never saw him again.

The muscle in Nathaniel's jaw clenches. "You'll remember this, I promise you."

His voice resonates through me like a caress.

I lean forward to press my lips against his, needing his mouth. He groans low in the back of his throat as my tongue darts between his lips, proving that he's not as in control as he appears.

His mouth is intoxicating.

His scent fills my head.

My power responds by flickering around us, glowing brightly in a thin thread like a ribbon curling around and between us in one continuous strand.

Last night, my release was nearly instant, a mere plunge of his tongue into my mouth. I seek that relief again, even though I'm not ready for the connection between us to end.

He refuses to open his mouth to mine despite my insistent kisses, a wild smile growing across his lips as his fingers slide out of me.

Taking hold of my hips, he finally uses his strength to put me where he wants me, angling my hips so he can slide inside me, drawing me down onto him with one strong thrust.

I gasp. Scream. Inhale. Don't know which.

Pure pleasure bursts through me. Starlight strikes the air, the ribbon snaking around his torso lighting up his chest and heart.

A thread of white light shoots through him, spearing across the gap between us and piercing my own heart like a needle, threading us together.

I arch back as he controls my movements by lifting and driving my hips to the rhythm he wants. Every beat strikes through me, breaking apart my foundations, shaking every doubt, every question from my mind.

"Aura."

The sound of my name on his lips, the curve of his mouth

as he speaks it, the rapid rise and fall of his hard chest beneath my hands, the wild dark in his eyes…

I wrench my hips from his grip, control the thrust, and shatter so hard around him that my world tears apart.

He tenses, pauses—then his fingers curl around my hips again as he crashes with me.

I drag air into my chest, my palms slick with sweat against his muscles, my fingertips slipping to his stomach as I ride the waves, ripples of pleasure that continue to ebb throughout my entire body for long moments after as I sink toward him.

At the last moment, the golden mark glitters at the edge of my vision and worry strikes through me that we smeared them.

The only mark I can see is the one above my heart.

It's in perfect condition.

"No smudges," I declare, meeting Nathaniel's stormy eyes.

"Fuck the smudges," he says, hooking my legs around his waist, wrapping his arms around me, and flipping me onto my back.

His hand rakes across the ink over my heart before he rears back to check his palm.

"Dry."

His lips curl up into a smile before his mouth crashes against mine, driving my lips apart, finally kissing me fully.

My thighs clench around him, making him groan. When his tongue plunges into my mouth, I arch and shatter again, this time low and soft, but just as complete.

Gasping for breath, I stare up at him, wide-eyed. My body is wildly out of my control, determined to shock me.

To shock him, too.

"Dark stars, Aura." He stares down at me before he leans

on one elbow to free up his hand and carefully brush his thumb across my upper lip.

The way he touches my mouth now is as if he sees it as some sort of weapon.

His eyelids lower a little as his smile becomes incredibly lazy. "If that's all it takes…"

"Yes," I whisper.

He draws me back into his arms, tangles his fingers in my hair, and starts all over again.

CHAPTER 15

I resist the urge to trace my finger across Nathaniel's jaw as he sleeps.

I'm curled up in his arms, our legs tangled, the weight of his upper arm heavy across my torso.

It must be close to lunchtime by now. Nathaniel has slept for a few precious hours, but I can't close my eyes, even though the room is as dark as he could make it for me.

He nailed rugs across the windows, took everything out of the room, made it as empty and uncluttered as possible.

But there's no stopping the glow between us and I refuse to shift to the far side of the bed.

Not only that... My mind won't let me rest. Every minute with Nathaniel now is precious. The Vanem Dragon said that by the time we fight, we will have walked a thousand miles in each other's shoes. We will understand each other's hearts and know the other better than we know ourselves.

Nathaniel wants me to fight for his people, to help free them from Cyrian's rule, but the question that burns me is: *What then?*

He stirs beside me, tugging me closer, his strong arms compelling me to curl up against him.

"Can't sleep?" he murmurs against my hair.

I shake my head. I often stay awake until after lunch. I'm used to functioning on as little as three hours of sleep each day, but I'll definitely need to sleep between the second and sixth hours of the afternoon so I'm ready to wake up at dusk when the sun sinks below the horizon.

He lets out a low, soft laugh. "Dark stars, woman. I was sure you were exhausted."

I smile against his shoulder, tipping my head back to see him. I can just make out the light playing in his eyes in the darkened room.

"We have less than two days left to fight Cyrian," I whisper.

He's suddenly awake. "Straight to the point."

I brush my fingers against his jaw, casting light between us as I pin him with my gaze. A Champion's gaze. "I've trained in strategy since I was ten years old. Whatever you plan to do, I've destroyed your timeline by invoking the Law of Champions."

I gesture in the general direction of the courtyard. "Are your people ready to fight?"

I roll back as he props himself up on one elbow, my light catching the shape of his broad shoulders and biceps.

"Yes," he says. "That's why I came for you. We've been working on the attack strategy for the last year, right down to the last detail. We plan to attack the castle under the cover of night."

"It has to be tonight," I say. "Tomorrow is too late."

He exhales slowly. "You'll help us?"

"Of course."

He pushes me back, looming over me, his voice fierce.

"You understand that my people will kill you if they find out who you really are?"

"I understand."

"And you're still willing to fight for them?"

I peer up at him. "Why are you so surprised? I'm your wife. Not to mention, I go where you go. Tell me what I need to know—what I need to do—and I'll do it."

He suddenly crushes his lips to mine but pulls back before the distraction becomes too much. He has already showed me that he's determined to learn every nuance of my body and my responses.

"We need my sister," he says. "She's an essential part of the plan."

He hasn't told me the details of the plan yet, but I trust that he will. I haven't met his sister and I'm filled with an unfamiliar flood of nerves. Until now, I haven't cared what anyone thought about me and it scares me that I suddenly do.

"Esther said your scouts were due back a while ago. They should have reported to you already, but nobody's come knocking on your door."

"They probably don't want to interrupt me," he says, but he doesn't sound convinced.

I reach up to place both of my hands against his cheeks. "You've been hiding your worry, but it's time to let me help you. Unless your sister and your scouts are eating lunch in the food hall right now, then we need to go out and find them."

He takes another look at me, a hint of admiration entering his eyes. "You're already thinking like a human commander."

"In Bright, I commanded three sets of guards—Day, Night, and Border. I knew everything about their movements and their whereabouts at all times. Scouts have designated reporting times for a reason—if they don't report in, then something's wrong." Again, I press my hands to his face. "Nathaniel, let me be an asset to you. You can use my skills."

His expression grows fierce and unforgiving. "You're already a gift to me, Aura."

My chest floods with warmth. The stroke of his hand down my side to my thigh fills me with another kind of heat.

Too soon, he says, "We need to get moving."

He pulls me with him off the bed, tugging me close. Despite his efficient movements, he drops kisses on my shoulders and neck as he throws open his closet and grabs some fresh clothing.

I catch sight of a multitude of weapons—more weapons than clothes, in fact—before he whisks me into the living area to scoop up the extra clothing Esther brought for me.

He passes me the water flask at the same time. "Hydration, bathroom, clothing, food. Then we check if the scouts are back," he says. "In that order."

I arch an eyebrow at him, prepared to let him boss me around, especially when he follows up his order with another disarming kiss on the corner of my lips.

Taking my hand, he seems perfectly comfortable prowling around butt naked in all his chiseled glory. Damn human is perfect from the top of his head to his toes.

Once we're back in the bathroom, we use the facilities without embarrassing each other—a skill we've had to acquire quickly.

Nathaniel casts a regretful glance at the bath as I pull on my new underwear. I've only got the bra half-clipped when he pulls me to his chest and places a lingering kiss on my lips.

"If we had time," he says, "I would fill the bath again and this time, we'd both enjoy it."

I step back before I decide it's worth the delay, securing the bra in place and pulling on the underpants before my need for his body overcomes my common sense.

I'm already glowing all over the place, spilling starlight across the bathroom in languid swirls.

"The marks won't wash off?" I ask, focusing on my question to push aside the heat building inside my body.

"The wedding ink is a kind of lacquer, water resistant," he says, pulling on the long, black pants and black shirt he chose. "My mother gave it to me before she died. It will wash off in time. But not too soon."

The clothing that Esther brought for me consists of the same fitted beige training gear they were all wearing. It's soft and supple, but I hesitate to pull it on.

"If there's a chance we'll need to leave Null to search for your sister, I should wear my armor instead of this," I say.

Nathaniel reaches for my black armor, which is slung over the chair in the corner. "Does your armor contain any active magic?"

I consider his question. "You're trying to decide if Cyrian will be able to sense it?"

He nods. "You would need to be close by, but your power will be like a beacon to him. We'll have to be very careful tonight."

"How close do I need to be to him before he'll sense me?"

Nathaniel shakes his head. "I'm not sure. Mathilda sensed you from a quarter mile away, but that was because of her acute sensitivity to pain. Cyrian doesn't have that ability. In fact… pain has no effect on him. I think you'll have to be in the same room as him."

He runs his hand over the shoulder of the armor. "But if your armor is magical, then he's more likely to detect you."

I reach for the suit. "Magic was used to harden the outer coating and make the surface blade resistant. But it isn't magical in the sense that it will activate to protect me. It doesn't store magic or anything like that. I think I'm safer in this than in human clothing."

Nathaniel nods. "I want you to be as safe as you can be."

I tilt back my head to meet his fierce eyes. "What if Cyrian finds out about the Law of Champions?"

Nathaniel's expression hardens. "He will torture you in every way possible without spilling a drop of your blood."

I reach up to Nathaniel's face, to the crease across his forehead and suddenly severe line of his lips. "I'm more powerful than he is—"

"He's human, Aura. Mathilda is a witch, so you could defend yourself against her. But you can't touch Cyrian. He's a human who has learned how to make dark magic a part of his soul. He's not a magical being."

Until the final fight between Nathaniel and me, I'm not allowed to hurt a human in any way. The consequence is my death.

Humans, on the other hand, can hurt me as much as they like as long as they don't spill a drop of my blood.

It's a cruel and lopsided aspect of the Law. It's designed to make my path as hard as it can be. Nathaniel spent the last day under the threat of death if he hurt a fae.

Now it's my turn to fear death while I'm surrounded by humans.

Surviving until the final fight is half the battle.

None of this was part of Nathaniel's plan. I was the one who invoked the Law and bound us to these rules.

If it weren't for the Law, I would be able to fight Cyrian

with all of my power—assuming the humans don't tear me apart first.

No matter how much regret I feel, Nathaniel's frustration must be a thousand times worse than mine right now.

My voice is bleak. "Then... how can I possibly help you tonight? He'll sense me when I'm nearby, which makes me a liability, and I can't use my power to kill him, which makes me useless."

"The same way you protected me from the wolves," Nathaniel says, his certainty grounding me and giving me purpose. "Your power is a shield. If you shield me from Cyrian's dark magic, I can kill him. But you must not use your power until I have a real chance. If we fail to kill him and he knows who you are, he won't stop until he's destroyed you."

I've felt more fear in the last day than I've ever felt in my life, but my fear has been for Nathaniel. Now, dread builds inside my stomach again. Mathilda predicted that both Nathaniel and I would experience pain in the coming hours.

I try to shake off my fears as Nathaniel's arms encircle me.

"I need to know one thing." I turn my eyes up to his. "If you overthrow Cyrian, who rules Fell country? For whom will you be fighting on the third day?"

His arms ease around me, the slightest hesitation. "That's up to my people. All I want is for them to have the freedom to choose." His grip tightens and shadows cast across his face again. "Even if their freedom only lasts a day."

"I understand," I whisper.

Yesterday, on the first day we met, we were Champions belonging to our monarchs, but today we will be shields for each other.

CHAPTER 16

*W*e finish the remaining food quickly and exit the hut.

I'm dressed in my armor again but leave the pelt behind this time. Our first goal is to find out whether Christiana and the scouts are back. If not, we'll return to Nathaniel's hut for weapons before we head out into Fell country to find her.

Outside, the distant sounds of training have died down completely. We pass the stables on our way to the food hall.

As we approach, a hubbub of noise spills through the wide doors of the hall along with the scent of the same vegetable stew that we ate earlier.

The hall is packed, the humans bumping elbows as they eat, their boisterous conversation washing across me.

As soon as we enter, Emily jumps up from her seat, disrupting the tall young man with light brown hair sitting next to her, who rushes to grab his bowl and save it from flying catastrophically across the table.

"Luciana Elect!" she shouts, oblivious to the chaos she nearly caused.

"Hey," the man exclaims, scooping a spoonful of food and flicking it at her when she ignores him.

"Keep your annoyance, Tom." She laughs and waves him away with her hand. "Luciana Elect. Over here!"

"I really need a shorter name," I murmur to Nathaniel, a smile growing on my face. "Do you see your sister?"

Despite shaking his head, Nathaniel wears a relaxed smile. "Go sit down. I'll find Esther. She'll know if Christiana's eating in her hut. My sister does that sometimes."

"Okay, but... stay within my line of sight," I say.

His chest rumbles with laughter. "If an invisible force knocks me onto my backside, you'll know why."

The Law of Champions binds us together so that we have to remain in each other's presence until the final fight. We have to eat, sleep, and breathe in the same space. The magic of the Law won't allow us to move into a position where there's an immovable object like a wall between us.

The first time I tried to leave Nathaniel's sight, I bruised my nose on the solid force that stopped me from taking another step away from him.

Keeping Nathaniel firmly in my sights as he strolls around the perimeter, I venture over to Emily. It's the farthest I've been away from Nathaniel since the Vanem Dragon bound us together.

She scoots along the bench seat, pressing up against Tom, who doesn't appear nearly as disgruntled about her proximity as he could be. She creates the barest space for me to perch on the end of the seat.

"Here," she says, reaching across the table to grab an empty bowl and start shoveling food from her own plate onto it. "You need food."

"Oh, no, please. I already ate."

"You sure? You should eat while you can," she says. "Esther will yell at us to do chores next."

I laugh. "Really. I'm fine."

Directly opposite me, another girl and boy sit. They appear a little older than Emily. The girl has wild, red curls that fall past her shoulders and the boy has identical hair and bright green eyes that tell me they must be siblings—possibly twins.

"Don't be an idiot, Emily." The girl snorts. "Esther won't tell Luciana Elect what to do."

While she speaks, her brother's hand darts across to her food, stealing the slice of bread right off of her plate.

"Anyone who has the ability to knock Nathaniel on his ass is not going to answer to Esther," he says, giving me a grin.

He doesn't seem to notice his sister steal his spoon.

She throws her head back. "Highlight of my day. I love Nathaniel, but damn, it's about time he met someone who can challenge him."

Her brother snatches her fork, but this time, her hand darts out, catching him in the act. The fork flips upward. Her brother catches it midair, only to have his sister boop his nose with his own spoon. He snatches the spoon out of her hand while she makes a grab for the fork.

My eyes widen as I watch their quick movements, their reflexes matching the fastest fae I've ever seen. They knock and snatch the flying utensils back and forth, even bouncing them off the table so fast that I can hardly follow their movements.

Emily's smile grows and she leans forward in anticipation.

"Hah!" The girl shouts in triumph as she plucks both the

spoon and fork from the air and hugs them close to her chest. "Victory!"

Her smile fades as her brother scrunches the entire piece of stolen bread into his mouth, grinning as he chews. "If you say so."

I can't help the laughter working its way into my throat. All around me, the humans are so relaxed, unafraid to show their feelings and be themselves. They've also shown me that they're skilled fighters.

My smile fades as I remember why I'm here. If Cyrian and his hunters are as violent and dangerous as Nathaniel said, then they'll need everything they've got to win a fight against him. Once Nathaniel finds his sister, he will need to prepare his people for the fight ahead.

I sense his presence beside me a moment before the teenagers fall silent. His big hand brushes my shoulder and he inclines his head toward the door. "I need you," he murmurs.

In the distance, I spy Esther hovering in the doorway, her anxiety visible all the way across the room. That can't be a good sign.

Emily wears a sweet smile as I rise to my feet. "See. He needs her." She sighs into her bowl, mumbling, "When will someone need me?"

Beside her, Tom nudges her shoulder, passing her his last piece of bread.

I stride with Nathaniel to the door, where Esther immediately ushers us outside.

Her voice is hushed and urgent, her posture tense as she hurries us along the path. "You were right, Nathaniel. I should have stopped Christiana leaving this morning."

Nathaniel responds with impossible calm. "Tell me what happened."

"When the scouts didn't come back I sent Geordie out with strict instructions to stay within the boundary of the Bitter Patch and use the spyglass to scan the fields. He just returned. He said he saw hunters only a quarter of a mile away."

Nathaniel tenses, but he keeps his voice moderated. "How many?"

"Three." Esther stalks the grass at the side of the path. "They've never come this far west before. I'd be less worried if Christiana weren't out there, but we haven't heard from her, either..." She stops Nathaniel and her shoulders slump. "Forgive me, Nathaniel. I should have kept her here."

Nathaniel places a hand on her shoulder, but it only seems to make her crumble more. She bites her lip hard and I sense how much emotion she's controlling. "I let you down."

"No, Esther. Nobody tells my sister what to do." His lips set into a regretful grimace. "Which exit did she use? East or west?"

"I'm afraid it was the east. She went out with the scouts, but I heard her tell them not to follow her."

"She probably thought Cyrian had something to do with my extended absence." Nathaniel studies the ground for a moment, but I can see his thoughts churning.

He raises his eyes and his expression is full of purpose. "This is what we're going to do. Luciana Elect and I will go out and find Christiana and the scouts and bring them back. Nobody leaves Null until we return. Remember that you're all safe here. It doesn't matter how close the hunters come. They won't see past the protective shields. They won't find you."

Esther rubs her forehead with the back of her hand. "I should come with you."

Nathaniel shakes his head. "You're needed here." He takes

her other shoulder in a firm grip, forcing her to meet his eyes. "I need your help getting everyone ready. Our timeline has moved up. Luciana Elect and I will be back before sunset. I need you to get everyone ready to fight."

Her lips part in surprise, but she suddenly draws a breath and stands straighter. "We're going to fight?"

Nathaniel gives her a determined nod. "Tonight."

The fear in her eyes disappears, replaced by the light of certainty. "We've been training for this for years. We won't let you down."

"I know you won't. Be ready to move at sunset." He grips her tighter. "But not if we aren't back by then. *Do not* come after us. Wait for us, do you understand? Don't leave Null without me."

She nods. "I'll make sure everyone understands."

"Good. We'll be back as soon as we can."

He catches my eye as he spins. I'm ready to match his stride, but I stop short when a woman I haven't met before appears around the side of the kitchen carrying two large baskets piled high with bread rolls.

She's older than Nathaniel but still youthful, her light brown hair pinned back at the sides but otherwise left to flow freely down her back. A boy of about five years old follows behind her, carrying a smaller basket of food. He has the same light brown hair and bright, curious eyes.

The boy shouts and drops his basket as soon as he sees us. "Nathaniel!"

Bread rolls topple but luckily don't fall out onto the path as the boy runs up to Nathaniel, who scoops him up with an "*Oomph!* You're nearly too big for me to pick you up, Jacob."

I sense the urgency thrumming through Nathaniel now— the need to keep moving—but he can't dismiss or ignore his people or they will sense his fears. I know only too well that the first job of a commander is to keep my people calm. They need to know that everything is under control.

"That's what Mom says." The boy hugs Nathaniel before he slides back to the ground so the woman can embrace Nathaniel and kiss his cheek.

"I'm glad you're back, Nathaniel," she says.

"Maggie." Nathaniel turns to me while I wait calmly beside him. Esther has also become a picture of serenity beside me, showing none of her former worry. "This is—"

"Luciana Elect." Maggie gives me a warm smile. "I'm Maggie, dear. Welcome to Null, where the food is simple and the company is… well… *boisterous* might be the best description." She inclines her head in the direction of the food hall, from which the sounds of revelry grow louder with every passing second.

"It's a pleasure to meet you, Maggie."

Esther clears her throat behind us. "Nathaniel needs to keep moving, but I'll help you carry the food to the hall," she says to Maggie.

"Thank you, dear." Maggie hands Esther one of the baskets, but she pauses another moment, her soft gaze passing across the mark on my face. "Ah, Nathaniel. That is the perfect variation of your name for your wife." Her eyes suddenly glisten. "Your father would be proud of you."

He squeezes her shoulder. "Thank you, Maggie."

She clears her throat, blinking rapidly as she becomes business-like. "I'd better get going before a rebellion breaks out over a shortage of bread."

She strides past us along the path but stumbles suddenly, reaching out to steady herself and knocking into the nearest fence post.

"Mom!" Jacob shouts, running to her side, nearly spilling bread rolls onto the path for a second time.

She quickly waves him off. "I'm fine, sweetheart. It's nothing. Too much time in the warm kitchen. Not enough fresh air."

Nathaniel catches my eye before he darts to her side. He takes her arm in his firm grip, urging her to look up at him. "Maggie?"

She bites her lip again, blinking rapidly and swallowing visibly before she says to Esther, "Esther, take my baby to the food hall, please?"

Esther gives her a rapid nod before she picks up the other basket and ushers Jacob away along the path.

Maggie swallows again as she waits for Jacob to disappear.

Nathaniel holds on to her arm and now it looks like she's leaning on him.

"It's the Rot," she whispers, her brown eyes turned up to Nathaniel's. "It's come for me early. A whole five years early. My baby boy isn't even six years old." Her hand shakes as she raises it to her eyes. "Oh, dear mother moon."

Nathaniel gathers her up into his arms as she starts to cry. His need to keep moving has been swamped by his shock and concern for Maggie.

She turns her face into his chest and his chin slowly drops to the top of her head, dark shadows descending across his expression.

"This shouldn't be happening so soon," he says. "How bad is it?"

"My legs are twisting," she says, drawing shaky breaths, still cushioned in his arms. "My arms are still functioning, but my speech sometimes comes and goes, which means it's already in my brain."

I meet Nathaniel's eyes over Maggie's head. I sense his thoughts like a storm growing around us.

I can heal her.

But I can't reveal my power.

All I can think about are the hatched bars of the cuts on his shoulders. Every person he's lost sits as a constant reminder across his skin. This woman—in fact, every single person in Null—is someone he cares about.

We need to go find the scouts and his sister, but my time here is limited. By the time we get back, we may need to move very quickly to attack the castle.

I'll never forgive myself if I walk away from Maggie now.

CHAPTER 17

"*M*aggie?" I carefully touch the older woman's arm, noting the clammy sweat on her forehead and the pasty color of her cheeks. "I can help you if you'll let me."

Nathaniel is suddenly tense. He gives me a firm, worried shake of his head and I easily read his thoughts. *It's too dangerous.*

I return his concern with what I hope is a determined expression that conveys my thoughts: *I can't stand by while someone you care about dies a slow and horrible death.*

Maggie catches my hand. "Dearest, I wish you could help, but there's no cure for the Rot. All I can do is prepare myself and make sure Jacob will be okay."

"I can heal you," I say, my declaration more certain than I feel.

I don't have the powers of a fae healer—I can't mend broken bones or heal cuts or burns—but I've healed fae children who were sick with an illness that appeared to be the Rot.

I've never tried to heal a human infected by it, let alone an adult, and for all I know the children I healed in Bright might have been infected with an entirely different illness.

Maggie's eyes slowly widen as she stares at me. "How?"

Nathaniel begins to speak—to deny what I said—but I plow on, a story slipping from my lips as easily as truth.

"Luciana was looking for a cure. She found a very old form of dark magic that might work." I hold up my hands so Maggie can see my palms. "She passed it on to me, placing the power in my hands. If you're willing, I'll need... uh... a well-lit room, a warm fire, and no distractions. Nathaniel can be there, but nobody else."

Maggie looks up at Nathaniel. "Is this really possible?"

His worry is carefully hidden. He gives Maggie a resigned smile. "I don't know if it's possible, but my wife is constantly surprising me."

Maggie takes glances between us, suddenly flustered. "I'm supposed to take more food to the hall—"

"We should act now," I say firmly. "Before the Rot gets worse."

I meet Nathaniel's eyes again. Another silent conversation occurs between us.

The worried crease across his forehead hasn't eased, but I press my lips into a determined line: *I have to do this. Before we run out of time. There might not be a tomorrow.*

The darkness in his eyes lifts.

"No distractions means the horde can wait for their bread." He whisks Maggie up into his arms. "My hut is the best place. Luciana Elect won't be interrupted there."

Relief floods Maggie's face as soon as Nathaniel takes the weight off her legs. She isn't old—many fae I know are much older—but at thirty-five years old in a society where nobody lives beyond forty years of age, her demeanor is that of a mother hen—even if she isn't my mother. She's done well to hide the Rot's effects for so long.

Nathaniel strides ahead of me up the stairs and across the porch to enter his home again.

"Fireplace please," I say to him as he sets Maggie down on one of the dining chairs. "And as many candles or lamps that you have to warm the space and counter the dark magic."

I don't need the warmth. What I need is for my bright starlight to be less distinct. Dark magic produces clearly dark light—like the light Mathilda used to try to see into my heart and the inky substance Nathaniel used to fight the Border Guards yesterday.

The more light there is around us, the less likely Maggie will be able to see the brightness of the light my power produces.

I catch her hands in mine, kneeling in front of her. Nathaniel told his people a story about his mother training a new generation of warriors so that myth could become reality.

Now I need to create a new story that will explain to Maggie how my hands can heal her—as well as explaining the color of my power if she sees it. Something that is just believable enough if she repeats it.

"This process of healing requires a careful balance between light and dark," I say. "The dark magic you see in my hands draws its power from the moon, so it will appear as white light, but make no mistake, it is powered by the dark. After all, the moon's light is brightest at night."

She gives me a nod, but her hands are shaking and this time, it feels like nerves. "I've never... Dark magic...?" She glances at Nathaniel for reassurance.

"Don't be afraid," he says. "You're safe here. Luciana Elect will never hurt you."

I run my hand over her forehead. The children I healed all had fevers. Maggie isn't burning up like they were, but her skin is damp.

None of the humans have rosy cheeks, but Maggie is particularly ashen. A close look at her lips reveals a delicate rim of purple around their edges, the same as the girl I healed yesterday.

I press the heel of my palm to her heart. It's definitely beating faster than it should be.

"I need to see your legs," I say. "May I?"

She raises her skirt carefully to her knees, but she glances away, as if she can't stand to look.

Her feet have started twisting in the wrong directions, her calves thinning out and bony. Dark bruises, the color of purple grapes, stretch from above her knees to halfway down her shins.

The bruises also surround her ankles when she removes her boots for me.

Nathaniel quickly finishes lighting the fire, setting up candles along the table beside us. As soon as he sees her legs, he drops to her side. "Maggie, why didn't you tell me?"

She presses her lips together. "I didn't want anyone to know. When my time came, before I couldn't walk anymore, I was going to leave a note and take my final walk through the Misty Gallows."

His hand tightens on her shoulder. With a final squeeze, he leaves her side and gives us space.

Taking a deep breath, I refocus on Maggie, knowing I need to act quickly now.

Ever since daybreak, my power has become finite. I have a reservoir and I've used up a lot of it already. Recklessly, in hindsight. My anger at Nathaniel—the conflict between us—

caused me to strike out. Not to mention, the impact of sharing my body with him...

I fight the blush spreading across my cheeks. Maggie is sitting with her back to his bedroom, but the sheets are still tangled, a tousled reminder of how I spent the last few hours.

"I need you to close your eyes for me now, Maggie," I say. "No matter what happens, don't open them. If you can, try to fall asleep. The more peaceful you are, the more likely this will work."

I wait for her to close her eyes, and then I do the same, seeking the light inside of me.

Nathaniel said my power has facets and each time I use it, I harness it in a different way. When I'm angry, it surges from my heart. When I need calm, it softens in my mind.

To use it to heal, I have to seek it from the cold expanse that lingers inside both my mind and my heart. I have to empty myself of all thoughts and emotions and reach beyond it, as if I'm touching the night sky.

Pulling the power down to my chest, I allow it to flow into my hand.

Maggie inhales sharply when I press my palm to her heart, but a quick check tells me she didn't open her eyes.

"Easy," I whisper, the same way Nathaniel calmed me when I was confronted by the mold moth.

I force myself not to fight the drawing sensation as her body soaks up my power. She is like thirsty, dry earth and my power is water. I will have to keep giving and giving until her pain eases.

Lowering my free hand to her knee, I sense her limb relax, the tension in it releasing.

She sighs, a gentle exhale, as I run my hand all the way to her ankle and then repeat the motion with her other leg, my power flowing into her body.

It is strangely cathartic that my power—which stems from a cold expanse—can fill a void inside this woman's body. There is so much empty in her, so much that has been sucked out, as if her soul is the only thing keeping her alive.

Just as I sense her entire body relax and I prepare to withdraw, a sharp twinge in my chest makes me flinch. I freeze, trying to sense the source of the pain.

My hand moves across her heart, a crease settling onto my forehead. A spot of darkness lingers inside her chest, a tiny pebble like a malignant seed planted inside her heart.

My lips part in surprise. That's where the Rot started, I'm sure of it. If I don't destroy it, she'll get sick again.

If it were the middle of the night, I wouldn't hesitate, but destroying a seed of dark magic is going to take most of my remaining power.

I tell myself it will be okay. Nathaniel doesn't need me to fight for him until tonight. Until then, I can't reveal my power anyway. And by then, my power will be replenished.

Taking a deep breath, I concentrate my light on Maggie's heart, warmth growing beneath my palm. I need to be careful not to hurt her as I press harder and release my power with a sharp *zap*—

To my surprise, her only reaction is a deep inhale. It sounds like the first clear breath she's ever taken, deep and extended.

Her eyes slowly open, a look of amazement in them. "Mother moon," she whispers.

I press my palm to her heart, my power vanishing. It's all gone now. I've got nothing left.

"Easy," I say to her. "You need to rest now." The children I healed had to sleep for hours to recover.

A quick knock sounds at the door and Nathaniel opens it to reveal Esther. "Is everything okay?" she asks.

"Everything's fine. Maggie just needs rest. Can you make sure she takes it easy for the rest of the day, please, Esther."

"Of course." Esther bustles into the room and wraps her arms around Maggie, helping her stand.

"Luciana Elect and I will head out now. Remember what I told you," Nathaniel says to Esther.

She gives him a determined nod.

Maggie's gaze remains on me as Esther leads her away.

The door closes behind them.

A combination of worry and anger floods Nathaniel's face as his big hands close over my shoulders. "That was dangerous, Aura. For so many reasons. I want to rage at you and thank you at the same time." His gaze softens. "You saved her life."

"Now we know that I *can* heal them," I say. "But I discovered something too. The Rot was a seed planted inside her heart, Nathaniel. I think it was put there. Could Cyrian be responsible?"

Nathaniel's grip tightens in alarm. "It could be some sort of portal into our lifeblood. A way to access our life's energy and drain it slowly over time," he murmurs. "But if that's the case, then... everyone could already be sick. He's already draining us. We only see the effects as we age."

I press my hand against his heart, but he covers my fingers with his. "Don't try to see inside my heart, Aura. You've already used up most of your energy. I watched your power drain out of you while you helped her."

"But I need to know," I whisper, closing my eyes and dropping myself into the empty space inside my mind before he can stop me.

The cold stream flows through my arm and into my hand, warming under my palm.

I gasp and lurch backward. Looking into Nathaniel's

heart is like staring into the sun, a bright flare that shoots warmth up my arm and into my mind. There is no take on his part. Only give.

His energy is blazing and brilliant and... could easily destroy me if I bask in it too long.

My eyes fly wide. "You're not infected. Not even close."

He drops a kiss to my forehead. His touch is reserved and constrained, as if he's trying very hard not to kiss me like he did in our bed. "Aura, you haven't slept and now you've used up your power. All of that is my fault—"

"Not entirely yours." My expression eases into a sultry smile as I push away from the table. "I'm fine. Let's go."

He rises to his full height. "Promise me you'll tell me if you need help."

"I will if you will."

He gives me perplexed smile. "Stubborn wife."

I arch an eyebrow at him and stride toward his closet. "Weapons," I say firmly.

It's time to go back out into the wilderness, but this time, I intend to lead the way.

CHAPTER 18

The Bitter Patch is quiet around us as Nathaniel and I finally exit into the fields beyond.

We stay low, traveling another half an hour before we reach a vast stretch of woods.

Nathaniel tracks the scouts' movements through the fields. His scouts must be skilled at what they do, because they barely leave a broken stem in their wake, but Nathaniel knows their usual path.

His sister is also a stealthy traveler. I pick up her path only once intertwining with that of the scouts in the middle of the field, as if they met for some reason.

Her footsteps were lighter and her footprints smaller. After that, her path disappears again until all three paths suddenly converge right at the entrance to the woods.

"Here." Nathaniel points to the faint tread in the damp ground at the edge of the trees.

I cast around carefully, spying the broken stems of wheat a little farther back in the field on our right. "Nathaniel. Look. She broke her careful path there."

"She wouldn't be so reckless unless something was wrong." He points from the distant broken wheat all the way to the patch where we stand now, his finger following her trail. "She was running. Toward one of the scouts who was located here."

I shiver as I step carefully inside the treeline, keeping my footsteps light.

The air inside the woods is as dank as it is in the Misty Gallows.

"There," I say, pointing at a disturbed patch of mud on the path between the trees. "There was a scuffle."

The quiet around us increases, the air whispering around me as I scan the creaking trees. It's nearly impossible for me to expand my senses now that my power is depleted. I vaguely register the crawling creatures beneath my boots but nothing more.

"Aura." Nathaniel's voice is a quiet breath behind me as his hand curls slowly around my arm, a warning touch.

I follow his line of sight upward.

My hand flies over my mouth.

Two bodies swing in the shadowy trees high above us.

The ropes creak and groan as they scratch against the branches.

"Hunters." Nathaniel draws a dagger from his harness.

Before we left his hut, we raided his closet. We both wear harnesses across our chests and backs, each carrying a bow, arrows, and an array of daggers. Swords are harder to run with, so we left those behind.

My hair is tied up again, this time into braids. I also carry my liquid daggers as part of my armor, but they'll be harder to access because of the harness strapped to my body. That isn't necessarily a bad thing—pulling out my fae weapons would reveal my race.

"Where's your sister?" I ask, a futile question since there are no answers in front of us.

He shakes his head. "Not in the trees. She's valuable. They wouldn't string her up. That's all I know."

A sudden, sick feeling swamps me. My senses are dull, but there's no mistaking the darkness creeping around us. Their presence is like a bottomless pit of darkness and I'm being sucked into it...

Nathaniel draws me slowly backward, step by step, as we back out of the woods onto the clearing at the edge of the field.

The Bitter Patch is far behind us—too far to reach in time and Nathaniel would never risk running in that direction in case he gave away the village it conceals.

"How many?" he whispers.

Each hunter's presence is like a void in my senses. "Thirty scattered out in the woods—approaching rapidly. They're fanning out so they can circle around us. If we should run, then we need to do it now."

"No." He growls. "These men enjoy the chase as much as the kill."

A cold chill travels down my spine. Even if Nathaniel hadn't warned me about them, the energy around the field and inside the woods is twisted, rotten, and makes my skin prickle.

I remind myself that I can't hurt them. But... dark stars... curbing my rage and fight reflexes around these men is going to be difficult.

Nathaniel draws me to a stop in the clearing. It's less than twenty paces wide but extends along the edge of the woods. "Don't draw your weapons, Aura. Remember the Law."

Still gripping his dagger, he relaxes his arms and shoulders, but it feels a lot like the moment when he prepared himself for the wolves to attack.

These men are a different kind of beast.

I raise myself to my full height, gathering my physical strength. I've trained for years to make myself strong in the day, not only at night. It's why other fae consistently under-estimate me. My armor is a defense. It will keep me safe. I just have to remember not to attack.

The silence stretches, but this time, I sense the hunters breathing.

Nathaniel side-eyes me before he raises his voice and roars, "Hagan Sever! Come out from the shadows."

The air swirls on our left before a man strides from the edge of the trees.

I stop myself before I take a step back.

He's the same height as Nathaniel and just as well-muscled, his bare chest broad and inked with runes that I can't decipher. I have no doubt they're connected to dark magic.

Two thick, rope-like scars twist and intersect across the right side of his ribcage while a wolf's head sits on his right shoulder from which a pale gray pelt descends down his back, partially concealing his right arm.

He's wearing black pants and carrying a row of daggers around his waist, but it's his face that really draws my atten-tion: a strong forehead, high cheekbones, and lips drawn into a merciless line.

He looks slightly older than Nathaniel, but maybe only by a few years. His black hair is cut close to his scalp on either side while the top is braided down the back.

Dangerous intelligence meets my gaze when I look in his tawny brown eyes.

"Nathaniel," he says, switching his focus away from me as

he draws to a stop a mere few paces away from us. His hand rests on his dagger's hilt. "It would have been better for you if you'd stayed gone."

Nathaniel doesn't miss a beat. "Be careful, Hagan. You don't want to take me on."

Hagan lifts his fingers from his dagger, splaying them carefully before he extends both of his arms out at his sides. "You're right, Nathaniel. We never had any trouble, you and I. But... I can't say the same for them."

One by one, thirty men appear out of the woods, rising from their hiding places concealed behind trees, some even swinging from the branches above us.

Many of them carry bows and arrows while the others hold daggers, hunting knives, and axes. Most have scars across their bare chests.

All of them wear pelts of different colors and furs—fox, bear, wolf. None of the other men reaches Nathaniel or Hagan's height or build, but the intense hunger in their eyes makes me shudder.

One draws closer to Hagan—a slightly younger man, maybe my age—with a completely shaved head and a dirty blond beard. He wears a pelt with two wolves' heads—one sitting on each of his shoulders. Their skulls are smaller than fully grown, which makes me think they weren't much older than cubs when he killed them.

I can't see the back of his pelt, but I assume it's sewn together down the middle.

Anger rises inside me. Nathaniel told me that killing more than one wolf is dishonorable. The way this younger man smiles at me tells me "honor" isn't in his vocabulary.

The others take up position around us, those with daggers standing closer than those with bows and arrows.

Nathaniel is deceptively relaxed as he watches them

maneuver into position. "Judging from the number of you...
you're here for me," he says to Hagan.

Hagan gives a single nod. "We've been ordered to bring
you to the King. Dead or alive."

"Why?" Nathaniel's demand is short and sharp, so sharp
that it makes the nearest men flinch. "I am the King's Shield.
Attacking me is treason."

Hagan returns Nathaniel's glare. "You crossed the border
into Bright, Nathaniel. Only traitors do that. The King has
stripped you of your position."

Nathaniel freezes beside me, his fist clenching around his
weapon.

Hagan reaches for his dagger.

This time, he doesn't appear afraid to use it. "You are no
longer the King's Shield."

CHAPTER 19

$\mathcal{N}$athaniel is a tower of rage beside me, anger bleeding into his expression.

His emotions aren't directed at me, but even so, intense guilt rises inside me. He never would have crossed the border into Bright if I hadn't invoked the Law of Champions.

My thoughts become frenzied. If the King has declared Nathaniel a traitor, what does that mean for the Law? What does that mean for the fight between us?

A sudden, strange wash of relief rushes through me. Maybe he won't be the one I have to fight... Or better, maybe the Law is now broken somehow...

One glance at Nathaniel's face tells me my relief is unfounded. I'm not sure why yet, but I sense everything just got a thousand times worse.

Drawing myself to my full height, I cast a dismissive glance at Hagan. "That may be so, but you were foolish to bring so few men to capture both of us."

His eyes quickly narrow at me, his gaze passing over my

armor and face. My golden mark will be plain for everyone to see, but my hair is still jet black.

I'm sure he would have sized me up before he even stepped from the trees, but now he's making a show of looking me up and down.

The younger man wearing the two wolf skins snarls at me, but he doesn't speak up. It's clear that Hagan is the leader, although the younger man edges forward in a way that indicates he wants that position.

"I wasn't expecting Nathaniel to have company," Hagan says. "Let alone a woman wearing the armor of a Warrior of Luciana."

The way the men focus on me tells me they all know what Hagan means. Nathaniel said that his mother trained them. She would have known each and every one of these hunters, along with their weaknesses.

If only I could acquire her knowledge right now.

Hagan continues to glower at me. "You don't look like much of a problem. Luciana chose wrong with you. You're not much more than a wisp of a woman. All of those weapons are going to topple you at any moment."

I tilt my head, carefully stepping closer to Nathaniel, demonstrating that my balance is just fine. "Appearances may be deceiving."

Hagan purses his lips as he studies my face, his gaze following the golden lines of Nathaniel's family name.

With a long exhale, he shakes his head. "Ah, but appearances are everything." He glares at Nathaniel. "You should not have made your feelings for her so plain by marking her, Nathaniel. Now the hunters will want to hurt her."

The man next to Hagan seems unable to keep his thoughts to himself anymore.

"Whore of Luciana," he spits at me. "You will scream when I gut you."

To my surprise, Hagan twitches, a hard scowl descending as he side-eyes the other man before wiping his own expression clean.

Beside me, Nathaniel quickly recovers, his lips pressing into a hard line before he raises his voice to a shout. "Any man who lays a hand on this woman had better be prepared to take his last breath." He points at the younger man. "That includes you, Tanner Snare."

The tension around us rises a thousand degrees, but Tanner throws his head back with a laugh.

"Why so possessive of your whore, Nathaniel?" he asks. "We'll take our turns laying more than a hand on her and you'll do nothing more than watch."

I'm sure I'm supposed to be afraid, but I've faced down worse than Tanner—Imatra's entire Day Guard and the fire they control that could have burned me to ash, just for starters.

I let Tanner's threats wash over me while I assess his stature. He's well-muscled beneath the pelt he wears, but the wolf skin serves to make him look larger than he is. I'll have to watch out for his speed more than his weight.

When I don't respond, his laughter turns to a glare and the silence around us intensifies.

A breath of wind stirs at the back of my neck. The man closest to my right licks his lips. The one next to him drags his dagger back and forth across the air in slow, illustrative moves as if he's practicing gutting me.

Other than Hagan, none of the men have focused anywhere other than my face, breasts, or pelvis. At the same time, several of them have edged closer while we talked, while others have quietly attached arrows to their bows.

These men are like the pack of wolves.

The two leaders are drawing our attention while the pack is preparing to strike from the sides.

Nathaniel leans toward me while he keeps Hagan clearly in his sights. "Remember: Evade and defend. Do not attack. Make no mistake, Aura: The Law still stands. The only difference is that my place in it has become volatile."

"Did you hear me, Nathaniel?" Tanner screams, his face red with rage. "We'll make your whore beg for mercy!"

Nathaniel rolls his shoulders and stretches his neck from side to side. "You can beg first."

From the corner of my eye, I sense the shift in the posture of three men standing side by side, each one holding an arrow taut to his bow. Their fingers flex and release.

The arrows are perfectly aimed at Nathaniel's chest.

Not today.

I'm already in position. I lunge toward Nathaniel, turning my shoulder as I press against his torso to cover his body as fully as I can with my own.

I don't have time to brace for the pain.

An angry scream roars out of me as the arrows hit my back.

My armor can't be pierced by human weaponry. Only the exposed parts of my body are vulnerable: my throat, face, head, and hands.

The arrows bury in the outer layer of my suit, the impact jarring through me and knocking Nathaniel off-balance.

He corrects himself before he falls, his arms whipping around my waist, and his eyes shooting wide as he registers the attack.

"Evade and defend." I gasp.

He plucks one of the arrows from my armor, his glare at

the men hot enough to burn them as his big fist closes around the wooden stem.

Darkness grows in his expression, anger twisting his lips as he snaps the arrow between his strong fingers.

At the same time, the remaining arrows drop from my back and clatter to the ground.

The inertia around us breaks.

Nathaniel spins to a man swinging an axe at him. I whirl to deflect the downward cut of a dagger held by the man who was air-gutting me moments ago and has now leaped at me.

The hunter drops to the side as I deflect a second blow, but another hunter is ready to take his place—this one holding a blade in each hand. At the same time, two more come at me on my right-hand side.

I dart and evade, using my armored arms—even my legs —to block the slashes they aim at my vital organs.

The huntsmen are as trained and coordinated in their attack as the Queen's guards.

As much as I can trust my armor to protect me, repeated blows in the same spot will eventually cut through.

The men target my heart, my lower back, and my stomach. Not to mention my throat, which is exposed. All I can do is take the blows to my body and desperately try to avoid the blows to my neck.

I can't return a damn strike.

As I duck and roll, Nathaniel flickers in and out of my view. He sends a man sprawling with blood streaming from his nose. Another man meets Nathaniel's fist and it sounds like a rock against the man's temple.

As the hunter falls, Nathaniel's blade flashes. The blood gushing from the man's throat as he drops at Nathaniel's feet tells me the hunter won't be getting up again.

Nathaniel steps over him to deflect the next attack. He's already disarmed multiple men and grips a hunter's axe along with his own dagger.

I don't have time to count the bodies, but they're piling up around him along the path. Some appear unconscious, but most are dead.

So far, Hagan and Tanner have stayed out of the fight, but they're watching carefully. Tanner gives a signal with his hand, but I'm not sure what it means. I've lost count of the hunters and their attacks.

Darting away from another man, I sense, too late, the arrows flying toward my back.

Too many of them.

I've acted as a shield at Nathaniel's back and the hunters are trying to bring me down.

CHAPTER 20

*P*ain shoots through my back ribs as the projectiles hit me all at once.

The barrage forces me onto my knees on the path. I swallow a deep scream, knowing that it will distract Nathaniel.

I'm too far away for him to help me.

I fight the pain, trying to scramble to my feet, but the butt of a dagger flies at me from the side.

Tanner has finally stepped into the fight, his arm swinging hard and fast as the heavy wooden handle hits my temple and knocks me sideways into the dirt.

By some miracle, it doesn't break my skin. At least, Tanner hasn't dropped dead, so I can only assume I'm not bleeding. Otherwise, the Law would have acted to kill Tanner on the spot.

I land on my side, fighting every instinct in my body that wants to hit back. I *need* to hit back. In any other fight, I would kick Tanner's legs out from under him and slit his throat.

I roll to the side before he can stomp on my chest.

Leaping to my feet, I attempt to dart to the side, but his boot connects with my already bruised back ribs, cracking across my torso and propelling me face-first into the dirt.

Tanner drops onto me and pins me down where I lie on my stomach, the sides of his pelt falling around me.

Driving the air further out of my lungs as he straddles my torso, he digs his grimy fingers into my hair and yanks my head to the side so I'm facing away from Nathaniel.

I can't see the fight anymore, and I can't throw Tanner off me without risking that he'll get hurt. He could merely graze his hands on the path and it would be my fault.

I've never prayed so hard that I would bleed. If a human spills a drop of my blood, their punishment is immediate death under the Law of Champions.

Surely, one of the arrows pierced my armor. Surely, my cheek is scraping on the rough path. Surely... the blow to my temple cracked open my skin.

Let me bleed.

Let him die.

Tanner leans over me, his lips close to my cheek. "People say that Luciana's warriors will be beautiful," he says, pressing so hard on my cheek that it feels like my cheekbone is going to pop. "You're the ugliest whore I've ever laid eyes on."

Now that I can't see Nathaniel, I don't know what's happening. All I have to work with are thuds, shouts, and the clashing of steel.

But as long as I hear all of that, I know that Nathaniel is still fighting.

Hagan is the only hunter in my view. He remains at the edge of the path exactly where he was when he first spoke to us.

He hasn't joined the fight against Nathaniel and I'm surprised to find that *I* am the subject of his attention.

Hagan's eyebrows are drawn down in an intense stare, his big hand twitching across the handle of his dagger while a muscle ticks in his jaw.

He's threatened to draw his weapon multiple times, but so far, he's restrained himself. I'm not sure what's going to happen when he finally joins the fight.

I also don't know what has caused him to feel so much anger right now—or whether that's his usual face. Probably, since he hasn't stopped glowering since he appeared.

Tanner tightens his hold on my hair, pulling my head back so far that I arch away from the ground. He may be a vile stink of a man, but his assessment of my looks is accurate. I am neither beautiful nor striking.

Whimpers of pain escape my lips.

Refusing to scream, I thump my fist into the dirt at my side, focusing on the pain in my hand instead. I have to find a way out of this. Some way to free myself that doesn't involve hurting him...

Tanner's lips drag across my cheek. "Why aren't you fighting me, ugly whore?"

"Be grateful that I'm not," I grind out between my gritted teeth.

His knee presses against the small of my back, making me moan as he compresses my stomach.

I can't stop the tears slipping down my cheeks. Thumping my fist into the dirt again is the only rebellious move I can make.

"Get on with it or get off me!" I scream, unable to suppress my pain any longer.

Tanner finally lets go of my hair to grab my arms, pulling

them behind my back and tying a coarse material around my wrists—some sort of rope.

"On your knees," he orders me, dragging me around so that I'm facing in Nathaniel's direction again.

I catch a brief glimpse of the aftermath of the fighting, gasping at all the bodies lying along the path, but I don't see Nathaniel.

Tanner shoves his boot against my lower back and drags my arms up and out behind me. He pulls my limbs so far back that I'm forced to double over my knees.

I curl up tightly, my view filling with the dusty ground. A completely submissive pose.

"Nathaniel!" Tanner shouts from above and behind me. "How does your whore like to—"

There's a sudden pause.

The tension in the rope increases as if Tanner jolted.

"Fuck," he whispers.

Footsteps thud toward us and a roar fills the air.

It's Nathaniel's voice, approaching at a rapid pace.

He sounds more violently angry than I've ever heard him, but he isn't forming words—only a shout that strikes through me as if his voice is a dagger inside my chest.

Pain sparks deep inside me, somewhere inside my ribcage, spreading through my body in a tumble of fear and dread.

The collision between Nathaniel and Tanner shudders through me.

Tanner holds on to the rope a second longer than he should, causing me to jolt upward with the force of Nathaniel's hit.

I crash back to the ground as the rope releases, but the fall is nothing compared to the rising fear inside me. A wild mix of terror and anticipation.

Rolling onto my side, I wrench at the bindings around my hands, unable to loosen them as I twist myself up onto my knees.

I turn just in time to see Tanner hit the ground.

Nathaniel looms over him still holding the axe he wielded before.

Tanner recovers quickly, leaping to his feet, but Nathaniel wrenches him around as if Tanner weighs nothing.

He drives Tanner back to his knees with a savage kick to his back, followed by a vicious fist to the side of his head that knocks Tanner to the ground. Nathaniel does it all single-handedly, still gripping the axe in his left hand.

Now that the younger man is lying flat on his back, concussed and not fighting back, Nathaniel plants his boot on Tanner's chest and allows the flat side of the axe head to rest down on Tanner's neck, waiting for him to recover consciousness.

Groans from all around me tell me that the other hunters are subdued—either injured or dead. Nobody is coming to save Tanner.

Nathaniel doesn't look at me. Blood runs down his arms and splatters his cheeks, casting crimson splashes across his face and neck.

I've heard about battle rage, even felt it, fought it inside myself, but Nathaniel's battle rage is beyond anything I've ever imagined.

My heart constricts inside my chest, the same sharp pain I felt before, and this time—now that I'm not doubled over—I can see the faint glow across my chest through my armor.

Golden light glimmers at the edges of my vision as if the sun is rising inside me, the most unexpected shine.

I hunch forward, unable to use my arms or hands, trying to hide the light until I realize...

It's not coming from me. It's a reflection off my armor.
Opposite me, Nathaniel's chest glows.
His heart shines as he roars. "You. Do not. Touch her!"

CHAPTER 21

anner coughs as he regains consciousness with a jolt.

He tries to grab the axe, tries to pull it from his neck and take control of the weapon, but Nathaniel swings it up and over his head.

It isn't the largest axe I've ever seen, nowhere near as big as Nathaniel's halberd and a far more simple construction of steel and wood, but it looks deadly sharp.

Every bulging muscle in Nathaniel's arms and chest tell me that he has the strength to cut Tanner's head clean off.

A cry of warning dies in my throat as Hagan runs up behind Nathaniel, finally joining the fight.

In a frighteningly simple move, Hagan wraps his left hand around Nathaniel's throat and drives his dagger toward the other side of Nathaniel's neck.

The blade stops just before it would sever Nathaniel's spine.

The move is so expertly carried out that it makes me wonder if Hagan derived his name from it. He has the strength to separate Nathaniel's head from his spine with one efficient stab.

Hagan's grip is so tight that Nathaniel is forced to alter his center of gravity, pulled slightly off Tanner, but he refuses to step off him altogether, his muscles straining as he remains firmly in place.

Hagan doesn't try to take the axe, which hovers dangerously above Tanner's chest while Tanner lies frozen and wide-eyed beneath it.

"Don't do this, Nathaniel," Hagan warns, his fingers tightening around the side of Nathaniel's throat. "You kill my half-brother and I'll have no choice but to end you."

Nathaniel responds with a growl as dangerous as a wolf's. "I've let Tanner live too many times."

Hagan shakes his head. "If you don't surrender, Christiana will pay the price."

The rage drains from Nathaniel's face, but his chest rises and falls with angry breaths. "Where is she?"

"At the castle."

Nathaniel's questions are abrupt. "Has Cyrian hurt her?"

"He will if we don't bring you back." The tip of Hagan's dagger is poised to plunge. "Like I said, Nathaniel, dead or alive. He doesn't care."

Nathaniel finally casts his gaze in my direction, meeting my eyes across the distance. The light I saw glowing from his chest is gone. It disappeared so quickly that I'm sure I must have imagined it. A trick of the murky sunlight here. Just the gleam of sweat across his shirt, nothing more.

Possibly for the first time, there's real fear in his eyes.

"I'll make sure nobody touches your woman," Hagan continues, lowering his voice as his focus shifts briefly to me. "She's proven herself worthy of your attention. If you come quietly, I'll make sure nobody molests her before we reach the King. I can't promise anything after that."

Nathaniel doesn't speak or move and his silence frightens me more than Tanner's abuse. I struggle against the ropes binding my hands as I sense many of the hunters recovering and rising to their feet around me. I'm not sure if they'll respect Hagan's orders or if, any second now, I'll have to fight off even more of them than before.

Very slowly, a storm grows in Nathaniel's eyes, but he suppresses it, his hand tightening on the axe and his focus lowering to the blade.

Hagan demands, "Do we have an agreement?"

Nathaniel grits his teeth. "Yes."

He pitches the axe into the dirt beside Tanner's head, making the younger man shout.

"Good." Hagan immediately releases Nathaniel and returns his dagger to its place on his belt.

Nathaniel leans down to Tanner. "If you come near her... even to speak with her... I will kill you. It won't matter if I'm in chains. I'll find a way. Do you understand?"

Tanner snarls up at Nathaniel. He jumps to his feet as soon as Nathaniel lifts his boot and lets fly with a string of curses in Nathaniel's face.

He only stops when Hagan grabs his shoulder and drags him away with a terse order. "Get the wagon. You'll ride with me."

To the other men, Hagan shouts, "Secure the prisoners! Gather up your weapons and get to your horses."

Nathaniel meets my eyes across the distance. He stands still now, his arms remaining at his sides as three hunters approach him. They're each bloodied from cuts and wounds. Unwinding ropes from their belts, they snarl curses at him as they wrap one rope around his neck and the other two around each of his wrists.

I try to get up, but Nathaniel motions with his flat palm for me to stay down. *Don't act.*

The sharp crack of a whip heralds the arrival of a wagon. Its wheels are whisper quiet, well-oiled, and the horses are sleek, black, and surprisingly healthy-looking.

The back of the wagon is a cage. It has a wooden wagon bed, but metal bars extend up and around it with a set of hinged cage doors at the back.

Tanner jumps from the seat to settle the animals while Hagan strides over to me. With a quick slice of his dagger, Hagan cuts the weapons harness from my body, taking possession of my weapons while he leaves the ropes binding my wrists intact.

"Up," he barks, yanking on my arm to hoist me to my feet. "Nobody will touch you, but that doesn't mean I'll tolerate trouble."

Wobbling as I regain my balance, I return his flinty stare. It's a shame I need to tip my head back to do it. It ruins the impact of my rebellious gesture.

Hagan drags me to the wagon while the other hunters collect their weapons around me. Many of them have cuts across their arms and chests. Bruises are appearing across the faces of others.

Hagan opens the doors of the cage, which swing wide on their hinges. I catch sight of a bundle of blankets at the far end, along with coils of rope and piles of chains.

I expect to have to climb in, but Hagan hoists me up again, this time into the wooden wagon bed, plonking me down on the left-hand side.

"Feet!" he orders, reaching for a coil of rope.

I place my ankles together and he ties them securely. "Be

grateful you get rope and not these," he says, dragging a set of chains from the wagon. Multiple sets of shackles are attached to them. I've never seen a set of chains like that until now.

I look up to find Nathaniel waiting at the end of the wagon. His weapons have also been removed. The hunters are pulling on the ends of his ropes, which dig into his neck and wrists.

"Get to your horses," Hagan orders them, forcing them to let go. His dagger slides through the knots, dangerously close to Nathaniel's neck, before the ropes fall to the ground.

Then he uncoils the chains, wraps the main portion around Nathaniel's waist, and secures a set of attached shackles to his wrists before locking them in place.

Nathaniel sits on the edge of the wagon while Hagan secures the remaining shackles around Nathaniel's ankles. The shackles rest outside of Nathaniel's boots, but he won't be able to kick off the shackles because of the limited length of chain connecting the ankle restraints to the chain around his waist.

I scoot along the wagon bed as Nathaniel swings his feet up inside the cage.

The doors close and the lock clicks.

Nathaniel slides up against the side of the wagon bed opposite me. The wooden sides are high enough for him to rest his shoulders against it. Above that, the cage's metal bars would allow me to stand up, but I'd have to stoop.

Hagan and Tanner take up seats at the front of the wagon and it jolts into action. I fall to the side as the horses take off with more speed than I was expecting. With my hands still tied behind my back, my balance is way off.

I land against the blankets. They're soft and surprisingly warm.

And breathing.

I recoil from the furry body I fell against.

Tangled in the gray blankets, two wolves lie sleeping. At least, I hope they're sleeping and not about to leap up at me. Their rising and falling chests indicate they aren't dead.

They don't stir. One of them looks exactly like the alpha female we fought this morning.

Tanner twists in his seat outside the cage. He catches me staring at the wolves and throws me a cruel smile. "They were howling this morning. They only do that when someone's going to die."

He turns back to the horses as they speed along the road.

I twist to Nathaniel and find him gesturing as much as he possibly can, urging me to come over to his side.

Sliding away from the wolves, I choose the far side of him, farthest from the front, scooching in close to his side so we can talk.

My hands rub against the coarse wagon wood and the back of my ribs ache from the pummeling I received from the arrows along with Tanner's boot. It's uncomfortable, but I make the best of it.

Nathaniel tilts his head to mine and keeps his voice low, a murmur beneath the sound of the wagon and the horses. "Are you okay?"

"I'm fine. You?" I don't like the look of the bruising around his neck or the cuts on his arms.

"Nothing that won't heal," he rasps.

"What about your sister?"

He's quiet and tense beside me. "She's in danger. So are you."

I drop my head to Nathaniel's shoulder, an overwhelming need to wrap my arms around him overtaking me, but it's not like I can do that right now with my arms bound behind my back.

I also have to be careful not to touch him skin on skin and accidentally glow.

"Yesterday, I broke the rules to save my brother," I whisper. "I know how important it is to protect family."

He's tense beside me. *"You're* my family. I made you a promise to protect you and I won't break it."

I search his eyes, hoping he hears me. "I trust you, Nathaniel."

He gives me a nod, but that is all.

I push at the fear that threatens to overtake me. Nathaniel warned me against going anywhere near Cyrian.

Now I'm on my way right to him.

CHAPTER 22

*W*e travel in the back of the wagon for at least an hour while the other hunters follow close behind on their horses.

The sun must be at its highest in the sky now, but the light never changes. The landscape morphs from fields of wheat to heavily wooded areas and then opens up into orchards again.

All along the way, humans are tilling fields, harvesting produce, or cutting timber.

Each time we pass through a village, moths rise up from roofs, fluttering into the sky.

Tanner bellows at anyone blocking the road to get out of the way. Children with pale faces run alongside the wagon when it's forced to slow down. All of them seem to know Nathaniel. He warns them not to get caught under the wheels and they run away again, shouting for their parents.

Adults with alarmed faces watch us pass by from darkened doors. They are all gaunt. More than a few are covered in furs, wearing the faces of foxes. Nathaniel told me those are the ones affected by the Rot to the extent that they don't show their faces anymore.

Finally, in the distance, a castle rises up into the haze. It's a monstrous collection of soot gray towers that soar higher than anything else around it—so high that I can only just make out the battlements before the towers ascend into the thick vapor that covers the sky.

We passed the last village a while ago, but there's another cluster of buildings farther off to our left. These are oddly pristine—white stone and russet-colored roofs. They're surrounded by neat rows of orchards.

The quick clatter of hooves breaks through my thoughts.

A woman on a bay mare gallops toward us along the path from the white buildings, her golden hair flying behind her.

As soon as he sees her, Tanner nudges Hagan, who draws the wagon to a stop, allowing the rider to draw level with the side of the wagon on which Tanner sits. The other hunters all pull up behind us, keeping their distance from the woman.

The newcomer's hair settles around her shoulders as she pulls to a stop. I can't help but stare at her—her golden hair and cornflower blue eyes. She looks just like Esther.

Tanner leans toward her. "Lady Ethel. What brings you to us?"

"I heard you had some unusual cargo." Her voice is sweet like sugar, practically oozing around us. "I had to see for myself."

Tanner twists in his seat, inclining his shaved head toward us. "Not such a hard catch."

Ethel casts her gaze in our direction, her eyebrows rising as she focusses on Nathaniel. "So it's true. *My, my.* How the mighty fall."

Nathaniel returns her gaze with a hard stare.

A faint crease forms in her forehead as she assesses me. She glazes over the mark on my face. "They look awfully cozy for prisoners."

Tanner scowls. "They won't be comfortable for long."

"Oh? Surely, Cyrian won't kill his Shield."

"Not his Shield anymore. And yeah... he might."

Ethel pouts at Tanner. "What a shame to waste Nathaniel's body when I could put him to work in my fields."

She suddenly grips Tanner's shoulder. "You will tell Cyrian, won't you, that I'd rather have Nathaniel work for me instead of casting his body to the beasts? I'm sure I can flog him enough for Cyrian's liking."

Her lips twist as she casts a distasteful glance at me. "The female, on the other hand... There's nothing pleasing about her at all. I couldn't even use her to entertain my guards."

Her gaze rakes down my body and her jaw drops suddenly. She squeezes Tanner's shoulder again. "Oh, but do tell Cyrian that I want her armor. Make sure he doesn't damage it, won't you? I haven't seen the likes of it since Luciana's days." She smiles prettily at Tanner. "You will tell him, won't you?"

He licks his lips at her. "Of course. I'll peel the armor off the whore's dead body myself. Just for you."

She bats her eyelashes at him. "If only I could come with you."

He laughs. "You know the rules. Only hunters and prisoners beyond the gates."

"A pity." Ethel pats his arm again before she steers her mare away from the wagon, circles it at a trot, and gallops away.

I make note of the way the hunters stay well away from her, even though she barely looked at them. She didn't speak with Hagan or acknowledge him at all.

He glares at Tanner. "Are you done licking her boots?"

Tanner smirks. "I've licked more than her boots."

Hagan doesn't look impressed. "Only fools go near that woman. You'll wake up with your balls in your mouth one day if you're not careful. She killed her own sister to gain favor with Cyrian."

Tanner's cursing is drowned in the sudden movement of the wagon as Hagan urges the horses back to speed.

The scent of the orchards lifted the sourness in the air, but the smell of decay becomes heavier as we approach the enormous gates in the outer wall.

Several guards patrol the battlements and one of them shouts an order to open the gates as we approach.

The large, iron spikes rise and the wall's dark shadow passes over the cage, dropping us into a cold chill as we pass through.

Nathaniel leans toward me with a look of warning in his eyes, but he doesn't have to speak. It will be a miracle if Cyrian doesn't identify me as fae. Then I'll need to fear all humans, not just Cyrian and his hunters.

Nathaniel's shackles don't reach far enough for him to grip my arm, but the intensity in his dark eyes is grip enough. I shiver as the fear I've been keeping at bay suddenly swamps me, but I remind myself who I am. Aura Lucidia. Commander of the fae army. The Queen's *traitorous* Champion.

A cold smile forms on my lips as we pass beneath the inner wall.

The wagon pulls to a stop in the middle of a courtyard while the hunters arrive behind us, jumping from their horses and handing them off to waiting guards.

Hagan jumps from the wagon's seat and strides around to

open the cage, stepping in and picking me up without a word.

I find myself gasping at the roughness of his movements, one arm pressed across the top of my head so I don't bang against the side of the cage while his other envelops my waist and knocks the wind from my chest.

We thud to the ground as he jumps off the back of the wagon, holding me tightly before he slides me to the ground with barely enough time to get my bound feet under me.

I slip in the sludge, forced to lean back against him before I find the side of the wagon with my hands so I can balance on my own.

"Stay there. Don't move," Hagan orders.

He turns to Nathaniel, who's already hobbling to the edge of the wagon before he sits and eases off the edge of it. The wagon bed springs up as soon as Nathaniel's weight lifts off it.

Farther back in the wagon, scuffling indicates the wolves are waking up. Hagan slams the doors shut, locking them again as the animals jump to their feet, their teeth bared.

Wrapping an arm around my waist, he yanks me away from the side of the wagon just in time.

The wolves race toward us, snapping their jaws, but they can't get through the bars.

Hagan's dangerous eyes meet mine as he continues to grip me like a bag of wheat.

Another group of guards runs from the gates, all carrying swords.

Suddenly, I find myself with wolves at my back, hunters at my front, and the circle of a wild man's arm around my waist.

My only ally, Nathaniel, stands chained and as angry as

the darkest star, his glare sharp enough to peel the skin off Hagan's face.

The hunters take up position around us while another guard strides between them carrying a set of chains—for me, no doubt.

He grabs me from Hagan, yanks me around, and takes hold of my bound hands, throwing me off-balance enough that I slip again, nearly losing my footing.

I bend my knees and engage every muscle in my body to stay upright so I don't end up bending over and giving these men a view of my backside. *Damn my bound feet!*

Hagan's hand snaps out to steady me from behind, sliding beneath my left arm and curling up around my chest, pulling me upward. His other fist wraps around the guard's arm. The man catches air as Hagan throws him backward.

"You don't want to touch this one," Hagan warns.

Even though Hagan now stands behind me, Nathaniel is in full view a few paces away. His lips are pressed together in a grim line, his glare a dangerous threat. He takes a step toward the guard, who immediately shoves the chains at Hagan and backs off.

It doesn't seem to matter that Nathaniel is bound. They still fear him. *Dear stars, they should.* Even I do. Sometimes.

The chains clatter on the ground as Hagan allows them to unwind. The sharp sound tells me that under the sludge, the courtyard must be made of stone—hard enough that any fall could break my bones.

Still holding me upright with one hand gripped under my left armpit, Hagan's big hand extends farther across my left breast than I'd ever allow if I had a choice, but he's the only reason I'm not a lump on the ground.

I crane my neck to keep an eye on his movements. Seeming oblivious about where his hand is resting, he slings the chains over his shoulder and pulls a dagger from his belt. He raises it high so Nathaniel can see it.

"To cut her bindings," he explains.

"Fine." Nathaniel's response carries a warning.

Still gripping my chest, Hagan reaches all the way down to slice through the rope around my ankles, freeing me.

His hand slides away from my chest as soon as I regain my balance. Then he drops to a knee behind me and slices through the rope binding my wrists.

The cord snaps and I expect him to step away from me, but he grips both my hands, easing them slowly back to my sides.

I suck in a breath as the blood flows freely through my arms in painful increments. Still, Hagan doesn't step away, pressing my arms at intervals starting at my biceps and working down to my wrists. The pain eases with every point of pressure he applies.

It seems like an unnecessary mercy and I'm not sure what to make of the unexpected kindness from this ruthless man.

The chains scrape against the ground before he drags my arms forward, clicking the shackles around them before wrapping the extension around my waist and bending to shackle my feet.

Tanner approaches but keeps his distance. "We need to move. The King's impatient."

I glance at Nathaniel. It will be a problem if the hunters try to separate me from him, such as sending us to different rooms. The Law won't let us separate.

I watch the men around us carefully as Hagan orders us to march. We can't walk faster than a shuffle, but when Tanner asks if they should unshackle our feet, Hagan gives him a look that tells him not to be an idiot.

We proceed in silence into the dark corridors.

I've never had to test my power against metal—my starlight can burn some substances, but steel is an unknown for me. What's more, I'd have to burn through my own armor to get to the chains since they're wrapped around my waist outside my suit. The idea of running around partially naked doesn't appeal.

Tanner leads us while Hagan takes up the rear. Nathaniel and I shuffle side by side. It's a painful ascent through dark, dank corridors lined with moldy tapestries and up endless staircases.

I count the minutes before we finally reach a wooden door. Whatever elegant design used to be carved into it, the surface now contains deep gashes that resemble claw marks.

Hagan thumps his fist on the door three times, pauses, and then thumps again.

The doors swing open. Tanner steps to Nathaniel's right while Hagan steps to my left, ushering us inside.

The room is brighter than I expected. From outside, the castle ascends into the haze that covers the sky, but I didn't imagine that above the haze, the light might be clearer. We must have climbed high enough now to have access to real light.

Weak sunlight slants across the floor through wide windows on the right-hand side.

Two wooden thrones sit at the other end of the room, both the same size as each other, their high backs rising far above their occupants' heads.

A man sits in one of the thrones, but he rises when he sees us.

Like the hunters, he's naked from the waist up, wearing only black pants that tug across his muscular thighs. Colorful runes cascade all the way down his right arm from his shoulder across his bicep and down to his wrist.

He wears silver bands on both wrists that gleam in the light as he scratches his chin. I can't see the color of his eyes from this distance—brown or nearing black—while his hair is black and his upper lip is shadowed by growth in a way that accentuates his lips.

I wasn't sure how to picture Cyrian, but I didn't expect him to appear as much like a warrior as he does.

I prepare myself for discovery as he strides toward us, ready for him to identify me as fae.

CHAPTER 23

Cyrian ignores me completely, his focus purely on Nathaniel as he draws to a stop in front of us.

I sense Nathaniel's surprise too, even though he quickly hides it.

We both expected Cyrian to recognize my power immediately. I don't know why he hasn't. Unless my power is so completely diminished right now that there's nothing to sense.

I should be relieved, but being so drained makes me feel even more powerless than I already am.

I sense Nathaniel's simmering rage as his focus shifts to the other throne.

A woman writhes on it. She's wearing mahogany armor in a very similar design to mine that covers her body from her neck to her ankles, but her feet are bare.

Her chestnut brown hair cascades down her sides, knotted in appearance, as if she's either been grabbed multiple times or she's thrashed for long enough to knot it herself. Possibly both.

Her full lips are pressed together and her face is pale in a way that tells me she's in pain but unable to scream. A bruise stretches across her cheek from her cheekbone to the corner of her lip.

Her likeness to Nathaniel is startling.

I was surprised by Ethel's cold beauty, but Christiana is gorgeous in an earthy way and her presence is powerful. I can feel her anger despite her pain. Whatever Cyrian is doing to keep her in her seat, if he lets her go... she will kill him.

Nathaniel wrenches so hard on his chains that they creak and groan as if they're going to rip apart, causing Tanner to glance at him in alarm.

"Cyrian!" Nathaniel roars. "We had a deal. I became your Shield. You leave my sister alone."

Cyrian meets Nathaniel's glare, appearing unconcerned. He's as tall as Nathaniel, possibly even larger. "You broke our deal."

"I crossed the border for *you*," Nathaniel says. "To kill the fae Queen."

Cyrian's eyebrows descend into a dark scowl. "Why would you do that? You have no loyalty to me."

"I went to Bright to end the war by wiping Imatra off the face of the Earth. I did it for my people."

It alarms me how convincing Nathaniel sounds, how forcefully the story spills from his mouth.

"Ah, for your beloved people. Of course," Cyrian says.

"I fought Aura Lucidia at the border," Nathaniel continues. "When I beat her, I forced her to take me to her Queen."

Cyrian's eyebrows rise as if he's finally surprised. "You fought Aura of the Lucidia?" He pauses. "And survived?"

"More than survived." Nathaniel growls. "I prevailed."

I keep my expression clear, not giving away any emotion

that might contradict Nathaniel's story while Cyrian narrows his eyes.

"But if you had succeeded, I would have sensed it," Cyrian says. "Killing Imatra would spill magic across both Bright and Fell."

Nathaniel's jaw ticks. "Imatra lives. But I know her weaknesses now. I infiltrated her people for an entire day. I know how to attack Bright." He takes a short step forward. "Let my sister go. Honor our deal. And I'll tell you everything I know."

Cyrian's gaze slides to Christiana. He rubs his chin. "Maybe I like your offer. But maybe I like your sister more."

His gaze slides to me as Nathaniel's fists clench.

Cyrian studies the symbol on my face and my armor. "Who is this?"

Hagan steps forward. "We found her with Nathaniel. She's one of Luciana's warriors."

Cyrian scoffs. "They don't exist."

"Clearly, I do," I say, challenging Cyrian's claim.

"You do not speak unless spoken to." Cyrian's fist flies out at my cheek, but I lean left to avoid it.

He quickly regains his balance, scowls at me, and then lets fly with a series of powerful punches, which I rapidly lean left and right and duck to avoid.

His attacks demonstrate skill—not as much as Nathaniel, but I'm surprised by how agile he is and how quickly he recovers. It confirms my initial assessment—he isn't a king who spends his days ruling from the throne. He gets his hands dirty.

"Hmph." Pulling back, he considers me with new interest, but the intrigued light in his eyes doesn't feel like a good thing.

To Hagan, he asks, "How did you capture her?"

"I caught her," Tanner announces, stepping forward and drawing Cyrian's attention.

"How?"

"She... uh..." Tanner grimaces. He licks his lips as if they're suddenly dry.

I didn't fight back when he captured me, and I can see him struggling to come up with a story that sounds good now that he's in the spotlight.

Hagan speaks up again. "She didn't fall easily. She took ten arrows to her body before she was overcome. After that, she was stunned for long enough to be bound and chained."

"Ten arrows." Cyrian casts a gaze up and down my body. His hands twitch at his sides as if he wants to poke every arrow wound. "Where?"

"Her back, my king."

Cyrian laughs. "You shot her in the back. Very clever."

"Cowardly, you mean," I say.

Cyrian arches an eyebrow at me. "You prefer a fair fight? Well, how about we make things fair then."

He points at Tanner. "You. Take off her chains. I want to see what she does when she's not bound." Cyrian takes a step closer to me, his eyes glinting in the pale sunlight. Up close, I see that they are chocolate brown, but with such thick black rims that they appear charcoal.

"I sense a fire in you, whore of Luciana," Cyrian says. "I might even be willing to swap you for Christiana."

Beside me, Nathaniel's fists tug at his chains so hard that they strain, but Cyrian appears unaffected. "Your wife or your sister, Nathaniel. Whom would you choose?"

Tanner's cruel smile grows as he removes the shackles from around my feet and hands. The chains slip away—and I'm free.

My instincts fire at once, screaming at me to help Christiana, distract the King, and unchain Nathaniel—but the intense friction in the room makes me pause.

Whatever I choose to do next could escalate the simmering violence I sense in Cyrian.

Christiana must be bound by a spell—I can only free her by using my magic, which is clearly not an option right now when I'm depleted. Everything else requires attacking a human, which I can't do. Except for freeing Nathaniel. I can certainly do that.

As if he reads my thoughts, Nathaniel gives me a quick shake of his head. As long as Christiana is bound by magic, we can't act.

Cyrian folds his hands in front of his chest, his biceps bulging as he waits for me to do something.

He slowly arches an eyebrow at me. A challenge to attack.

I picture myself spilling his teeth across the floor, the satisfying thud of my fist against his cheek, and the shock that would wash across his face. All in my imagination.

The silence grows.

His eyebrows lower and his expression fills with disappointment when I don't make a move.

With a sigh, he turns to Nathaniel. "I'm a man of action. If you had assassinated Imatra, I would have hailed you a hero of the people. But you failed."

Nathaniel draws upright as Cyrian approaches him again. Despite telling me not to act, Nathaniel pulls at his chains, the links clattering and creaking.

"What's more," Cyrian continues, seeming unaffected by Nathaniel's growing anger. "I don't believe that you fought Aura Lucidia and won. Not by yourself. If ever there was a fae for whom myth is a reality, it's her. She is the first fae beside Imatra whose violent reputation has spread across

Fell country. Nobody beats Aura Lucidia—not even her own people."

He suddenly points at me, an accusing finger, and I startle.

Does he know who I am? Has he been playing us all along?

"*She* fought Aura Lucidia for you. Didn't she?" Cyrian shouts. "Only a female Warrior of Luciana would have a hope of challenging the fae Queen's Champion. That's why this woman is with you now. You conspired with her to get you across the border, but then you failed. You should have sent her to kill Imatra instead."

Nathaniel has become very still, but he suddenly seems extremely aware of my position and Christiana's, his perceptive gaze traveling the arc of the room before returning to Cyrian.

The King steps away from him. "Our deal is off. You remain a traitor to the throne. I will, however, allow your sister to say goodbye to you before I have you flogged to death."

He continues without taking a breath. "As for this woman… I'm intrigued by her. I will keep her until she bores me." He half-turns back. "Which could be sooner rather than later at this rate."

Cyrian turns his back on us with another wave of his hand.

Inky light spills from his fingers and slides through the air toward Christiana. I freeze, shocked by the ease with which he called the dark magic to himself. No spells or incantations or sacrifices. He simply waved his hand.

I shudder as I consider the seed of magic that lived in Maggie's heart. If that's where Cyrian's power is coming from so readily, then it's no wonder the humans are being wounded under its life-draining force.

Up on the throne, Christiana jolts against her chair, pressing into it and turning her head to the side, trying to avoid the dark light flying toward her. Cyrian said he was going to free her, but I guess she's experienced enough of his magic to believe that he could be lying.

Judging by the way she braces, the magic headed her way could mean an increase in pain instead.

I fight every instinct in my body that tells me to dig deeper than I have before, to seek the last possible shreds of starlight in my bones and use them to break the spell.

If Nathaniel gave me any indication that I should make a move, I would do it regardless of the danger.

The light settles across Christiana's body, falling around her head and shoulders like a blanket.

She inhales sharply, her eyes widening, and her cheeks filling with color.

Instead of hurting her, the magic appears to release her, after all.

Leaping upright, she wobbles before she recovers her balance.

Gasping in a breath, she releases it with a fearsome scream. *"You. Fucking. Liar!"*

She flies from her seat, but not at Cyrian. Not even at Nathaniel.

Hagan is her target.

CHAPTER 24

*H*agan stands his ground as Christiana charges at him, her bare feet flying across the floor and her hair sailing behind her.

Cyrian doesn't make a move to stop her, settling back onto his throne and watching her with a smile that indicates she entertains him.

Closer to me now, she is somehow littler, more fragile than she appeared from a distance, but she rams into Hagan at full speed, hitting his chest with her fists.

"You promised me!" she screams. "You promised to keep my brother away from the castle! If you had any respect for my mother, you would have kept him safe."

Hagan takes her pummeling with a growing scowl.

When her fists have no effect on him, her open palm cracks across his cheek in a fierce slap.

She has as much impact as if she'd slapped a tree. She raises her hand again, but Hagan catches it before she lands another blow.

"Do not take your anger out on me, woman," he says.

"*Woman?*" she shouts at him, her scathing gaze raking across his face and chest. "How dare you call me 'woman'? You filthy hunter. Look what you did with the honor my mother gave you."

While Hagan grips Christiana's wrist, Tanner launches into action, grabbing her waist and dragging her away from Hagan.

Nathaniel jolts a little, but the look on his face tells me he trusts that his sister can handle herself right now.

She elbows Tanner in the stomach, spins, and punches his face, knocking him on his backside before she flies back at Hagan. Hagan strides toward her at the same time, a deep glower growing on his face.

"She never should have trained you!" Christiana shouts as they hurtle toward each other. "She never should have taken you in. She should have left you in the ditch where she found you. She treated you like her own son and this is how you repay—"

Oomph. The breath knocks audibly from her lungs as Hagan tackles her, gripping her around her middle and hoisting her up over his shoulder—the one without the wolf's head.

He roars above her shouting. "Your mother would want—"

"What?" she shrieks at him, regaining her breath. She thumps his broad back, but her fists meet the pelt instead. "What would she want? You fucking bastard. You don't care what she would have wanted."

Hagan deposits her roughly back onto the empty throne right next to Cyrian's and turns his back on her.

For a second, I think she's going to leap after him, but she stays seated.

"Fuck you, Hagan Sever," she whispers, her hands forming fists beside her thighs. "You never cared about us."

He pauses in his stride, his usual glower deepening before he swings back to her. "Do not test me, woman."

"Or what? You'll put me in the King's lap? Maybe you'll hold me down when he—"

Cyrian snaps his fingers and Christiana lets out a scream, doubling over her stomach before her cries subside to whimpers. She curls up in the chair, tears leaking down her cheeks.

Nathaniel lurches beside me and Hagan stiffens, his back very straight as his fists slowly clench at his sides.

Luciana trained all the hunters—which includes Hagan. Christiana must have once trusted Hagan, but the betrayal in her eyes now is sharp and angry.

The King presses a hand to his heart, his chest vibrating as he laughs quietly. "You see, Hagan Sever, this is why I like Christiana. Being around Nathaniel's sister is like poking your hand into a fire. You know you're alive every time you get burned."

He leans across the arm of his chair, only inches from her face, smiling at her. "She fights me every step of the way. I like *fight*."

Christiana's hair falls across her shoulder as she twists toward Cyrian. Her cheeks are pale and her chest rises and falls slowly.

"I know you do," she says to him.

Her left arm suddenly swings in an arc toward his chest.

Steel flashes in her hand. A dagger is gripped in her fist.

With a sharp, strong thrust, she drives it at Cyrian's heart.

With a shout, Cyrian's hands fly up between his chest and the dagger, dark light bursting from his fingers and shielding him.

The dagger halts an inch from his heart.

His angry shout mixes with Christiana's scream of effort, their voices echoing around the room while the dark magic hums around them.

Where did she get a dagger?

Hagan jolts and checks his belt—there's an empty patch where one of his daggers is missing. She must have stolen it while she was screaming at him, a clever and brave move while everyone was distracted.

Beside me, Nathaniel suddenly roars, pulling his arms outward. My eyes fly wide when the chains creak and snap, breaking apart. Chain links pop and scatter across the ground.

He's free.

Ignoring Hagan, he spins toward me instead of Christiana.

I only realize why when I sense Tanner creeping up behind me, his dagger raised.

With a roar, Nathaniel barrels past me, lowering his shoulder just as Tanner slashes at him with the hunting knife. Nathaniel's shoulder punches into Tanner's stomach. With a swift shove, he flips the younger man up and onto his back.

Tanner lands with a thud and Nathaniel doesn't stop.

He runs toward Hagan, who stands between him and Christiana. The two men face off for a split second before Hagan throws a crushing fist at Nathaniel's face.

To my shock, Nathaniel takes the blow, but at the same time, he whips his chain around Hagan's chest and arms, dragging him away from Christiana. With a savage kick, he pulls the chains tight and forces Hagan to his knees, knocking him out with an elbow to his temple.

I leap into action too. My target is Tanner and his array

of daggers. He groans on the ground, rolling onto his side, momentarily facing away from me as he attempts to rise.

Timing my approach, I somersault over him one-handed and snatch one of his daggers as I fly across, landing at a crouch in front of him.

His eyes are glazed—a sign of concussion—but even so, he draws a wobbly breath, freezing at my sudden appearance. He can't stop me from grabbing a second dagger. My hand darts forward before I backflip away from him, holding the weapons.

Leaping back to my feet, I run in an arc around him and speed toward the thrones.

Hagan slumps to the floor, unconscious, as I draw level with him and Nathaniel. Now that Hagan's down, Nathaniel jumps to his feet and plows toward his sister.

Up on the throne, Christiana screams as she pushes the dagger with both her hands, trying to breach the force of dark magic Cyrian is using to protect himself. Sweat drips down her face and her arms shake with effort.

Cyrian isn't fairing much better. He grits his teeth, the dark light spilling up across his face making his eyes appear black and his eye sockets sunken.

He's pinned where he sits, caught behind the shield he created.

"Luciana!" Nathaniel shouts. I hear the question in his voice.

He crashes into the throne, adding his weight to Christiana's.

He needs me to break through Cyrian's shield so that they can kill him.

I try to calm my mind as I run, trying to find the cold expanse where my power lies, but there's nothing but weak sunlight and moldy air. I scream with frustration, hot tears burning my eyes. "I'm sorry!"

All I can do is distract Cyrian and hope he spreads his power too thin. I drop to a knee, raise my arm, and fling one of the daggers I stole from Tanner as hard as I can toward Cyrian's face.

The blade spins through the air and thuds into the wash of dark magic protecting the King.

I don't expect it to pierce the magic—if it had, I'd be dead—but the movement forces Cyrian to divide his power and attention between my dagger and Christiana's, weakening his concentration.

"Take the daggers!" I shout, flinging the next knife at Cyrian's forehead.

It thuds into the wash of magic, distracting Cyrian enough that his angry gaze rakes over me. His magic is spread too thin to deflect the new dagger and maintain the same barrier between him and the first blade.

The color drains from his face when Christiana's knife descends another inch, finally pressing against his heart, but it still doesn't pierce his chest.

Nathaniel grabs both of the daggers I threw at Cyrian, plucking them from the air in front of Cyrian's face, drawing back his arms and driving them, one by one, toward Cyrian's chest.

The blades stop right before they would pierce his skin, frustratingly close.

Nathaniel pushes with all his might, his biceps bulging with strain, but no matter how hard he and Christiana try, the daggers can't seem to break through.

"You can't win, Nathaniel," Cyrian gasps, straining behind the dark light. "You'll die like your father—stabbed in the back. No... Even better..."

Cyrian grins, a garish sight as he gasps for breath in the effort to maintain his magical shield. "Flogged. Your stomach cut open and bleeding... like Hagan's was... But who will barter for your life like you bargained for Hagan's?"

Shocked, I swivel toward Hagan and the two rope-like scars cutting across the right side of his ribcage. Cyrian did that to him and left him alive because of something Nathaniel offered in return.

Hagan begins to stir, dragging at the chains draped across his chest as he regains consciousness, while Tanner also stumbles to his feet behind him.

Thudding sounds on the steps outside tell me the other hunters will soon flood the room.

There's so much darkness around Cyrian, dark magic that Nathaniel and Christiana are fighting with everything they have.

It's taking all they've got and I have no way to help them. I've got nothing at all. All I can do is step between them, preparing to defend them against Hagan and Tanner.

The hum of Cyrian's dark magic grows louder behind me. His teeth are bared. "I will do whatever it takes to kill you, Nathaniel. Even if I have to do it slowly."

As he speaks, a new wash of dark light spreads along all three blades that are aimed at his chest. The light ascends from their tips to their handles, rapidly progressing toward Nathaniel's and Christiana's hands.

Nathaniel jumps back, but Christiana continues to push on her blade, screaming at Cyrian until Nathaniel grabs her, wrenching her away from Cyrian before the dark light touches her skin. "Get back! Don't let it touch you."

Just as she lets go, her blade crumbles into dust, falling around Cyrian's feet.

She fights against her brother's hold. "He'll kill you!"

"I won't let him kill *you!*" Nathaniel shouts at her. He grips her shoulders in his big hands. "Christiana, I can't lose another person."

She stills, her head tilted back to see him. "You have to be prepared to lose me, Nathaniel. Otherwise, how will we ever be free?"

She suddenly chokes and falls to her knees, her face draining of color. Nathaniel catches her in his arms, but she shakes her head, this time in a way that indicates she can't speak.

Cyrian rises to his full height behind her, ash wafting around him. A burning smell fills the air and the warmth of the sunlight shining through the windows is suddenly sickening.

"Well, that was illuminating," he says.

He brushes the ash from his coat before he points at Tanner. "Bring my whip, but let's make this flogging public."

Tanner gives a swift bow and strides from the room, smiling cruelly at me as he veers closer than he has to. "You'll die soon, whore."

I ignore him, keeping my focus on Cyrian.

The King's pointed finger swivels to Nathaniel, who holds Christiana. "The people will see what happens to someone who betrays their King."

CHAPTER 25

*H*unters pour into the room, filling the space all around us.

They're carrying spears this time, perfect to poke us in any direction they want us to go.

With a satisfied smile, Cyrian grabs Christiana's arm, wrenching her away from Nathaniel and dragging her toward the door.

He throws an order back over his shoulder. "You will do everything I say now, Nathaniel. Or I will snuff the life out of your beloved sister."

Nathaniel's expression is blank in a way that scares me.

Hagan, too, wears an unbreakable mask absent of all emotion.

Cyrian pauses at the door to spin back to me. "You will also do whatever I tell you, whore. Now, follow me. If you make any sudden moves, Nathaniel's precious sister dies."

I'm Aura of the Lucidia, you stinking pile of dung.

Yet here I am, completely shackled, even though I stand free of chains.

Christiana whimpers as Cyrian drags at her hair.

Nathaniel catches my arm as he strides toward me, propelling me along with him as the hunters converge behind us. They aim their spears at my face, poking dangerously close to my eyes.

Hagan strides ahead of the others, walking immediately behind us as we retrace our steps back to the courtyard in silence, broken only by Christiana's whimpers.

Cyrian glances back every time he hurts her, making sure Nathaniel understands what's at stake.

When we exit the building, we find the rest of the hunters —the wounded ones—sitting in rows on benches around the sides while women wearing tattered dresses apply salve and bandages to their wounds.

As soon as the King appears, one of the guards shouts to alert the others and the hunters rise to their feet.

The women rise too but keep their eyes down. They're all thin, their faces clean, but their cheeks are hollow-looking. None of them looks any older than thirty.

Hagan steps forward while Christiana glares daggers at him.

"Gather the villagers!" he shouts to the hunters. "There will be a public flogging of..." He trails off, turning to Cyrian. "What is Nathaniel's name now?"

Cyrian grins. "The same as Christiana's: *Displaced.*"

"There will be a public flogging of Nathaniel Displaced," Hagan shouts. "Get to it. The King is impatient."

The hunters immediately disperse, some of them running on foot while others head to their horses.

Tanner reappears from the side of the courtyard, carrying a whip with a long, wooden handle and two tails. Each tail is intertwined with metal barbs. Each barb has a small claw at the end of it, designed to rip open flesh.

One hit will be enough to tear someone open.

He smirks as he bows and hands it to the King.

Cyrian takes the whip, carefully folding the tails so he can hold them without gouging his own hands.

Standing beside the King, Hagan fixes his gaze on a point in the distance, but his fingers twitch at his sides. The scars across his stomach suddenly look more prominent.

Cyrian grins at Nathaniel. "You know the way to the whipping post. Get walking."

Christiana kicks Cyrian while his attention is diverted, but he evades the blow, running his hand down her arm. Dark light spills from his fingers, making her stiffen. She jolts upright, her expression blank and compliant.

The hunters come at me with their spears, poking me in the back. Nathaniel draws me quickly to his side, drawing me along the path.

"Where are they making us go?" I whisper.

"To the White Walls—the buildings we passed on our way to the castle. There's an arena there. Cyrian wants my death to be a spectator sport."

I glance back at Cyrian, who shouts at us. "Separate them!"

My gaze passes to Hagan as he strides toward me. I'm unable to tear my eyes from the thick scars across his stomach until one of the hunters jabs his spear at me, trying to force it between Nathaniel and me.

I picture myself shoving the spear back in the hunter's face and breaking his nose—right before Nathaniel does exactly that. The hunter yelps, blood streaming down his hands as he clutches his face.

At the same time, Hagan plows toward me, dipping his shoulder the same way he did before he tackled Christiana.

I backpedal, glaring at him. "Throw me over your shoulder and I will leave you unable to have children."

"I'll take my chances," he says, hoisting me up and over like I'm a damn sack of grain before he hits his stride, whisking me away from Nathaniel.

Behind me, one of the hunters slams his fist into Nathaniel's stomach. Another cracks him over the head with the butt of his spear.

My stomach lurches with fear that they've knocked Nathaniel unconscious, but he rises to his feet, groggy and bleeding as he stumbles along the path again.

I grimly consider that the hunters were preparing to give me a beating too before Hagan whisked me out of their way.

His quick stride puts distance between us at an alarming rate and I can already feel the tug as I travel farther from Nathaniel—a gap wider than I've experienced since yesterday morning.

"Slow down," I snap. "Or Nathaniel will want to break your neck."

Hagan's rough voice growls back. "Who are you to Nathaniel?"

I scowl at Hagan's back. I thought it was obvious from the markings on my face. "I'm his wife."

He makes an unhappy noise in the back of his throat. "Nathaniel disappeared for a day, claims to have infiltrated Bright, and returns with a wife. You are more than you appear."

When I remain silent, he continues. "If I can sense that there's something different about you, then Cyrian can too. You need to be careful."

The furrow in my brow deepens. "Why are you warning me?"

"Because I owe Nathaniel a debt. It's the only reason I didn't kill him this morning when I could have."

"What happened between you?" I ask quietly.

"That is not your concern." Hagan's voice changes. Angry. Sharp. "All you need to know is that nobody escapes Cyrian's power. *Nobody*. So I ask you this: How far will you go to save Nathaniel's life today?"

Pain spears through my heart so sharp, I can't control it. I'm wary of being honest. For all I know, he could be fishing for information—to see if I have a plan of escape up my sleeve. Hagan has proven himself to be unpredictable and my instincts are frustratingly silent about his motives.

I crane my head to see Nathaniel. He's far enough back that he can't hear us. He's recovered his footing, even though he's slower than normal because of his wounds.

Even from this distance, I can see that a trickle of blood runs from his temple to his chin, sustained during the scuffle with the hunters just before.

His focus appears split between me, the hunters, and his sister. Behind him, Cyrian continues to pull Christiana along like a puppet while Tanner gloats at the side.

My response is quiet. "I will do whatever it takes to keep Nathaniel alive."

Hagan stops walking and slides me to the ground more carefully than I expected. He grips my shoulders and forces me to meet his tawny brown eyes. "Then you truly are his wife."

I'm astonished by the sudden honesty being shown to me by this brute of a man, but it draws me to question his motives too. "When you brought Nathaniel here, you knew you were bringing him to his death. You did it because Christiana is in danger. What is she to you?"

"You ask too many questions," Hagan says, his expression closing off.

I rub my forehead in exasperation, but he spins me around to face our destination "We're here."

I face a solid wall made of smooth, white stone with three arched doorways carved into it at intervals. A white pebbled pathway leads through the center entryway into what appears to be an enormous courtyard covered in the same gleaming quartz stones. The pebbles are cut with sharp edges, not smooth, so that walking on them with bare feet will hurt.

Hagan glowers at me before he releases me and strides back along the path.

Left unexpectedly free and alone, I quickly assess my surroundings and the chances of escape.

Neatly-spaced trees fill the space around me. They would be easy to run through, but their trunks aren't wide enough to provide cover.

If Nathaniel could break free of the hunters, he could run with me, but Christiana is still bound by Cyrian's dark magic and we can't leave her behind. Maybe if he grabbed her and was able to carry her with us, I could break the spell once my magic was stronger—but Cyrian currently controls her every movement. There's no doubt in my mind that he is able to make her fight her brother against her will.

The only way to free her is for me to use my power in a sustained way—to burst through the dark magic and maintain a shield around us—which is impossible right now. Which means... I'm back to my state of powerlessness.

Above me, the sun is a hazy outline. The fact that I can see a silhouette at all tells me that the sun is at its highest. Even if I hadn't used up my power, I'm now at my weakest.

Tears of frustration burn unexpectedly at the back of my eyes. The only way I can help Nathaniel and Christiana right now is to use my body in any way possible.

Even if it gets me killed.

CHAPTER 26

I watch Hagan stride back along the road toward
Christiana, his boots kicking up the dirt as he
leaves the quartz path.

Nathaniel grabs his shoulder before he can walk past,
forcing Hagan to grind to a stop.

Nathaniel says something I can't hear, but his gaze is
narrow and his whole body is tense.

Hagan glowers something in return that looks equally
aggressive before he wrenches free of Nathaniel's hold. It's
like watching two dragons threaten each other.

No other human I've met so far meets Nathaniel's stature
and strength—not even Cyrian—but Hagan does, and it
unsettles me.

There's definitely a lot of history between Nathaniel and
Hagan, and I'm not sure where Hagan's true loyalties lie.
From what I've seen, his sole purpose may simply be
survival.

Hagan continues toward Christiana, bows to the King,
and then scoops her unceremoniously into his arms.

Cyrian scowls but gives a dismissive wave that releases Christiana's stiff body. She relaxes within Hagan's hold, her head turning in to his chest and her legs folding across his arm. He slows his pace then, remaining beside the King.

It dawns on me that her feet are bare.

If she walked along the pebbles, she'd cut her soles to shreds.

Hagan closed off when I tried to pry open his thoughts about Christiana, but if he didn't care about her, he would let her walk through the courtyard as she was.

A pretty voice behind me makes me spin back to the White Walls. "Look who's unchained."

Ethel's eyes glitter like cruel, blue gems. She stands in the center of the archway, dressed in a pair of pure white pants with a wraparound-style white top that is cut low at her neckline to reveal a substantial amount of cleavage.

"Only the truly powerless walk to their execution unchained," she says, leaning toward me as if she were my conspirator. "That's Cyrian's gift. He picks away at your defenses until he finds your true weakness. Then he slowly dissects you, slice by bloody slice, until you don't know he's killing you."

"What's your weakness?" I demand to know.

"Oh." She smiles. "My weakness is that I enjoy seeing others in pain. It's symbiotic with Cyrian's goals. That's how we coexist so harmoniously."

She stands aside as the hunters reach us and shove Nathaniel toward the opening in the wall beside her.

She clicks her tongue at him. "What a waste to do away with you so quickly."

She wafts past him, briskly striding all the way back toward Cyrian, calling out to the King as she goes. "Are you sure you won't reconsider your decision, my darling Cyrian?

I'm sure I could stretch out Nathaniel's torture to your satis-
faction."

Cyrian pauses as she approaches—along with Hagan,
who stops in the middle of the road still holding Christiana
—but they're far enough away that I don't hear Cyrian's
snide response.

Nathaniel avoids another spear shoved at his back as he
grabs me and pulls me toward him. There's a storm in his
eyes. "If I die, you'll be released from the Law. Kill
whomever you have to so that you can escape. Promise
me."

The nearest hunter wrenches him away from me. "Stop
talking!"

"No! Nathaniel!" I reach for him, but a hunter rears up
behind me, his grimy hand snapping around my neck and
yanking me toward the left-hand side of the courtyard, away
from Nathaniel.

Fear strikes through me as the hunters drag Nathaniel
into the center of the courtyard. A crystal-white whipping
post sits in the middle. Every splash of blood will be visible
on these white pebbles.

About five paces opposite the whipping post is another
tall post, but it's not as wide in diameter and I'm not sure
what it's for. Elevated seats surround the yard. It's like the
Coliseum in Bright except on a much smaller scale.

Until this moment, I was sure Nathaniel had a plan, that
there would be a way to escape, but now my heart is
cracking.

Has he thought through every option and come up with
nothing? Was Hagan trying to warn me that there is no
escape when he asked me how far I'd go to save Nathaniel?

I refuse to accept it.

My belief that I'm afraid for Nathaniel simply because I

want to be the one to kill him is no longer true. He's a part of my heart and I won't let him be ripped away from me.

Just like the room in the castle, two thrones sit on the right-hand side of the courtyard, directly opposite where I stand. They're positioned so that they have a clear view of both posts. The thrones are white—pristine like everything else—and made of stone.

Hagan carries Christiana to the throne on the right and sits her in it, guiding her sleeping head to the armrest. He waits for Cyrian to take a seat on the other throne before he leaves Christiana.

Then he strides toward me, wrenching me away from the hunter, whose grimy hands were sliding around places on my body where they don't belong.

"What are you doing?" I snarl. "Nathaniel's about to die and you're tying me up?"

"Like I said: Nobody escapes Cyrian." Hagan drags me to the second post, wrapping rope around my wrists and tying the other end of it around the post.

I'm now tied on a kind of leash, standing only five paces away from Nathaniel and the whipping post. The hunters are trying to force Nathaniel's arms behind his back so they can tie them around the post, but he isn't making it easy for them.

This is not an ordinary whipping, where his back will be cut open. Cyrian clearly intends to rip Nathaniel apart, starting with his stomach.

I wrench at the rope around my hands while Hagan grips me.

"Wives get to watch their husbands die," he says. "It's Cyrian's way."

His expression is closed off now and I know I'm not going to get anything from him.

He spins toward Nathaniel, who has fought his way free.

One of the hunters falls to the ground, his neck broken. Another doubles over as Nathaniel's boot meets his stomach. Blood sprays when Nathaniel's next kick shatters the man's jaw.

Nathaniel is two steps off the plate, charging toward me, when Hagan rams into him, evading a crushing blow to his head and knocking Nathaniel up against the whipping post hard enough to make it shudder.

Four hunters run up behind Nathaniel to pull his arms back and tie his wrists before he can free himself from Hagan's grip.

On the throne, Cyrian appears completely unfrazzled. He orders one of the other hunters to retrieve the dead hunter's body and drag it off to the side. Then he hands Tanner the whip.

"You," Cyrian says to Tanner. "Gut Nathaniel on my command."

Tanner grins as he strides toward the whipping post, measuring out the distance to determine where he needs to stand—halfway between Nathaniel and me, but off to my left to account for the arc of the whip's tails.

Once he's happy with his position, he allows the whip to uncurl, its metal barbs rasping against the stones on the ground.

Nathaniel's chest is rising and falling rapidly. He pulls hard enough against the ropes around his wrists to make the post shudder again. He broke his chains earlier today, but if the hunters have tied the knots properly, there will be no slipping them.

"Nathaniel!" Cyrian calls. "Consider what's at stake if you continue to struggle." He grabs Christiana's sleeping head, lifting it above the stone armrest as if he's going to bash her skull against the rock while she's under his spell.

Nathaniel exhales and inhales. He stops struggling, his focus firmly fixed to the ground.

Ethel saunters into the arena as a commotion grows outside, heralding the arrival of the remaining hunters and the villagers they brought with them.

They enter directly into the viewing stalls and I can only guess that the other two arched entryways contain stairs leading directly into the seating areas.

There are hundreds of villagers, more than I expected, a mix of women, men, and children. All of them are pushed and shoved along by the hunters. Like the women tending to the hunter's wounds earlier, they are clean but visibly malnourished, their clothing varying shades of beige.

Many of them have scarred arms or legs, even the children. But one thing they have in common is that they all look to Nathaniel and many of them are crying, even the men.

Whatever he says about his people loving his mother, they love him more.

When they finally settle into their seats, Cyrian rises.

"My people," he says, smiling up at them. "I make the rules clear. As long as you obey me, I will provide you with work and food. For those who break the rules, punishment is swift and just."

He turns to Nathaniel, rage filling his voice. "Nobody breaks their promises to me. Not even Nathaniel, who was once mighty among you. Now he is nothing. Today, you will watch him die!"

CHAPTER 27

athaniel meets my eyes across the distance and his gaze compels me to look at him.

Despite the threat to his sister, he strains at his bindings again, one last effort to break free.

The way he's looking at me... it's as if he wants to race across the distance and throw his hands over my eyes and cover them. To cover my ears and protect me from everything that's about to happen.

As he points at Nathaniel, the King's silver wristbands gleam and his dark eyes flash. "Nathaniel was once your hope for the future. But his father betrayed you. All of you! He led our army to slaughter and for what?" Cyrian peers at the crowd. "Empty claims of glory."

He strides across to Nathaniel, pauses, and then lashes out with a fist to Nathaniel's stomach. Nathaniel takes the beating, groaning and spitting blood onto the stones, breaking eye contact with me.

Cyrian glides back to his throne. "It's time to clean the

stain from our history. But first... Nathaniel, I will give you one mercy. I will release your name."

He raises his hands, dark light swirling across his fingertips. He snaps his fingers and I sense something release—some sort of magical lock.

Opposite me, Nathaniel drags a breath into his lungs, his knees buckling before he rights himself.

"My name," he breathes.

He meets my eyes again across the distance and his expression changes. The hard, determined angles disappear, replaced by the intensity he showed me this morning.

A faint smile lifts his lips that heats me all the way to my toes. He danced with me, told me he wanted me to trust him, drew his name on my face, defended me, promised to help me whenever I ask, treated me like an equal, respected my feelings and my strength...

Whatever Nathaniel's real name is—whoever he is—he is more important to me than anyone has ever been.

Cyrian smiles. "Once Nathaniel is dead, Christiana will be my wife. Now that I've released her name, she can join me on the throne." His grin broadens. "True power will then be mine."

He points at Tanner, giving him a firm nod. "Gut Nathaniel."

Tanner is already stepping into position.

"Prepare for death, Nathaniel Displaced," Tanner says, grinning back at me across his shoulder. "Your whore will join you soon."

Up in the stalls, villagers press their hands over their children's eyes. A woman in the bottom row is openly sobbing, but a hunter hits her in the face with the butt of his dagger. She whimpers and covers her mouth with her hand.

Nathaniel hasn't dropped his gaze, focused on me. Only me. Not the King. Not his sister.

Since dawn yesterday, I connected with him in ways I never expected. It doesn't matter that he's human or that we are destined to be the end of the other.

He has done everything to keep me safe—to keep my identity hidden.

Now... I'm the one who can save him.

Tanner raises his arm, preparing to swing.

I spin so that my back is to the throne and snatch the liquid dagger off my left hip. Twirling back, I pull the rope taut and slice through it.

In the same movement, I slap the dagger back onto my hip so fast that all anyone will see is the flash of a blade—and that I'm free.

My hands are still tied at the wrists, but I can move the way I need to.

I time my leap. Envisage the distance in my mind and exactly where I need to be.

Shouts rise up from the hunters as I dive toward the ground, somersaulting twice and flipping back to my feet.

The whip's deadly tails fly through the air toward Nathaniel's stomach, but I rise up right where I want to be— directly between the whip and Nathaniel.

Tanner shouts, but it's too late for him to adjust.

The lower tail strikes across my armor, dragging across my upper ribs. The upper tail strikes high across my shoulders, the final barb flicking out and catching my chin.

The claws tear through my armor, but the resistance is just enough—the material just strong enough—that the whip doesn't gouge my body, leaving bloody scratches beneath the torn material instead.

Nathaniel roars behind me. I hear the fear and pain in his voice.

He can't see my face, won't know if I'm okay, will picture me gutted instead of him, but I can't turn around while Tanner is still standing.

Ten paces away, the King shoots to his feet. Hagan is also poised to act—although his focus is on Christiana.

All I've done so far is to take the first strike. I'm not enough of a threat for the King to attack me. Yet.

Tanner recoils, sweat dripping down the side of his face.

"Bitch!" he spits, dragging the whip through the stones. "Your armor may protect your body, but I'll rip off your face."

I press the first two fingers of my left hand against my chin.

They come away coated red.

"A drop of blood," I whisper, holding my hand out toward him.

His eyes are already blank.

The whip drops from his hand and his legs buckle before he collapses onto the stones.

He falls so hard that he smacks his head on the jagged stones and blood quickly pools beneath him.

"No…" Nathaniel wrenches at the whipping post as I spin, snatch my dagger from my hip again, and slice through the ropes binding his wrists.

I slap my dagger back to my hip, but the movement was more obvious that time and I'm bound to have been seen doing it.

Cyrian screams from the side, staring at Tanner's body. "What dark magic is this?"

Ethel has turned pale, her hand clutched to her heart, frozen as she also stares at Tanner.

Up in the stands, many of the onlookers have jumped to their feet while the hunters reach for their weapons to subdue them.

I only have moments before chaos breaks out.

I grab Nathaniel's arm, pulling him close. "I'm sorry I can't help your sister. But I won't let you die. We have to run. *Now.*"

Nathaniel glances back at his sister. "Christiana—"

"I can't help her, Nathaniel! We have to come back when I'm stronger."

He grips my arm, refusing to budge. "She might not be alive later!"

My grip tightens, my heart wrenching for him. He's telling me that Cyrian could kill her before we return, but I have to make him understand that it's a chance we have to take. "If we stay, we *all* die."

Blood is smeared across his face. His clothing is torn and bruises and welts have formed across his chest and thighs.

The fight drains out of his eyes as I continue to grip his arm, unwavering in my determination to save him.

He gives me a single nod.

I don't let him rethink, pulling him into a run. He's injured, but I'm relying on his adrenaline to keep him moving.

The doorway is only a few steps away when a wash of dark magic fills the air in front of us, rushing around us like a storm and blocking our path.

Cyrian's voice roars. "Stop! You will not leave."

The dark light thickens across the doorway, a barrier that appears impossible to get through.

We skid to a stop, but I'm not afraid to test the magic, reaching my hand toward it.

I jolt away from it. It's pure malice. The heat burning off its surface tells me it will burn me alive if I touch it.

"There's no way out," Cyrian calls, prowling toward us. "Nobody gets away from me without paying whatever price I ask. You know that already, Nathaniel."

Nathaniel's grip tightens around my hand as we swing back to Cyrian. Up in the stands, hunters stand with arrows pointed at our hearts, but Cyrian shouts, "Do not kill them until I tell you to!"

He stops beside Tanner's body, bending to study the younger man's vacant eyes.

"Death by blood," Cyrian murmurs, a curious crease forming across his forehead.

He rubs his chin as he mumbles to himself. "Death without a weapon or even physical contact. Death by drawing blood... What magic is this?"

His sharp gaze pins me to the spot as he rises and stalks me, his boots crunching loudly in the silence. "The answer lies in you. Or rather..."

His fist darts out, snatching at my hip.

He pulls off one of my liquid daggers. His eyes light up with triumph.

"A fae blade." The darkest smile crawls across his face. "You are not human."

Shocked murmurs from the onlookers fill the space around us.

Christiana still sleeps, but Hagan rises slowly to his feet. He sensed there was something different about me. The way he looks at me now turns me cold.

Nathaniel said that the humans would tear me apart if they found out I was fae. Hagan handled me gently before, but there's no chance of that now.

The hatred in his eyes makes me shudder. He looks at me as if *I* am the monster.

Nearby, Lady Ethel is pale with rage. "Kill her!" she screams.

The hunters look to Cyrian, but he continues to stroke his chin, appearing deep in thought.

Nathaniel's grip is painfully tight around my hand, a warning not to speak, although I don't see how we can hide my identity much longer.

Cyrian leans in quietly and drags a cold finger down my cheek, his fingernail pressing against the golden symbol drawn on it.

I freeze to the spot, but not because I'm afraid.

It's the first time he's touched me.

My senses explode as darkness floods my body, an assault of rage and vengeance. I try to take a breath, fighting the need to strike out against the dark magic suffocating me.

Cyrian is speaking, but his voice is muffled in my hearing as I fight the onslaught of darkness.

"If you are fae, what sort of fae are you? And why aren't you using your power against me now?"

His arm darts out. Thick fingers wrap around the back of my neck as he shoves me to my knees. Using his other hand —the one with the dagger in it—he flings a barrier of dark light between Nathaniel and me to keep Nathaniel at bay.

As soon as the barrier is in place, Cyrian drives my dagger at my neck, stopping an inch before he would impale me.

I grit my teeth, my head bowed to the ground under the weight of his fist and my inability to fight back. "Do it! Spill my blood!"

"You will tell me your name," he says.

"No."

His fist tightens around my neck. "You will tell me your name… or I will burn Nathaniel alive."

Cyrian drags me upright so I'm facing Nathaniel, ripping at my hair and making me wince.

The dark magic that formed a barrier across the door has curled inward to meet the barrier between us so that a rim of magic now surrounds Nathaniel—a rapidly closing circle of dark light.

Cyrian's fingers close painfully around the back of my neck, tangled in my hair so hard that my scalp burns. "Tell me your name."

"You don't want to know my name!" I scream at him. "You don't want to know who I am." I grit my teeth at him. "Because then you will know that your days are numbered."

He shakes me. "Answer me or the next thing you hear will be your husband's dying screams."

I inhale.

It feels like my final breath—because I'm out of time.

"My name is Aura Lucidia!" I scream. "I am the fae Queen's Champion. The only Twilight fae. Killer of humans. Destroyer of souls."

All my anger burns inside me as I glare at him. "Even my own people hate me."

Cyrian's fingers splay wide against my neck, carefully untangling from my hair as he takes a backward step.

But I'm not finished.

I have one final promise that I know in my heart to be true. "If you hurt Nathaniel, I will destroy you. No matter what price I pay."

CHAPTER 28

$\mathcal{T}$he dark wash of Cyrian's power drops so suddenly that my ears hum.

The maelstrom around us vanishes, returning the courtyard to its garish whiteness.

The King stands very still, an ominous silhouette against the backdrop of dazzling white.

The villagers remain in their seats, clinging to each other while the hunters stand guard among them.

The humans fear me now, even more than they fear Cyrian, but the look on their faces when they take glances at Nathaniel is heartbreaking.

He brought me here.

The question in their eyes is undeniable: Has he betrayed them? Why would he draw his family's name on my face—a name that, by all appearances, means more to them than Nathaniel has ever revealed to me.

Why would he fight with me when I am their mortal enemy?

Cyrian's shrewd gaze passes over Tanner's body again.

"One drop of your blood killed him," he says. "That can only mean... the Law of Champions has been invoked."

Nathaniel's presence is a strong force at my back as Cyrian pitches my dagger into the ground at his own feet.

He points at Nathaniel. "You have proven yourself untrustworthy to your King and to your people. I can't rely on you to fight for me under the Law."

I sense Nathaniel's tension growing.

Another disturbing smile grows on Cyrian's face. "I invoke the Three Chances!"

I don't know anything about the old law, so I have no idea what he's talking about. I'm sure it couldn't be any worse than the situation we're already in.

"What are the Three Chances?" I demand to know.

Cyrian's eyes drag across me as he paces slowly around us. Nathaniel draws closer, his chest pressed to my back.

My adrenaline is still high, but the pain of the cut across my chin is seeping through and I fight to ignore it. I can't allow such a small pain to distract me now.

Infuriatingly, Cyrian doesn't answer me. Instead, he snarls at Nathaniel. "You changed her hair and painted her face. You thought you could hide her from me. You thought you could hide the Law from me."

He leans in close enough that the dank scent of his skin makes me shudder. "What is your weakness, Aura Lucidia?"

I'm not surprised that Cyrian doesn't know everything about me or my power. When Nathaniel first fought me, he wrongly assumed that I controlled all of the elements of nature.

I had to explain that every fae belongs to either the Sunstream or Eventide classes. The Sunstream fae control powers related to the seasons—my brother, Evander, is a Frost fae who controls wind and ice while Solstice fae control heat and fire. Sunstream fae sleep at night like humans do.

The other class of fae—Eventide fae—control the elements of night and spirit, including healing powers or the ability to commune with animals. I am an Eventide fae, which is why, very soon, my energy will be drained completely and I'll need to sleep.

I'm already way past needing rest.

Nathaniel draws me into his side. "You invoked the Three Chances, Cyrian," he says. "The clock is ticking. Or are you too afraid to take the first chance? All of your hunters are here. What's stopping you?"

Cyrian's face grows red with anger. "When was the Law invoked?"

"Yesterday at dawn," Nathaniel says.

Cyrian's glower deepens. "Then I only have half a day." He lifts his eyes, casting a dark gaze around the arena and raising his voice as he addresses his men. "The Law of Champions was invoked without my knowledge or the chance to endorse my Champion. That gives me the right to replace Nathaniel. To do so, I summon the Three Chances: three steps that must be satisfied before the start of the final day of the Law—before dawn tomorrow. If the steps are not completed by then, Nathaniel remains my Champion."

I shiver, but this time, it's in anticipation. If Cyrian can replace Nathaniel, then that means we don't have to fight.

A glimmer of hope grows inside me. This could be how we can both survive the Law…

Cyrian continues. "The first chance: I will call for volunteers. One of you must step forward of your own free will to challenge Nathaniel for the glory of becoming my Champion.

"The second chance: You must fight Nathaniel and defeat him. Then you will be worthy to become my new Champion and carry the strength of my name."

He gleams at the hunters. "Who is willing to volunteer—"

"You forgot the third chance," Nathaniel says.

Cyrian grinds his teeth. "I didn't think you would want the reminder."

"Don't spare my feelings," Nathaniel says, a dangerously cynical tone in his voice.

A cold smile settles on Cyrian's lips. "The fight between Nathaniel and the challenger will determine who has the right to be my Champion. However, if Nathaniel doesn't die in the fight against his challenger, then the third chance must be satisfied. To finally break the Vanem Dragon's seal, Nathaniel must die some other way."

Cyrian smiles at Nathaniel. "If you're still alive after the fight, anyone can try to kill you."

"Anyone but *you*," Nathaniel says. "From now until the Three Chances are exhausted, you can't touch me." He surveys Cyrian with a cold calm. "That's the real chance you take, Cyrian—that you can find someone strong enough to end me for you."

Ignoring him, Cyrian spins to his hunters. "Who will volunteer for glory?"

The hunters glower down at us, but more than one of them glances at the dead man lying at the side of the arena—the hunter whose neck Nathaniel broke. He wasn't a small man, not so easy to kill. Yet Nathaniel ended him in a heartbeat.

The silence grows thicker.

A deep crease appears in Cyrian's forehead.

"The problem with asking people to fight for you is that they have to want to," Nathaniel murmurs.

Cyrian's scowl eases as he addresses his men. "You've seen the benefits Nathaniel enjoyed as my Champion. He had access to sunlight. *Real* sunlight above the haze. Fresh air and fresh food every day. The freedom to come and go. Who wants that?"

Several of the hunters lean forward. Cyrian hasn't ordered any of them to volunteer and they seem only now to trust that he can't.

"We can't enjoy it if we're dead," one calls out.

The others shout their agreement. "If you want us to fight Nathaniel, you've got to offer us more—"

"I'll do it."

The quiet declaration comes from the side of the courtyard.

Hagan steps away from the throne, his previous hatred shuttered as he considers Nathaniel and me.

"Hagan Sever." Cyrian grins. "A true contender."

Hagan stops and folds his enormous arms across his chest, returning his focus to Cyrian. "I want something in return."

The King arches an eyebrow at him. "You get to be my Champion and enjoy all of the benefits that come with that position. That should be enough for you."

"Not even close." Hagan gives Cyrian a slow shake of his head. "The risk is high. The men who've seen Nathaniel's true strength are long dead and buried. Even if I win against him, I will face Aura Lucidia in... what? Less than two days? She has bright magic on her side. I need more than glory and sunlight for a day."

An angry hum sounds in the back of Cyrian's throat. "What do you want?"

"I want Christiana."

Cyrian blinks at him. "You can have her. Take her. Do whatever you want with her. Bring her back—"

"No." Hagan takes a threatening step forward. "I want her for myself. Mine for the rest of my life, however long that is. Without any interference from you or any other man." He glowers at Cyrian. "You will make her my wife and give me complete control over her."

Cyrian purses his lips in thought, then just as suddenly makes a decision. "If you defeat Nathaniel in battle, Christiana is all yours."

"You will give her to me now."

Cyrian's lips twist and his eyes narrow. "I have a better idea. There is one more step that must happen before the fight can occur. The Vanem Dragon must come to Fell country to seal the challenge and bind you to fight Nathaniel."

I startle, but Nathaniel holds me tightly. The Vanem Dragon has never crossed the border into Fell.

I can't imagine the dragon flying all the way from the mountains on the north of Bright into the darkness here.

"You may have Christiana after the dragon has bound you to the fight," Cyrian continues. "That way, I know you can't back out. You will then fight and kill Nathaniel before dawn."

"Agreed," Hagan says.

"Very well." Cyrian turns away from Hagan to announce to the crowd. "We await the dragon! The battle will be held in the Ditch once Nathaniel and Hagan are bound. In the meantime... it occurs to me.... that starlight only shines at night."

He swings to Ethel, who has finally ventured out from behind the throne. "When was the last time you opened up Luciana's old greenhouse, Lady Ethel?"

She flicks her hair behind her shoulder, her face screwed up in disgust. "That old place? Not for years. I have no use for flowers. Or sunlight, for that matter."

Cyrian gives me a cruel smile. "Sunlight is exactly what I want."

CHAPTER 29

*W*e exit the courtyard surrounded by a ring of hunters.

I stay close to Nathaniel, brushing the back of his hand with mine.

I have no power left, so I won't glow. Even if I did, it wouldn't matter. My identity is public knowledge now.

Ahead of us, Hagan carries Christiana away after Cyrian ordered him to return to the castle to rest and eat.

I sense Nathaniel's disquiet. Christiana wasn't awake for any of the interaction. I don't think Cyrian will dare hurt her now that Hagan has bargained for her, but I worry about what Hagan will tell her when she wakes up.

The flash of hatred Hagan showed me burns in my memory. The villagers look at me the same way.

The remainder of the hunters usher the villagers from their seats. Cyrian shouts at the hunters to ride out as far as they can and order people to come to the Ditch tonight.

"I don't care if they freeze while they wait! I want everyone to witness Nathaniel's downfall," he says. "In the meantime, Nathaniel can't run. The Three Chances tie him to me until the chances have run their course."

Cyrian continues speaking as he gleams at me. "Aura Lucidia, you are bound to Nathaniel and Nathaniel is bound to me. And soon enough, Hagan will be bound to both of you."

Cyrian leads us toward the back of the arena and through a maze of white buildings directly toward another enclosure that looks a lot like the first arena.

Although it's the same color as the other buildings, it's made from irregular stones, not polished and smooth, and it's much larger in diameter.

"That's the Ditch," Nathaniel murmurs. "It's an arena dug out of the ground. There are enclosures under our feet."

"For what?"

"Humans. Animals. Cyrian built it for his own entertainment."

We walk for another fifteen minutes before we come full circle back to the castle, this time not to its gates, but to a stone building that's built up against the castle's outer wall.

It looks like a cottage—except that its roof is made entirely of glass. One portion of the glass is smashed, leaving it with a jagged hole in the middle. The windows have been boarded up, so it's impossible to see inside.

Cyrian heads toward the outer castle wall to a large, metal wheel with a lever attached to it. A chain rests around the wheel—some sort of pulley system that ascends up the side of the outer wall and then across to the castle wall.

I study its path all the way up until the haze is too thick to see farther.

"Behold," Cyrian says with a cold twinkle in his eye. "Not magic, but science."

Nathaniel's hand tightens on mine as Cyrian slowly turns the lever. The chain creaks, catches... and unsticks.

Sunlight spears through the haze directly through the roof of the greenhouse. It's bright and golden, as pure as the sunlight in Bright.

I force myself to stay where I am, squinting in the sudden glare. I'm not the only one. The hunters lift their hands to shade their eyes and even Lady Ethel takes a step back, with a whiny, "Too damn bright."

Cyrian's rough hand clamps around my arm. "Get inside."

Sudden movement at my side makes me gasp.

Nathaniel's fist snaps out, cracking across Cyrian's jaw.

Cyrian hits the ground as Nathaniel looms over him. Golden light spills from Nathaniel's chest, mingling with the sunlight pouring around us.

The King stares upward, rubbing his jaw. "That was a bad move, Nathaniel."

Nathaniel shrugs. "It was overdue."

"Get them inside!" Cyrian shouts, spitting blood into the dirt as he rises to his feet.

Now that Christiana isn't here, Nathaniel doesn't seem afraid to lash out. The first hunter who lays a hand on me meets Nathaniel's fist. The second hits the ground. None of them seem prepared to use their daggers near me after what happened to Tanner.

Cyrian's rage increases as he watches the hunters' futile attempts to force us into the greenhouse.

"Enough!" he bellows. "Throw them in and barricade the door. No water. No food. The Vanem Dragon won't arrive before sundown. They don't come out until then."

Four hunters run at us at once. One attempts to barrel into me Hagan-style, but I sidestep so that he thuds into the stone building instead. He only just gets his shoulder up so he doesn't break his own neck.

Sadly, I find that I side-stepped into the middle of the doorway.

Dark stars. My reflexes and instincts are dull with fatigue. There's no way I can sustain a fight with these men.

The others jab their spears at Nathaniel, finally pushing him through the opening with me.

The moment he steps through, they slam the door shut and Cyrian screams for wood to nail the opening closed.

Sunlight beats down on my head and shoulders, sapping my strength.

Pain fills my body. Instant. Cruel. Heat floods the entire space and I'm already burning up in it.

I wobble over to the wall and lean against it. The glass ceiling doesn't cast a single shadow. Squinting upward, I seek the source of the sunlight, finding the glare originating from a structure far above us.

"There are reflective silver panels on top of the castle," Nathaniel says, scooping his arm around my waist as he lifts me and studies our surroundings, squinting hard to see in the glare. "This greenhouse was once a place of miracles. People came here for healing, not torture."

Echoes of beauty exist all around me. Pale blue tables stand at angles while intricately carved clay pots lie over-turned and cracked, their terracotta shards mixed with the husks of dead plants.

Nathaniel quickly checks my face, peering into my eyes as I try to focus on him. In the bright light, the deepening circles under his eyes fade, a trick of the light that makes him look well-rested.

He's as fatigued as I am.

"You need to sleep," he says, focused on me. "You'll get through this if you sleep."

He props me against the wall, sweat already dripping down his face as he presses his hand briefly to my cheek. "I'll make shade. We can sleep under it."

I inch my way along the wall, determined to help him.

As soon as he sees me following him, he takes hold of my hands again, urging me to stay still. "You need to conserve your energy. Let me do what I can to help us both."

My vision blurs as he drags tables into position, turning three onto their sides with their legs facing outward. He rapidly positions them with their corners touching before he upturns a fourth table and places it over the top, forming the beginning of a shelter. The opening faces away from the beams of sunlight streaming in from above.

Judging by the thudding sound outside, Cyrian has everything he needs to barricade us in now.

Climbing the wall, I force myself to move. "Is there any chance they'll come in here sooner than they threatened?" I ask, lowering my voice. Air puffs in from the cracked roof, the door bangs once more, but then it's very quiet and I'm not sure how far sound will travel.

"Cyrian will leave us in here to sweat as long as there's sunlight. He'll only come and get us before sunset if the Vanem Dragon arrives sooner."

"Is that likely?"

"The Vanem Dragon can choose to arrive when he pleases," Nathaniel says as he slides a second overturned table into position across the top of the shelter to complete its roof. "But it won't be soon. Hagan and I can only fight once the dragon binds us. Cyrian then has from that moment until dawn to make sure I die."

He kneels in the opening and removes his shirt, his head disappearing and his voice muffled as he ducks inside. "The longer the dragon waits... the less time Cyrian has to end me."

I can't endure my armor in this heat. The black material is attracting the sunlight and trapping the warmth against my skin—it's designed for winter frosts, not the summer sun.

My hands are slippery with sweat as I tackle the clasps at the side, finally peeling the suit off my arms and down to my waist as I stumble toward the shelter.

I need the shade or I'm going to pass out.

Moaning with relief, I drop to my knees and slip into the shadow of the shelter.

My groan is loud enough to startle Nathaniel, who's wiping out the base of the shelter with his shirt. At my sudden appearance, he jumps and bangs his head on the table above him.

"Are you okay?" I twist in the entrance, my suit sitting awkwardly around my waist as I reach for him, trying not to bang my own head. "Show me."

He winces at me, rubbing his scalp but refusing to turn his head for me to see where he bumped it. His gaze flickers from my naked stomach all the way up past my human underwear to my eyes. "I'm fine. It was just a bump."

There isn't enough room to sit upright in the shelter, so I drop onto my back and lift my hips off the ground to peel the armor over my backside.

I vaguely register Nathaniel pause in the entrance and can't imagine how provocative my pose is right now, but he's demonstrated more respect and care for my body than I thought possible.

Tipping onto my side, I shimmy the suit down my legs

one by one. As soon as I kick my boots off, the armor finally slips from my body.

I shove the boots into the corner above my head where I can grab them easily, bundle the armor under my head, close my eyes, and sigh out an exhale.

The floor is gritty, it's not nearly as dark as I need it to be, but inside the shelter is a whole world better than outside it.

"Thank you." I sigh.

"Don't thank me, woman."

His response is unexpectedly gruff. I crack open one eye to see him.

"That word means something more here, doesn't it?" I ask. "When Hagan called Christiana *woman*, she nearly tore his head off. What does it mean?"

A wonky and unexpected smile softens Nathaniel's face before he slides into the space beside me, pulling the final table over the gap at our feet, an awkward task.

"It means *mine*," he says, lying down beside me. Not touching. "You need to sleep now, Aura."

The beating sun made me feel like I was going to pass out —all I could think about was getting inside the shelter and surviving the glare.

Now that I'm safe, all of my questions resurface.

I follow the contours of Nathaniel's face, his shoulders, muscles, the dirt clinging to the droplets of sweat dripping down his skin.

He turns away from me, a resolute movement, seeming determined to shut down all conversation.

All it does is remind me of the crisscross of scars on his shoulders, along with the remains of the symbols inked beneath the scars.

"Who are you?" I whisper.

"A traitor," he says. "A human who fell in love with a fae."

My eyes widen as heartache fills my chest. I remember the way his people looked at him when my identity was revealed. They were shocked. Confused. The foundations had clearly shifted beneath them. They didn't understand why he hadn't killed me.

I slide toward him, slipping my arm around his waist and pressing up against his back. "I'm a traitor too."

He turns in my arms, allowing me to hook my leg around his hip and nestle my head in the crook of his arm. He strokes my back before he tips my chin. "We have the same wounds again."

Yesterday, he and I ended up with nearly identical cuts on our left arms from wounds sustained during different battles.

Today, we both have bruised ribs in nearly identical places—again, sustained during different battles and for different reasons. Nathaniel's back is bruised because of his charge into the tree. Mine is bruised because of the arrows that hit me and because Tanner kicked me when he forced me to become acquainted with the dirt. Both of our chins and chests are cut.

"I don't have this one," I whisper, hovering my palm above the cut on his forehead.

He gives me another wonky smile. "I won't allow this one to happen to you."

My lips find his, brushing the shape of his skin. "Nathaniel, please tell me about your name. I know Cyrian released the spell that was stopping you from speaking it. I felt the dark magic lift."

He stiffens in my arms, but I clasp him tightly, refusing to let him go. "Yesterday, you said that if you told me who you are, I wouldn't trust you. But that was then. This is now."

He reaches out to brush the hair from my temple, his

thumb grazing my cheek, but his lips are drawn into an unforgiving line, merciless.

It's the same way he looked at me when he first saw me.

"To answer that question is to tell you all the things I don't want you to know about me. All the answers you want, but none of what you need."

"Who are you to say what I need?" I ask, trying to quell the frustration rising inside me. "You've known me for a day and a half. You've barely scratched the surface."

"You're right." He nods, but it's a suddenly angry movement. "There's so much more I want to know about you, so much more I need, but there's no time. I need a lifetime to understand your thoughts and your heart. But I don't have it. All I have is now. I don't want to lose you in the few hours I have left."

I study his face, the hard lines of his jaw, his broad shoulders, bare arms corded with muscles, and the way his dark hair falls across his cheeks.

Even lying in the dirt with me, I'm reminded that he's dangerous. He beat every hunter who came after him today. But the only person he didn't beat is the man who is going to fight him this evening.

A sudden shiver runs down my spine. "Is Hagan capable of killing you?"

"We trained side by side. He knows every move and strategy that I know. He knows my weaknesses like I know his."

Until now, I haven't once considered the possibility that Hagan will kill Nathaniel today.

Suddenly, sleep is the last thing I need. The next hours with Nathaniel may be the most important hours of my remaining life.

I need answers and I'm not prepared to wait any longer.

I tighten my arm around his waist and clamp my upper leg across his hips, not caring about the dirt and sweat.

His arm flexes around me, dragging me even closer, his hand resting flat against my spine.

"Aura?"

The sound of his voice and the nearness of his body trigger every need inside me, but I refuse to be distracted.

I tilt my head back to meet his eyes.

"Tell me," I whisper. "Everything."

Nathaniel strokes the hair from my cheek, his fingertips lingering on the shape of my neck. I don't think he's going to speak, but then he says, "My true name... is Exalted."

I tip my head a little, pursing my lips in thought. Human names represent status and occupation, so... "*Exalted* means...?"

He is very quiet and still. "Highest."

"I don't understand."

His fingertips rest on my neck lightly. Precariously. "To be the highest is to be above everyone else."

I give a little laugh because what he said is obvious, but he still hasn't answered the riddle of his identity. "Higher even than the King?"

Nathaniel's speech is careful, cautious. He watches my face as he speaks. "Cyrian wasn't born into the royal line. He was my father's Champion. When my father died, Cyrian became the caretaker of the throne until I was old enough to—"

"Stop." I draw back from him. Fear rises like a tide inside me. My speech is as stilted as his was calm. "Your father was the King."

"He was."

My heartbeat slows, but it's like the pause before a storm begins to rage. "You're telling me that Cyrian stole the throne. That you're the rightful heir."

My heart pounds hard inside my chest. "You're the Fell King?"

"I am."

CHAPTER 30

*F*ear. Too much fear rises inside me.

When Nathaniel came for me, he planned to convince me to help him overthrow Cyrian.

Now I know that means he wanted me to help return his Kingdom to *him*.

But before he could carry through, I invoked the Law of Champions.

Now, the fight between us is for control of both lands.

We're fighting on behalf of our monarchs, but if Nathaniel is the true King of the Fell Kingdom, then that means...

I'm frozen in his arms. "You have everything to gain from my death."

He starts to speak, but the darkened space spins around me, and I can't stop talking, can't find my foundations. They've been ripped out from beneath me. "Even if you win for Cyrian, he doesn't have the right to rule. You can claim your birthright. If you kill me, you will have power over everything—"

"I don't want power over everything!" His response is loud enough to break through the buzz in my ears. "I just want freedom for my people. I want them to wake up to a day without fear, to know that they're cared for and safe from harm."

His arms tighten around me, but I struggle against him, trying to get free. "You need me to die."

"No—"

"That only happens if I die!" I scream, wrenching against him. "You only get justice for your people if I'm dead. That's the only way."

"I don't want—"

"Don't want what, Nathaniel? Don't want me to die?" Tears leak down my cheeks. I sense them slide across the marks Nathaniel made with the wedding ink—*golden* wedding ink, the kind a king would use to mark his queen. "That's a fool's wish."

He opens his arms, letting me go.

I bang up against the other side of the shelter so hard that I nearly topple the table above us.

A beam of sunlight streams in and I edge away from it.

The burn across my skin draws another thought to my mind. A horrible, clawing, heartbreaking thought. "Did you make me fall in love with you so I would choose to die instead of fighting you?"

His eyes widen. Pure shock. "You know I didn't. Hating you would be far easier. If I hated you, I would have killed you already."

"But you wouldn't." A laugh tears out of me. Cruel. I don't even sound like myself. "You need my help to overthrow Cyrian first. *Then* you can kill me."

Nathaniel is completely frozen opposite me, not even a breath.

Then he sucks in air, and his chest rises and falls far too fast, his inhalations hitching as if he's in pain.

He suddenly presses his palm against the location of his heart. "I made you a promise, Aura. I promised to protect you—"

"And to fight me on the final day."

"I won't let you die! You're my wife—"

"Then let's do something about that." My fingers rub in the dirt beside me, gritty and harsh.

I lurch into a sitting position and slap the granules against my face, rubbing as hard as I can against the symbol he drew on me, scratching as deep as I can into it.

The pain barely registers.

I'm angry. And afraid. More afraid than I've ever been.

When I thought that Cyrian was the rightful King, I could balance out the future in my mind. Imatra and Cyrian are both cruel and reckless with their power in different ways. Neither would make a peaceful ruler of both lands. But Nathaniel... his people love him, respect him, trust him. Maybe a little less right now, but they will come to trust him again. He would treat them with fairness and justice.

He would make a *good* King.

Even for the fae. He may not love them like he loves the humans, but he would treat them fairly.

Tears fall down my cheeks because I know... in my heart... that Nathaniel has to live and I have to die.

My hands are shaking. My face hurts. I've rubbed too hard across my temple and now I'm bleeding.

"There," I say, my voice catching. "Now we have the same wound."

He didn't try to stop me, but I sense the storm in his emotions. He withdraws to the other side of the shelter. The light on my side is brighter now that I displaced the table.

"You're breaking my heart, Aura."

I rotate toward the wall before my tears turn the dirt to mud. "Better to break now than when you have to kill me."

The light from above me glints in my eyes. It reminds me of the glow inside Nathaniel's chest when I looked into his heart.

The sun will carve a path toward the horizon soon. Then I'll be strong again.

I'm sure I won't be able to sleep, but emotional exhaustion has drained me. Somehow, my eyes close and I welcome the deep oblivion.

Darkness presses in around me.

The cold expanse in which I sleep squeezes my chest, freezing me in the *nothing* where I belong.

I'm dreaming. I know I'm dreaming, but even in the dream, it feels so real.

Pain bursts inside my mind, dark light tearing through the nothing and curling around me like a hook, ripping through my chest, my body, dragging me down where I don't belong.

I drop like a stone, burning through the cold expanse, unable to fight back, screaming as I fall.

I hit solid ground and the world explodes around me. Bright white light tears across my vision, expanding my senses, rippling outward in waves so massive, it's like the world is an ocean and I am a storm crashing across its surface.

A woman runs within the wash, racing toward me, a crimson glow around her silhouette so bright that it obscures her face.

She carries a blade in her hand.

When she drops to her knees, I realize that I'm lying on the ground and the ripples rolling across the world are spreading across the sky above me.

Her dagger glints as she raises it, sharp, curved, its target certain: my chest.

I can't fight. Can't breathe. Can't move.

An angry, golden light grows behind her, a male form holding a swinging blade strong enough to cleave off her head.

It carves a space through the wash toward her neck, the symbol etched into it burning into me: the sun and the moon.

He's too late.

The woman's hands are already splattered with my blood.

I wake up screaming, my cries rebounding off the surface of the overturned table that I'm facing.

My palms are pressed flat against it and my power blasts it across the room, shattering wood, sending shards spiraling into the air.

The two tables that lie above me drop without the support beneath them. My reflexes kick in and I roll backward into the safe space—the triangle that the fallen tables now form.

Nathaniel's arms clamp around me the moment I hit his body in a full-length collision, my back pressing to his front.

My heart is pounding—a wild thud—but it's still beating. It hasn't been ripped out of me.

The dream wasn't real.

Even though the man's blade really does exist. It's the only weapon Imatra ever seemed afraid of when she saw it in Nathaniel's hands yesterday. His father's halberd.

Outside our shelter, everything is quiet again. Dark too,

telling me that night has fallen. The air is much cooler, drifting through the cracks in the shelter and easing the heat.

My armor and boots are now outside the shelter, since the tabletops have fallen short of their location.

The cold trickle of power through my chest means the moon will dominate the sky very soon.

"Aura?" Nathaniel asks.

"Your father was there when I woke up fifteen years ago," I say, drawing the only conclusions I can from the dream, spilling my thoughts more quickly than I probably should. "Imatra wanted to kill me, but he wanted to kill her."

Nathaniel doesn't say anything. He promised to always tell me the truth and I'm slowly learning that means sometimes he will choose silence rather than lie to me.

"What now, Aura?"

He asked me the same question this morning. In answer, I placed my hand in his and followed him into the dark, but I won't do that again.

"Now I will keep you alive," I say, preparing to shimmy out of the small space.

"That's all?" he asks.

I can't tell if his question is angry or sarcastic. As if he's saying that keeping him alive will be an impossible task.

Peering over my shoulder, I try to read his expression, but his face is in shadow.

He can't hide in the darkness from me.

I allow my power to shine, casting light across his face. He looks drawn, still slightly groggy, making me suspect that I woke him from a deep sleep when I screamed.

"You could have rolled in the other direction," he says, a challenging statement of fact. "You didn't have to roll into my arms."

I snap forward again, scowling into the cramped space.

When the tables toppled, I could have darted toward my clothes and ended up outside the shelter, not plastered up against Nathaniel in nothing but my underwear.

A retort rests on my tongue, but I inhale his scent before I can let my scorn loose.

Even sweaty and dirty, he smells like sex and heaven. In that order.

Squeezing my eyes shut, I try to forget what his hands can do to me, what his lips can do to me. When I don't immediately pull out of his arms, they ease around me.

His lips press to the sensitive spot on my neck just behind my ear, making me shiver to my core.

"You scrubbed my name off your face," he whispers. "You want to break us apart and put as much distance between us as possible, but it won't work, Aura."

His gaze burns me as he says, "We're bound together, body and soul. My heart to yours."

CHAPTER 31

*N*athaniel's fingers splay across my bare stomach, his big hand allowing his fingertips to brush across the top of my pelvis, slow strokes that burn through to my center.

"You can't get to my heart through my body," I snap. "Not this time."

"I want to get to your mind, Aura. Your beautiful mind. That part of you that has already reasoned through every outcome of the next one and a half days and come to a single conclusion."

I shiver again, but this time, it's fear. Our second day will soon be over. I want to claw back the time and return to Null. Stay there and never leave.

"You believe that there is only one path now, but that's not true," he says. "Every minute, every breath we take, we have the chance to change the course of the future."

The conviction in his voice tells me he believes what he's saying, but I can't allow any hope to cloud my judgement.

I turn in his arms, cautiously and awkwardly. He's as

dirty and sweaty as I am, mud smeared across his cheeks, dust glistening on his chest.

"You're not the only one who has choices to make, Aura," he says. "I can't ask you to trust me now. Or believe me. But I won't stop trying."

The space between us glows again. My power is returning with a vengeance with every breath I take. As strong as that makes me feel, my hand trembles as I press my fingers to my face. I ground dirt into my wounds. The most reckless thing I could have done.

I lower my hands, pressing them against his chest, but he doesn't take advantage of the contact like I thought he might.

"You said the dragon will take as long as possible to get here," I say. "Do you still think that?"

He nods. "Midnight is my guess. In the meantime, Cyrian will leave us here because he wants us as weak and dehydrated as possible, but there's something he forgot about: a water pump in the corner of the greenhouse."

We need to hydrate. I give him a quick nod, preparing to wriggle downward. He beats me to it, withdrawing his arms to maneuver himself slowly toward the opening, feet first.

He pauses as his head reaches the level of my stomach and then my pelvis, dropping two quick kisses on either side of my hips, his palms grazing my thighs as he continues on his way.

By the time I wriggle out of the shelter, he crouches next to an obstruction of pots piled in the corner of the greenhouse. He carefully shifts them out of the way.

The water pump he reveals is like finding gold, but when he pumps it… nothing happens.

He spins to me, grinning. "Wait for it…"

The ceiling suddenly opens up like storm clouds. Water sprays around me, misting across my skin.

Nathaniel bends to the pump again. "If I turn this dial..."
He pumps the lever again and this time, clear water pours
from the spout. "It comes directly from the spring, so it
should be safe to drink."

He rinses out a cracked piece of ceramic with enough
depth to form a cup, filling it and handing it to me before he
finds one for himself.

I fill and refill the bowl until my thirst is quenched, nearly
bursting with how much water I drink. As I lean back against
the wall with relief, I startle to find Nathaniel stripping off
and hanging his clothes carefully over the table.

He steps directly in front of the pump, turns the dial
again, and pumps the lever. A moment later, a cascade of
water pours from the ceiling onto the spot where he stands,
drenching his body and washing off the first layer of dirt.

It also washes off the blood.

I worry at my lip when I can finally see his wounds. Cuts
across his arms and legs. He winces as he carefully washes
out the wounds, pumping the lever again.

I stride across to him. "Here. Let me."

My hands brush his as I take hold of the pump and give it a
good push. It takes a bit of effort, but it's nothing I can't handle.

He considers me quietly—but his silence feels a little
dangerous—his gaze shadowed in the growing dark before
the water cascades down his damn perfect body again.

I allow myself to glow a little as night thickens outside so
that Nathaniel can concentrate on washing out his wounds.

The sun must have sunk well below the horizon now—I
can tell because of the falling dark—but there's nothing to
see beyond the glass ceiling above us. No visible stars. Right
now in Bright, the stars would be sparkling like diamonds
scattered across the sky.

"Was last night the first time you saw the stars?" I ask. I pump the lever again as I search the sky above us, hoping to see the moonlight that I crave.

"No."

His arms crash around me, pulling me against his body under the stream of water.

I gasp as the liquid plasters my hair to my face, washing across my head and shoulders, soaking through my bra and underpants.

I tip my head back, my breasts pressing against his chest, my legs straddling his thigh.

"The first time I saw starlight was when I saw you," he says, dragging me up against him so that I have to arch up on my tiptoes to keep my feet on the ground, completely reliant on him to retain my balance.

The water stops flowing, but I'm already soaked. It's hard to care when all I feel is the pounding of my heart and the heat of his body.

One arm still wrapped around my waist, he places me firmly back on my feet, then leans to the side and pumps the lever one-handed, causing another cascade of liquid to wash over me.

I tip my head back, close my eyes, and let it flow.

His arms slip away from me. "Wash now, woman."

He shakes out his hair and stands to the side, butt-naked and dripping, controlling the pump to keep the water flowing.

I let it wash through my hair first, then across my shoulders before I remove my underwear and check over my wounds—scratches across my stomach and cuts on my face that I can feel but not see.

He surprises me by holding out his hand for my wet

underwear, wringing it out and slapping it across his shoulder.

He gives me a cocky grin. "Your clothing will dry faster with my body heat."

"What about me?" I ask, giving him a challenging stare. Completely reckless given the distance I'm trying to put between us. He hasn't bothered to dry himself off and there's nothing resembling a towel in sight. "How am I going to get dry?"

He looks me up and down, a brazen glance. "Hmm."

He gives the lever a pump without taking his eyes off me, but this time, he reaches above my head to fill a ceramic container to the brim. The water resumes its cascade around me as he strides away to the nearest table, turns it the right way up, and throws the water over the top of it.

What a strange thing to do...

I watch him carefully as he returns to the shower, fills the pot again, and repeats that three times until the water runs clear off the top of the table.

Then he comes back a fourth time, carrying his dirty shirt with him, and edges his way under the water so that I have to step out of the flow.

He washes his shirt out—again until the water runs clear.

There's still enough heat inside the greenhouse that I'm not cold—even with the cracked opening in the ceiling.

Returning to the table, he spreads the shirt and my underwear out flat across it as if he's expecting the sun to come out any moment and dry them.

I can't help the laugh that bubbles to my lips. Watching him concentrate on his task makes me think this is how I must have looked last night when I carefully lay myself down on the surface of the Spinning Lake to see the diamond in its depths. Completely absorbed and determined to carry through with my goal.

"I don't see how that answers my question," I say, unable to keep the smile out of my voice.

"No," he agrees. "But this might."

He prowls back to me, and this time, his heated gaze burns across my every curve.

A shiver runs to my toes, but I stay where I am and wait for him to reach me, my head held high, water dripping down my body.

He reaches across my shoulder, takes the length of my black hair in his big hands, and squeezes the water out of it, then he allows my hair to drop against my back again.

I cast him a questioning glance.

He gives me a half-smile that makes my heart miss a beat.

With tantalizingly slow movements, he slips one arm around my waist and hooks his other beneath my backside, bending his knee and angling it between my legs.

Slowly, he draws me upward.

His voice rumbles in my ear. "The door to the greenhouse may be closed, but all you need to do is say *no*."

I tip my head back to see him. Washing ourselves was necessary. This is not. A completely unnecessary drain on our energy, in fact.

"You have to fight soon," I say.

"And?"

"You need to conserve your energy."

He drops a kiss against my ear that makes me shiver. "Dark stars, Aura. If I have an hour left alone with you, this is how I want to spend it. If you're objecting on your own behalf, then say so and I'll stop, but let me make my own choices about what's best for me."

My lips part and my cheeks burn. "Am I still your wife?" I

press my palm to what must remain of his family name after I scrubbed off the ink. "Did I change anything when I did this?"

"Does it make a difference?"

I shake my head: *No.* "My path is yours. And yours is mine. Until one of us is dead."

It doesn't seem to matter how much I try to keep Nathaniel at a distance, to keep him away from my heart.

I find myself spinning back to him. His body. My body. The glow from his heart and the glow from mine.

He crushes me up against him, his lips finding every reachable part of my face, neck, and chest as he carries me to the table.

CHAPTER 32

*B*y the time Cyrian's hunters tear the barricade off the door, the light in the sky has changed to an eerie white glow that tells me the moon has risen fully.

Nathaniel and I are dressed and as ready as we can be for whatever's coming our way.

We stand back from the doorway, quiet and prepared.

Even though my armor is ripped across my stomach and chest, I still carry one remaining hip dagger as well as the sword concealed across my shoulder. Luckily, Cyrian doesn't know enough about fae armor to know that the dagger I used earlier is not my only one.

Nathaniel is dressed in his long pants and shirt again—even though the material is also ripped and, in his case, damp. I'm worried about the cold when we leave the greenhouse. I haven't spent a night in Fell country to know whether the temperature drops as severely as it does in Bright.

I want to ask him about the humans in Null—they will be waiting for us to return and preparing to fight, but when I try, the words stick in my throat—and not because I'm nervous.

"What about Null?" I finally manage to ask, trying to shake off the block in my mind that stops me from even thinking about the human army. In fact, it's been hard to even remember them since I left Null.

Nathaniel gives me a wry smile. He watches me practically chew my words as I speak them. "Nobody who leaves Null can speak about what is there." He shakes his head, scowling as he chooses his speech. "But I'm sure it's fine."

It's hard to place an interpretation on what he said—I'm hoping he means the humans are safe and will stay where they are. They shouldn't attack the castle tonight because there's no safe plan of attack while the Three Chances are in play.

The back of Nathaniel's hand brushes mine, the barest connection as the clattering at the door increases and it's finally flung open.

"Out!" One of the hunters shouts. He's one of the few whom Nathaniel didn't beat bloody earlier—a large man with a scar that meanders down his left arm from his shoulder to his wrist. I heard the others call him "Snake" and it seems to match his personality as well as his scar.

Snake lifts a bottle of water to his lips as he stands in the doorway, blocking the exit despite his order. I think he's trying to goad us into trying to take the flask because he expects us to be dehydrated.

We've concealed the water pump again, but the scent of rain fills the greenhouse, fresh and dewy. He doesn't seem smart enough to notice.

Behind him, ten other hunters hold burning torches that cast garish shadows across the animal heads sitting on their shoulders.

"No Cyrian this time?" I ask, not seeing the King among them.

Snake grins. "You're his entertainment while we wait for the dragon."

I tip my head, unimpressed, and allow my magic to glow around my fingers. Its calming light won't harm anyone, but Snake jolts backward in case it touches him.

"We'll see about that," I say, catching Nathaniel's hand and spearing through the gap Snake's sudden step back created.

If we need to fight for our safety, I would rather be outside in the open to do it.

Starlight glows brightly around both of us, but I have to be careful about how much I allow it to touch Nathaniel. If the hunters see that it doesn't hurt him, they'll figure out it won't hurt them, either.

Snake recovers quickly, moving into position and ordering the other hunters to surround us. The opening in front of me closes far too fast, but at least we're outside the greenhouse now.

Snarling, Snake pokes his spear at me. "You're going back to the White Walls. Lady Ethel wants to play with you."

I hide my shudder, taking comfort in Nathaniel's presence at my back. Ethel told me that her weakness is enjoying other people's pain. Nathaniel said that if Cyrian found out I was fae, he would torture me to the full extent he could without shedding a drop of my blood.

The longer the dragon takes to arrive, the longer Nathaniel stays alive. But it also extends the time that Cyrian has to make my life unbearable.

Snake leads the way back to the White Walls.

When we arrive, we find that the arena has been cleaned up. There's no sign of the bodies or the blood. The stones are pristine again. Torches are attached at intervals around the walls to light up the space, although there are no spectators this time.

Cyrian reclines in one of the thrones. A large, brown pelt falls across his shoulders with the head of a bear encasing the back of his head, its jaw framing his forehead.

Nathaniel said that Cyrian was his father's Champion. Cyrian must have been physically strong—he still is, although his fighting skills have given way to his reliance on magic.

I have no doubt Cyrian killed the bear himself, but whether he did it with or without dark magic is another question.

Christiana sits rigidly on the throne beside him. It's impossible to tell for sure, but it doesn't look like Cyrian's controlling her with dark magic this time.

She's wearing a glittering black dress, low cut and fitted. A black pelt with white flecks rests around her shoulders and a chunky diamond necklace plunges from her throat to her cleavage.

Her glistening brown hair is piled on her head, a few wisps trailing past the darkening bruise across her cheek. Torches on either side of the thrones accentuate her pale cheeks and catch the diamonds.

If it weren't for the bruise, she would look like Cyrian's Queen, not his captive. Her gaze immediately seeks Nathaniel, the deep worry in her eyes making my heart squeeze.

When she looks at me now, her lips press together in a firm line and the tension around her eyes increases.

Her fingers tighten around the armrests of the throne, as if she's restraining herself. I can only guess her emotions. She wanted to strike Hagan for bringing Nathaniel to the castle and putting him in danger, so her feelings toward me must be beyond angry: rage that I'm fae, fury that I will fight Nathaniel under the Law, hatred that I'm the reason he's captive now.

And beneath it all must be confusion about why he doesn't treat me with hatred.

As Snake draws to the side of the arena behind us and the other hunters enter the stands, I quickly assess the rest of the area.

Plush lounge chairs with blood-red coverings have been brought into the arena, located on either side of the thrones.

Ten other people sit in them, drinking from crystal goblets. They're all dressed in fine clothing and wearing glittering necklaces and bracelets—even the men.

One of them is Lady Ethel, so I guess the others are somehow part of Cyrian's Court, that they've gained favor in one way or another like she has.

A shadow moves at the side of the arena. Hagan is dressed in simple black pants and a shirt, similar to Nathaniel's clothing, but he's also wearing his pelt to stay warm, the wolf's head appearing even more vicious in the flickering lamp light. A row of daggers rests around the belt at his waist.

Hagan's eyes narrow with anger as his gaze rakes over my cheeks. He steps forward as if he's about to say something, but Ethel jumps to her feet, interrupting him.

She's holding a set of chains consisting of links that appear to be covered in velvet.

"Oh, good," she says as she zeros in on me. "You're finally here to entertain us. I really don't know why Cyrian left you to boil for so long."

Cyrian grins in the background, a cruel smile. He doesn't seem to mind Ethel's verbal jab.

Ethel pauses in front of me before she begins to circle us.

"My, my, look at your face. What an extraordinary quarrel you must have had to wipe Nathaniel's name off your body."

I don't know what I look like right now, but I can imagine how ugly I appear with the remaining scratched flecks of gold lacquer combined with all the bruises and scratches on my face.

Ethel runs her hand down my arm and across my stomach, pouting at the rips in my armor. She wanted it for herself and now it's ruined.

She turns to Nathaniel where he stands directly behind me. Her fingertips glide across his bicep.

His fist snaps out the moment she touches him, but she darts beyond his reach.

"Feisty!" she exclaims before she spins to Hagan. "Keep Nathaniel busy, won't you, Hagan?"

Hagan snarls. "Do your own dirty work."

Ethel's jaw drops, exaggerated outrage shooting across her face as she clasps her chest. She lets out a dramatic laugh. "Well, I never!"

At the side of the arena, Cyrian shoots to his feet, grabs Christiana's hair, and wrenches her in Hagan's direction.

Christiana screams before she clamps her lips closed, half-standing, visibly swallowing the rest of her cry while Cyrian stares with cold eyes at Hagan.

Nathaniel twitches beside me and I don't miss the unspoken communication between him and his sister. His worry. Her pain. But she grits her teeth and remains silent.

Hagan responds to Cyrian's threat of violence against Christiana by lowering his head with a snarl, his fists clenching in a brief pause before he shrugs off his pelt and strides forward to take a swing at Nathaniel. Nathaniel backsteps to avoid the blow, but it drives him away from me.

When Nathaniel tries to get back to me, Hagan shoves him farther away.

As soon as Nathaniel leaves my side, Ethel pounces, stretching out the chains toward me.

I step to the side to avoid her, but I bump right up against a large body.

"Got you," Snake whispers, his hands clamping around my arms.

Ethel's chains sweep around my arms before slithering around my waist and then my feet as I struggle against them. I sense the dark magic in them now, which guides them around my body without effort on Ethel's part.

A second later, I'm whisked into the air, parallel with the ground, my body arching painfully because the chains drag my arms and legs up higher than my torso.

The pressure nearly dislocates my arms, and I scream as my body jolts and swings.

"Aura!" Nathaniel breaks free from Hagan and charges back to me, but the chains whisk me high above his head out of his reach.

I try to stop my scream at the wrenching pain and instant panic shooting through me.

Cyrian laughs. The lords and ladies lean forward, anticipation filling their faces, and Ethel plants her hands on her hips.

"Stand back, Nathaniel," Ethel says. "Or it will be so much more painful for her."

My tears of pain drop all the way to the stones below me.

At the edge of my vision, I catch a flash of pity on Christiana's face before she hides it. Cyrian released her the moment that Hagan obeyed Ethel.

Now Christiana grips her armrests again, her hair messy around her face, several strands stuck to her wet cheeks.

Despite her hatred of my people, I guess she can still empathize with my pain.

As I swing in the air, my limbs on the verge of dislocation, I tell myself I'm not beaten. Dark magic is controlling the chains, but I can break through it.

I can defeat the magic keeping me suspended, even if I might not be able to destroy the chains themselves—or untie them.

Nathaniel's dark eyes, his face upturned as he continues to stand beneath me, will me to try. His arms twitch and I know he'll catch me.

I close my eyes and draw on my power. Carefully. Slowly. Preparing myself for the fall as soon as I break through the magic—

A crackle of lightning in the distance makes my eyes snap open with shock.

It's a sound I haven't heard all day, but it's as familiar to me as the sound of my own name.

It's Treble.

CHAPTER 33

*M*y thunderbird breaks through the haze far above me, his beautiful blue-gray feathers glowing and rippling with lightning.

A single sweep of his wings cracks across my hearing, his thunder thudding in the air and drowning out the shouts below me as he pins his wings to his sides and dives right for me.

With only seconds to prepare, I flood my body with my power, starlight bursting from my chest and raging through my arms and legs.

The chains disintegrate, bursting into flames a moment before Nathaniel drops to his stomach and Treble soars beneath me.

I drop safely onto Treble's back.

There's no way for him to land, but I have to remain within Nathaniel's sight at all times. Otherwise, the bond between him and me will wrench me right off Treble's back and onto the ground.

"Up, Treble!" I scream.

Treble is already banking left, circling around Nathaniel's location so that I remain within his sight—but only just. With every beat of his wings, I feel the bond tugging at me, pulling me in Nathaniel's direction on the ground.

A barrage of arrows flies at us, but Treble is trained to avoid all projectiles. He darts left and right as fast as he can.

While the hunters try to shoot us from the sky, Cyrian's hands are also outstretched, dark light flying toward us.

My power glows around Treble, protecting him from the dark magic while I shoot as many arrows out of the sky as I can, careful only to aim up so I don't accidentally hit a human.

I want to lean over Treble's neck, breathe in his power, expand my senses with the comforting sounds of his thunderous heart, and cry at his undying loyalty.

I have no idea how long he's been circling above the haze or whether he just arrived. He saved me from a nasty fall. But now he's in danger.

"I'm going to jump off now!" I shout to him. "You have to fly away before they kill you."

Treble's answer is to bank again, turning against the direction I was preparing to jump so that I jolt against him instead.

He's refusing to allow me to leave his back.

"No, Treble!" I shout, my heart breaking that Treble is refusing my command. "You have to go!"

A gasp as another gust of wind—a much more savage blast—knocks me flat against Treble's back.

At first, I think it's Cyrian's magic finally breaking through mine, but then...

An enormous fire-red dragon drops from the haze above us.

The Vanem Dragon's wings spread across the sky so far that it looks like the night sky has turned to blood.

The wind he causes with his descent pushes and drags at me so wildly that all I can do is cling to Treble so I'm not knocked from his back.

On the ground, the lords and ladies, along with Ethel, have dropped to the ground, clinging to their diamonds, their screams drowned in the storm. The hunters have also dropped to their knees but are still trying to fire at us.

Cyrian shouts at his men to lower their weapons. "Don't harm the Vanem Dragon!"

As soon as they stop firing at us, Treble dives toward Nathaniel.

There's barely any room to fly through the arena, let alone to land in it, but Nathaniel's already running, darting glances across his shoulder as he judges where Treble will touch down.

I hold my breath as Treble's feet graze the pebbles and Nathaniel leaps, catches Treble's wing, and swings himself up behind me. His weight settles in behind me, a familiar presence on my thunderbird.

Treble takes off again without missing a beat.

I catch Christiana's shocked expression, Hagan's shuttered gaze, and Cyrian's rage as Nathaniel's arms close around me.

As we rise into the air, soaring toward the Vanem Dragon's position, I want nothing more than to fly above the haze and leave everything behind. To see the stars again. I want to tell Treble to fly us far away from both Bright and Fell—to escape together, all three of us.

But the Vanem Dragon has landed on the road beside the orchard, and Treble flies straight for him, drawn to the dragon's power.

The dragon's arrival moments after Treble tells me that they flew here together. I'm grateful for that, because it means that the dragon will keep Treble safe while they're here.

Treble sets us down twenty paces away from the Vanem Dragon as the dragon thuds to the ground and folds his wings against his sides.

Nathaniel and I quickly descend along Treble's wing, stepping down to the road. We take a knee in unison, our heads bowed to show our respect to the dragon.

Moments later, the sound of running feet meets my ears.

Hagan and Christiana appear on the other side of Treble. Hagan immediately takes a knee, but Christiana rips the diamonds from her throat and pitches them along the road, where they scatter.

Her chest heaves as she stares, eyes wide, from her brother to Treble, and then to the dragon.

She glances behind her—confirming that Cyrian isn't here yet—before she pelts toward Nathaniel and throws her arms around him despite his kneeling position.

He catches her, rising to a half-crouch, hugging her tightly.

Her cheeks are wet with tears, but her angry brown eyes pass to me and her speech is rapid. "Nathaniel, what the fuck? That's Aura Lucidia! What are you doing with her?"

He grips his sister tightly. "The Law of Champions—"

"I don't care about the Law," she whisper-shouts. "I care that you drew our family name on her face. You would never do that unless she means something to you, but she *can't* mean anything to you—"

Nathaniel breaks through her speech. "I need you to trust me, Christiana."

She tugs away from him. "I can't trust *that* creature." She points at me. "I will never trust her after what she did."

The dragon cuts them both off with a roar directed toward Cyrian, who strides down the road toward us with his hunters behind him, all of them carrying torches.

"Cyrian Deceiver!" Angry flames puff from the dragon's mouth as he speaks. The ground shudders as he stamps his foot and shakes out his wings. "Do not keep me waiting!"

"Vanem Dragon," Cyrian sneers as he draws to a stop without taking a knee. "You will do what I want—"

"How dare you summon me to Fell country!" the dragon shouts, flames licking around his lips as he lowers his head and thuds across the earth toward Cyrian.

"I invoked the Three Chances. You will honor the Law!" Cyrian shouts back, standing his ground.

Fire builds within the dragon's mouth as he halts only inches from Cyrian, the dragon's body dwarfing Cyrian so badly that the human looks miniscule.

"I do not honor the call of a liar and murderer. A traitor to his own King," the Vanem Dragon says.

The hunters keep their distance, their weapons firmly put away. They won't want to get too close to the dragon or anger him by making themselves a threat.

As Cyrian blusters, the dragon swings back to Nathaniel.

The creature's voice lowers. "But I will honor the call of Nathaniel Exalted. Speak, Bright Heart, and explain what has happened. I will believe what you tell me."

CHAPTER 34

*M*y heart suddenly hurts.

The dragon is giving Nathaniel the chance to deny what Cyrian said, but Nathaniel would never lie to the Vanem Dragon—not even to save himself.

Nathaniel slowly raises himself up to his full height, drawing Christiana behind him. "The Three Chances have been invoked. The first step was satisfied: Hagan Sever has volunteered to challenge me of his own free will."

The dragon makes an unhappy noise in the back of his throat. Deep sadness grows in his eyes. "Your heart never allows you to lie, Nathaniel Exalted. Even when the answer is dangerous to you."

The dragon takes a prowling step toward Hagan. "Rise, Challenger. Does Nathaniel speak the truth?"

"He does," Hagan replies, drawing to his feet. "However, I struck a bargain in exchange for volunteering. With respect, I ask for assurance that the agreement will be honored."

The dragon peers at him. "With whom was this bargain struck?"

"With King Cyrian."

"What were the terms?"

"Once sealed, Christiana Exalted will be mine. Nobody can interfere, not even the King."

Beside me, Christiana stands stiffly, her lips pressed together into a hard line.

Her rage is quiet, indicating that she knows all about the bargain but will not accept it without a fight.

The dragon's head rises slowly, an air of caution growing around him as he considers Hagan. "Your bargain will be secured once the Three Chances are sealed. King Cyrian can't break the deal. Nathaniel can't interfere. Neither can Aura. As for Christiana... she is free to make her own choices."

"Understood," Hagan says.

The dragon sighs. "Then step forward."

Hagan strides toward the dragon and so does Nathaniel, leaving Christiana with me.

I allow my power to glow softly around us so that Cyrian can't try anything, but she shudders, drawing her arms close to her sides to avoid coming into contact with my power. I guess she has no reason to believe I won't hurt her.

Nathaniel and Hagan turn to face each other, meet in the middle, and grip arms the same way Nathaniel and I did yesterday.

"Before I bind you and seal the Three Chances, I will make the rules clear," the dragon says, giving them both a stern look. "Nobody may interfere in the fight between you. To ensure magic is not used to help or hinder you during the fight, the seal between you will repel magic, whether it is dark magic or fae magic."

The dragon glares pointedly at Cyrian before swinging to

me, his expression softening but no less firm. "This rule applies until dawn breaks."

He returns his attention to Nathaniel and Hagan.

"You were once brothers," the dragon says to them, carefully exhaling a ring of flame that encircles their arms. "You are now bound to fight until one of you yields or dies. This fight will determine if Hagan is worthy to take Nathaniel's place as Cyrian's Champion. If Nathaniel yields, then he must subsequently die before dawn—either by Hagan's hand or someone else's. Whether Hagan is worthy or not, only Nathaniel's death will grant Hagan the right to take Nathaniel's place as Cyrian's Champion."

I shiver as the flames fade. The seal was created far too quickly.

Dread builds inside my chest as Nathaniel and Hagan release each other, their shoulders stiff.

Christiana's expression zigzags between anger and fear, but the longer she focuses on Nathaniel, the more her face fills with misery.

Cyrian shouts as he strides forward. "You're done here now, Dragon. You will leave Fell country—"

"Consider your time on this Earth limited, Cyrian," the dragon says, cutting Cyrian off with a snort of hot flame. "When you invoked the Three Chances, you triggered a disturbance in the glitter field that was felt by every fae in Bright—especially Queen Imatra."

I'm surprised by this news. The glitter field is the border protection system between Fell and Bright. A bulb of deadly glass rests at the top of every stem of glitter grass. Any living creature that disturbs a bulb is cut to shreds by its exploding shards.

Nathaniel and I only survived running through it together because, for a reason I've never been able to explain, the glitter field changes when I touch it, becoming harmless and green like soft grass.

Cyrian laughs. "Why should I be concerned about that?"

The dragon's lips draw back into a snarl. "Because parts of the glitter field became airborne. Several glitter bulbs drifted into Fell country and exploded in the mist. Others drifted into Bright."

I take an involuntary step forward, my eyes wide. "Was anyone hurt?"

"No, dear one," the dragon says to me, his expression softening.

"But how did it happen?"

The Vanem Dragon shakes his head, a worried light entering his eyes. "This afternoon, I sensed the invocation of the Three Chances and rose from the mountains with the thunderbirds. The Border Guards saw us rise across the distance too. At the same time, they also saw a single moth rise out of the Fell mist and fly into the field. The moment the moth touched the glitter field, the stems reacted, sending bulbs into the air."

I struggle to understand what the dragon's telling me. At the moment that the Three Chances were invoked, the dragon rose up and so did... a moth?

Cyrian laughs, scorn dripping from his voice. "You expect me to believe that a mold moth flies into the glitter field and it mysteriously causes the field to send out explosive bulbs—"

The dragon ignores Cyrian's laughter, lowering his head to me, his brown eyes softer than I've ever seen them. "Your brother, Evander, saw it with his own eyes. He said the moth was glowing like starlight. You wouldn't know anything about that, would you, Aura?"

A glowing moth?

"I'm at a loss," I whisper.

But as I think back... I remember the moth early this morning that cleaned the dust off my hand... the dust that seemed to come from inside me when I stayed too long at the burn site...

I have no way to describe that event or to explain how it could all be connected to the field, but I meet Nathaniel's eyes across the distance between us.

His lips are parted and a curious crease forms across his forehead. He must remember the moth too.

"A mystery, then," the dragon says, finally releasing me from his gaze.

I speak up before he can turn away. "Is Evander okay?"

"Imatra continues with her plan," the dragon says, giving me a warning glance. "But, yes. For now, he is safe."

Right before I ran from Bright, the Queen proposed to make Evander her husband—despite Evander's love for the Eventide fae, Talsa. I took Imatra's proposal as a threat to Evander's life—a way for the Queen to gain leverage over me.

The dragon turns to Cyrian, his fierce eyes becoming hard and cold again—a creature of immense power. "Imatra declared the bulbs were created by dark magic sent by the Fell. She is gathering her army and preparing to defend Bright against you. Consider yourself lucky that the Law of Champions is invoked, Cyrian. If not, you would have felt her wrath already."

Cyrian scoffs, folding his arms across his chest, returning the dragon's glare with a hard stare. "Be gone, dragon. We have a fight to start."

Sadness fills the dragon's eyes as he swings to me again. "I will see you again, Aura. Whoever wins this fight between

Nathaniel and Hagan will meet you in battle on the third day. I pray the outcome doesn't break your heart."

I can't stop the shiver that racks me. This morning, Mathilda warned me that my heart will be torn apart before the beginning of the third day, but I refuse to believe it might be because of this fight.

The dragon backs away from us before he sweeps his wings and rises into the sky, the wind from his wing beats knocking us all off-balance.

I lower my center of gravity to stay upright as Treble nudges my back, resting his face against my cheek before he, too, lifts into the air.

My heart aches as I watch him disappear into the haze. I'm glad he's safe—that the Vanem Dragon is looking after him—but it's like watching my oldest friend leave me behind.

Cyrian is already striding toward us, his cruel eyes glittering. "Time to throw you in the Ditch."

CHAPTER 35

$\mathcal{N}$ ow that the dragon is gone, the hunters' savagery returns.

Snake grabs me around the back of my neck to propel me along the path while the other hunters crowd Nathaniel, shoving him after me.

Hagan steps in Cyrian's path before we've gone more than a few paces. "You will honor our agreement."

Cyrian snarls before he casts an angry glance at the sky. Judging by the absence of light, we're now approaching midnight. Dawn is only a few hours away. He will be anxious about timing now.

After an angry pause, Cyrian snaps. "Christiana's yours. Now let's go—"

Hagan spins away from him, striding toward Christiana, whose eyes fly wide. "Wait... *now*? Like hell I'll let you touch me, you filthy hunter."

Her fist flies out, whacking Hagan neatly on the chin, but he catches her hand before she can thump him again, scooping her up against his chest, one arm around her waist, the other gripping her hand.

Nathaniel wrenches free from the hunters, his own fists clenched as he paces like a caged animal. He can't stop any of it. Neither can I.

Christiana attempts to kick Hagan's shins despite her tight skirt, but he only winces before he spins her away from himself and pulls her back in again.

She freezes up against this chest, her eyes even wider. "What are you doing?"

Hagan is extraordinarily calm, but the ticking muscle in his jaw indicates he's deadly serious. "Marrying you properly."

A storm grows on her face, anger washing through the set of her lips, sharpening the glare in her eyes. "I don't think so, you ugly, great—"

She wrenches against his hold, trying to free her hand, but he resolutely grips her wrist, never letting it go as he continues with the dance.

I can see now, watching from the outside, how beautiful the dance could look—how close he holds her and how often she could choose to step away from him, returning to him instead—but not in this case.

Every time Hagan spins and pulls Christiana back to him, her dress sparkles, catching the firelight in a dangerous flicker before she wallops him—a fist to his face, his chest, his stomach—so hard that she flexes her fingers and shouts against the pain that must be shooting up her arm every time. "I will *not* marry you!"

I wait for her to grab one of the daggers at his belt, and I'm surprised when she doesn't. Then I realize that she can't.

Hagan is destined to fight Nathaniel and nobody can stop that from happening. Christiana can't kill or wound Hagan even if she wants to. Even her fists must be landing without impact right now.

Cyrian startles me when he whispers at my shoulder. "If I'd known how entertaining this would be, I would have given my permission a long time ago."

A retort rests on the tip of my tongue, but I edge away from the King, wary of his proximity and deciding now is not the time to draw a violent response from him.

Hagan drops Christiana into the final move—the sultry bend—and then the dance is over. She's tried every physical assault she could to free herself.

Now he has to draw his name on her face.

Still gripping her with one hand, his muscles bulging as she fights him and pulls with all her strength, he eases one of his daggers free, awkwardly sliding it tip-up one-handed before he pricks his forefinger on it.

The dagger clatters to the dusty road as he pulls Christiana off her feet, hard up against his chest. She plants both her palms against his shoulders, turning her face away.

It's over in five strokes.

On her left cheek, he draws a single line of blood down the middle with two branches on each side at the top like a 'Y' with two extra spokes.

Her chest heaves when he finishes his task. "You will never own me, Hagan—"

"You will do what I say now." Hagan growls, his tawny eyes raking over her face and the mark he drew on her. "Do you understand?"

"I will *not*!"

He grits his teeth. "You are my wife and you will obey me."

"Fuck you!" She shoves against his chest, but this time, he lets her go so abruptly that she stumbles.

She flails and tries to regain her balance, stumbling back a few steps before she right herself and stares up at him in surprise.

She lurches back when he takes a threatening step toward her.

"You will go now," he says.

A confused crease forms on her forehead.

She teeters on the spot, taking glances at Cyrian and then Nathaniel before she returns her focus to Hagan.

Near to me, Cyrian tenses, an unhappy snarl on his lips. Nathaniel is also on alert, the flash of his dark eyes telling me he's as shocked as Christiana.

"You are my wife," Hagan says. "You will do as I say. I'm telling you to leave and never let me see your face again."

She blinks at him, her lips pressed together, latent tears trickling through the blood on her cheek. "You're... setting me free?"

"Did you not hear me, woman?" Hagan's voice rises to a ferocious roar. "*Get out of my sight!*"

Christiana is frozen and pale. "You don't want me to see the fight."

"I won't let you watch me kill your brother."

Her eyes fill, glossy with tears. "Then don't do it."

"Enough!" Hagan grabs her, his big hands closing around her upper arms, but she doesn't fight him this time.

"You're mine," he says. "You will go or I will choke the life out of you."

"You won't hurt me," she whispers, meeting his eyes.

"Don't test me, woman."

"*Woman,*" she murmurs quietly, resolutely, before she shakes her head. "I won't go."

Beside me, Nathaniel stirs, takes a careful step. "Christiana. You need to leave."

Her brown eyes flash to him. "No, brother..." She shakes her head, defiant tears dripping down her cheeks. "I won't."

Nathaniel is suddenly angry, his voice rising. "This isn't about you or me. It's not about what we want. You know that! You have to be safe."

Her face crumples. "But—"

"Go. *Now.*"

Reaching up to place her palms over the backs of Hagan's hands, she draws his arms away from her shoulders, holding on to one of his palms a moment longer than she needs to as she searches his eyes.

He is cold and blank now, no emotion at all.

Freeing herself, she runs to Nathaniel, hugging him, a sob dragging from her mouth before she spins to me. "Do not let my brother die. I can't be the person he wants me to be."

She hitches up her dress while the hunters press in around us. Deftly darting between the men, she disappears into the night.

CHAPTER 36

*M*y focus returns to Nathaniel as the hunters compel us to move—back past the White Walls toward the arena Nathaniel pointed out this afternoon.

When we reach the White Walls, Cyrian splits away from us with several hunters while Hagan remains with us, following slightly behind so I can't see him without turning back.

When we reach the western side of the Ditch, an opening yawns in it that I didn't see earlier. It appears to lead down into the dark bowels of the building.

Snake shoves me inside into the dim lighting. There are only a few torches along the way, leaving much of the walkway in shadows.

The path descends at a gentle slope with levels dug out at intervals. I hesitate at the first one, glancing left and right at the rows of cages contained on each side before Snake pushes me forward again.

My stomach feels hollow. I'm starving and filled with dread. The scent of fear sits heavy in the air as we descend.

When we finally reach the lowest level, low keening meets my ears. Growls. Moans. Human or animal, I can't tell which.

Directly in front of us, a large, arched opening is covered by both a wooden hatch and a set of metal bars. The wooden barrier has the effect of dulling the sounds from outside and obscuring our view of what awaits us.

I sense many people beyond the gate.

As Hagan steps up beside us, Snake orders the other hunters to open the gates.

The wooden hatch rises first, letting the sounds in—as well as the light. Then they raise the metal gate.

Firelight floods the arena ahead of us, burning torches sitting all around its walls. The space is about one hundred paces long and slightly less wide—an oval shape. A combination of dirt and sand covers the ground, uneven and clumped in places.

The arena isn't as large as the Coliseum in Bright, but what it lacks in size, it makes up for in danger. Thick, metal spikes jut from the walls at both shoulder and ankle height. Running into them will be fatal.

Two snarling wolves are chained at either side, their ropes long enough to reach a wide radius that will pose a danger if the men step within the wolves' reach.

I recognize the animals as the ones that traveled in the wagon with us this morning—one is the female we fought, her nose an inky black contrast to her blue-tinged fur. The other has pale charcoal fur and a white-flecked tail.

Three other doorways lead into the arena at ground level —one on each side of the oval shape. They're covered by large, arched, wooden hatches like the one we passed through.

High above us, the viewing stalls are packed with humans, but unlike the arena in Bright, they are deathly quiet. Low murmurs. No cheering. Many of them huddle together against the cold.

A wooden stand sits in the center of the arena, filled with weapons of all kinds. As we leave the underpass behind and enter the arena, I'm able to finally see the stands behind us.

Cyrian sits on a throne on a dais similar to the one Imatra has in the Coliseum. He's no longer wearing his bear pelt.

The seats closest to him are filled with lords and ladies, including Lady Ethel, who appears to have recovered from the shock of seeing the dragon. A new crystal goblet dangles from her fingers as she leans toward one of the other men, deep in conversation with him.

Hagan strides ahead of us, but Nathaniel catches his arm when we're well clear of the hunters, who remain behind in the underpass.

Nathaniel grips tightly enough to make Hagan jolt to a stop and glare at him.

"Thank you," Nathaniel says, his voice low.

Hagan presses his lips together in an unhappy line.

He points to the thick scar roping across his stomach. "The day Cyrian had me whipped for disobeying him, I should have died. Instead, I woke up alive and healed. Nobody ever said why, but I know it was because of you. For some light-forsaken reason, you struck a bargain for my life. Now I've repaid my debt."

"Freeing Christiana was about more than repaying a debt," Nathaniel says, a dangerous tone in his voice that demands truth.

Hagan shakes him off. "Don't mistake my intentions, Nathaniel Exalted. There is no path to redemption for me. Christiana is my only source of light. A hellish, fiery sort of light, I'll admit, but light still the same. She hates me. Rightfully so. But I did it for her."

Hagan casts an angry glance back at me, his eyes narrowing as he fixates on my bare cheeks again.

He scrutinized me the same way when we arrived at the White Walls this evening.

"You will explain to me what happened to your face, Aura Lucidia," he says.

I bite back a reply that I don't need to explain anything to him.

"I ate dirt," I say, deciding on a sort of truth.

For some reason, Hagan's glower deepens. "To deliberately wipe a man's name from your face before the ink wears off is to dishonor him."

Damn.

My heart sinks. I wanted to put distance between Nathaniel and me, not publicly shame him. No wonder Ethel looked so delighted when she saw my face.

Revealing nothing of the regret I feel, I cover my emotions with the cold expression I learned to wear in Bright. "That's a human law. I'm not human."

Hagan steps up to me, lowering his line of sight to mine. "You're damn right you're not human. But you will pay under human law for the crime you committed."

I'm immediately on my guard, but not because of his threat. What he said sounds a lot like Christiana's accusation earlier. She pointed at me and said she would never trust me after what I did.

My eyes narrow in thought. All humans hate me because I'm fae. I'm their enemy. But the way Hagan looks at me... the way he spoke... it's as if he's referring to something more specific.

"What did I do?" I demand to know, even though I'm wary of the answer.

Hagan's jaw clenches. "You killed the only woman who ever gave me hope."

Confusion rises inside me. "Who?"

Before Hagan can answer, Nathaniel steps between us.

"Enough talk. It's time to fight," Nathaniel says, planting his clenched fist against Hagan's chest, a firm threat.

Hagan grits his teeth, his focus shifting from Nathaniel's fist up to Nathaniel's face. What he sees there seems to unsettle him. "She doesn't know, does she?"

Nathaniel shifts, half-turned to me. Shadows grow in his eyes, the same way they always do when he's keeping secrets from me.

His hair falls across his face like a boundary past which I can't step. "It's not your place to tell her, Hagan."

Dread builds inside me as I glance between them. *Tell me... what?*

"Fuck that!" Hagan shouts at Nathaniel, shoving Nathaniel off himself. "She was important to me too."

Hagan grabs my arm so fast that he nearly dislocates it, wrenching me to the side.

I fight my instinct to retaliate as the tension rises in the stands above us. At the edge of my vision, the King leans forward, gripping the railing, but he doesn't demand that the fight begin.

The fact that Cyrian is allowing us to continue talking can't be a good thing. Neither is the smile growing across his face. I'm sure he's too far away to hear us, but Hagan's aggression toward me will be plain for everyone to see.

"Aura Lucidia," Hagan says, dragging me close enough that I can see the blood pounding at his neck, sense the thud of his heart. "Destroyer of hope. Killer of the weak. A cowardly murderer."

My eyes widen as his hatred for me is fully revealed. Only

deep pain can cause this sort of rage, the kind of pain that won't ever heal.

"Who did I kill?" I whisper, needing to know the answer, even if I can never atone for it.

"You killed the woman who pulled me from the dirt. Who gave me purpose. The only mother I ever knew." He shakes me, his fist unbearably tight around my arm, but I hardly feel it.

"Nathaniel carried her into the Misty Gallows," Hagan says. "But I followed them. I watched you kill our Luciana. Our Paloma Exalted. You cut her down in a single strike and then dropped her in the mud as if she were nothing important."

He beats his free fist against his heart, furious tears in his eyes. "She was important to me!"

My heart is cracking. "Paloma... Exalted..."

I seek Nathaniel three steps away, hoping to discover that Hagan is telling me lies.

Nathaniel's shoulders, his fists, every part of him is beyond tense. Beyond wild. Beyond pain.

"Hagan," he snarls. "You had no right."

There is no triumph in Hagan's voice, no glee, or joy. Only pain, gripping and hooking into me in a way that will never let me go.

"You killed Nathaniel's mother," he says.

CHAPTER 37

*E*very limb in my body gives way, my weight dropping so fast that I fall to my knees, barely staying upright.

Hagan lets me go, stepping away from me, his anger unyielding.

The torches around the arena are suddenly glaringly hot, the air freezing cold. Sharp contradictions.

I press the heel of my palm to my heart, but I feel nothing. My heart has stopped, the breath pausing in my chest.

Yesterday morning, I was about to cut Nathaniel's throat and he asked me...

Am I braver than my mother?

I hunch over my chest, my hands finding the dirt, digging into it and filling my fingernails with grit.

I assumed someone else killed her, but who else could it have been?

There is no atoning for this. No redemption. No way back.

"Aura?" Nathaniel's body casts me into shadow.

He kneels in front of me, reaching for my chin, my cheeks, trying to make me look at him. "She asked to die by your hand. She was proud. Strong..." His voice breaks. "The Rot had reached her brain. She couldn't walk, was losing her speech. She asked me to take her to the forest. She wanted a warrior's death. You gave her that."

"That's not the way Hagan and Christiana see it."

"They need someone to blame. You struck the final blow, but listen to me, Aura. Even at that moment, there was no darkness in you."

Closing my eyes, I try to block out the echo of Nathaniel's shout yesterday. I told him that his people didn't have to suffer. That I could heal the ones who came to the border to die.

He told me... *Even fate isn't that cruel.*

My whisper is cold, my breath catching in my throat. "I could have healed her."

"You didn't know that then."

I want to scream at him for being so calm, so forgiving. I want to lash out at him for not telling me himself, for letting me hear it from Hagan.

I want to rage at him for carrying his mother to the border. For choosing to place her under my sword.

I want to hate him for not hating me.

Nothing he can say will take away my guilt. I hurt him and his people and I did it without thinking.

I don't even remember her.

Slowly reaching up to my hair, I place my hands on either side of my head and allow my power to shine, burning at the sap that turned my locks black.

Nathaniel sucks in a quick breath, lurching away from me when I press too long and the ends of my hair catch fire, the sickening scent filling the air before I catch the thick strands and smother the flames beneath my palms.

I don't care about the heat. All that matters is that my hair is white again.

Now there is nothing left that makes me appear human.

"You have to stay alive," I say, raising my eyes to Nathaniel's, speaking clearly so that Hagan will hear me too. "No matter what it takes."

"Aura—"

"You may have bargained for Hagan's life once, but it's your life that will give your people their freedom." I draw to my feet and back away from Nathaniel, my body numb, but my thoughts clear. "You will do whatever it takes to stay alive."

Nathaniel returns my steady gaze. His clothing is ripped and torn. He's bruised and beaten, but he's still the most mesmerizing man I've ever met.

The soft edges of his expression become hard, determined. I glimpse again the rage he showed when Tanner threatened me. The inner warrior he tempers with reason and justice.

I may have scratched his name from my face, but he is a part of my life I can never erase or replace.

"Stay alive," I whisper. "I need you to stay alive."

Even if it means that I will face him in a fight to the death. I need Nathaniel to live.

Nathaniel inhales, filling his big chest, his muscles flexing before he gives me a nod. Then he spins and strides toward the weapon stand, quickly collecting a weapons harness, tying it around his chest and waist and filling it with every blade it can hold.

I back toward the gate we came from, but I veer toward the snarling white-tailed wolf on my way, checking out the length of its chains and ascertaining that they're secured to the wall—unbreakable.

Up in the stands, Cyrian's booming voice suddenly demands our attention. "The Three Chances are in play!" he shouts. "The traitor, Nathaniel Displaced, has been challenged by the strongest of my hunters, Hagan Sever. This is a battle that is long overdue."

He waits another beat for Nathaniel and Hagan to turn to him.

Then Cyrian raises his hands above his head, his silver wrist bands glinting. "Let the fight begin."

My heart leaps into my throat, anxiety shooting around my body, but I'm surprised when Hagan and Nathaniel take a step away from each other.

They both take a knee, heads bowed, the same way Nathaniel's trainees show respect to each other before they fight—the way Luciana taught them.

Up on the dais, Cyrian falters a little. It's clear from his glower that he didn't intend for the two men to show each other any respect.

Hagan rises to his feet. "Son of Luciana," he says to Nathaniel. "I will respect your strength by fighting with my own."

Drawing to his full height, Nathaniel gives Hagan a dangerous nod. "Brother, I expect nothing less."

Neither man has drawn a blade.

Hagan nods.

His fist flies out at Nathaniel and it's like watching a bear move—except this bear has rocks for paws.

Nathaniel ducks and returns the hit. Hagan avoids it, but Nathaniel's arm is already swinging back, his elbow colliding with Hagan's cheek.

Hagan ducks under the next hit, landing a walloping blow

to Nathaniel's stomach, another to his shoulder, and then charges under him, crushing his chest and driving him back across the ground.

In retaliation, Nathaniel's fists slam onto Hagan's back, then his stomach, forcing a gap between the two men.

They both take a second to recover before they charge at each other again. Their blows are crunching and rapid. Every single hit makes me wince, sending a shock through my heart. Within seconds, they're both bleeding from splits across their cheeks and lips.

Yesterday, I would have watched their fight with clinical interest—assessing their strengths and weaknesses, studying their techniques, figuring out whether they favor a particular arm or leg. But today...

Today, all I want is for the fight to end and for Nathaniel to be standing at the end of it.

I back away from the battle, digging my fingernails into my palms so hard, it hurts.

Edging toward the wall, I'm in danger of hitting a spike, but it's nearly impossible to remain still. I force myself to pace back and forth, unable to take my eyes off the two men.

Especially when Hagan draws his sword and drives Nathaniel dangerously close to the female wolf on that side of the arena.

The two weapons clang and glint in the firelight while the animal snaps at Nathaniel's back.

Nathaniel retaliates with equal force, beating Hagan back toward the center of the arena before he slices neatly across Hagan's bicep.

I hold my breath, but the wound doesn't appear deep enough to cause any real damage and Hagan moves as if it never happened.

My heart is in my throat as I pace in the dirt, my

breathing alternating between rapid and halting as Nathaniel and Hagan continue to fight, both of them now gripping a dagger as well as a sword.

Nathaniel nearly impales Hagan's shoulder.

Hagan nearly cuts off Nathaniel's arm.

The two men are equally matched. The outcome is going to come down to stamina. Sweat drips down both their faces, soaking their shirts.

Nathaniel is surviving on minimal sleep and has spent the last day and a half fighting for his life. He's at a distinct disadvantage the longer the fight continues. Hagan will aim to wear him down...

My magic hums in my ears, needing to be released, but I can also hear the crowd, murmuring and pointing. Louder than before.

Nathaniel's name is on their lips.

He is their rightful King. Their leader. Their path to freedom.

A change in the air warns me a moment before Cyrian steps forward, takes hold of the railing, and leaps from the dais.

A shot of dark light spreads across the air beneath him, slowing his fall so that he lands safely on his feet.

For a second, I think he's going to try to interfere with the fight, but his focus is purely on me.

His hands shoot out as he strides toward me. Dark light spears across the distance, a great wallop of it colliding with my stomach, lifting me and driving me back toward the spikes jutting from the walls of the arena.

Starlight floods my body. With a defiant flash, I free myself from the grip of his magic and drop back to the ground, inches from the nearest spike. Too close for comfort. Too close to the wolf.

I duck and roll out of the animal's path, jumping to my feet as it snaps at me. I'm now closer to Cyrian than I want to be.

Across the way, I sense Nathaniel split his attention, seeking my position.

Hagan takes advantage of the distraction, driving his dagger toward Nathaniel's chest. Nathaniel leaps back just in time to avoid the blow.

My muscles tense. Any distraction could get Nathaniel killed and I'm guessing that's Cyrian's intention.

Cyrian's mouth splits into a wild grin as he continues to stride toward me.

"I've been waiting to get you alone," he says. "It's just you and me now, Aura."

He waves his hand at the crowd. "And a thousand people to watch you break."

CHAPTER 38

"You think that my magic can't hurt you," Cyrian says, coming to a stop close enough to push me dangerously near the wolf at my back.

I curl my fingers into fists, fighting the need to retaliate and show him just how strong I am.

I remind myself: *Defend, don't attack*. And above all, I can't allow Nathaniel to be distracted.

Despite the chill, Cyrian's wearing a short-sleeved black shirt that fully exposes the colorful runes cascading down his right arm. They appear to shift and slide across his skin as dark light plays in his eyes and around his torso.

"You have no idea how much power I control," he says. "I have access to the life energy of every human heart. Every beat gives me more power."

"By killing your people slowly!"

He shrugs. "The Ebon Rot is a byproduct of draining their bodies and minds."

Rage builds inside me at the pain Cyrian has caused the humans, but my head lifts defiantly. "But not Nathaniel."

Cyrian scowls. "For reasons that evade me, I've never been able to infect him. But... let's see how long *you* can resist me..."

A trickle of black light wafts across the air between us, brushing up against my neck. It leaves a burning sensation that startles me and makes me gasp.

"Imagine the pain you just felt magnified a hundred times," Cyrian whispers. "It would take all of your starlight to counteract it. But then you would distract Nathaniel and put him in danger..."

Cyrian circles me as my hand itches to draw my liquid sword or my dagger, but a blade won't do me any good.

"I can reach inside your mind and burn your senses without even leaving a mark," Cyrian continues, running his hand across my shoulders before I quickly step beyond his reach, whirling to face him.

We've now switched places and he stands closest to the wolf.

Cyrian smiles. The chains holding the wolf suddenly break.

The animal leaps at him first, but it yelps and darts away when it comes into contact with the dark light covering his body.

The wolf spins and launches itself at me instead.

Cyrian expected me to use my magic, but my reflexes are at full speed. My liquid sword is in my hand. I dart left. The animal skids past me, one claw dangerously close to disemboweling me through the rips in my armor before I swing and jump at it, landing on it from behind and driving the sword into its neck.

The whole move is completely silent.

The kill strike is clean and the wolf slumps beneath me.

I take a deep breath, preparing to face Cyrian again, when

EVERLY FROST

a clutching sensation grips the back of my neck, pulling me to my feet.

"Very good, Aura," Cyrian whispers, leaning across my shoulder, far too close for comfort. "But how will you cope when I take hold of your insides and make you feel like I'm ripping them out?"

I gasp as burning pain rockets down my spine. He hasn't touched me, but dark light swirls around my torso now, sinking beneath my armor, gripping my arms, legs, and ribs.

"That's your bones," he says, circling me again as pain shoots through my body. His hands glitter with dark light as he extends them, turning and twisting them in the air around me. "Next your stomach and lungs."

I double over, kneeling in the dirt beside the dead wolf as the burn spreads through my abdomen, a fire like no other eating at my stomach and spreading upward.

I gasp a breath. Then another, each one like inhaling flames and smoke.

"And finally..." He bends beside me, grabbing my left shoulder and forcing my torso upright. "Your heart."

He dares to slide his palm across my upper left breast and I'm grateful that my armor forms a barrier between us.

Mercifully, this time, the pain doesn't worsen.

A hint of confusion enters Cyrian's eyes. He tilts his head, taking glances at my chest and then my face, searching my eyes.

A short laugh escapes his lips.

"Aura," he asks. "Where is your heart?"

CHAPTER 39

I stare back at Cyrian in confusion, my vision blurring with the force of the pain burning inside me.

I try to focus, replaying his question in my mind, but it doesn't make any sense. My heart is where it's supposed to be—*inside my chest*.

Cyrian suddenly grabs my hair. Pain explodes across my scalp at the sudden pressure, but at the same time, he seems to lose his concentration and the pain elsewhere in my body eases. Not much, but enough for some clarity of thought to return.

His voice is sharp. Deadly. "How do you exist?" He shakes me so hard that it feels like my bones rattle. "What *are* you?"

I grit my teeth at him. I don't understand what he's talking about, but I do know who I am.

Finally, I have some understanding of my place in my world. If he'd asked me a day ago, I would have defined myself as Imatra's Champion. Then as a traitor and an escapee. But now...

Grabbing his hand and shoving it away from me, I return his hard stare. "I'm Aura Lucidia, the brightest of the Bright Ones. I'm Nathaniel's wife. And I'm the reason you'll be dead in a day."

A hint of worry enters Cyrian's eyes, but he gives me another shake, a snarl on his lips that makes him appear more wolf than man. "Let me tell you a story about life and death, Aura. And then we'll see how certain you are."

His momentary distraction is over. Dark light gusts across my arms and legs, burning pain dragging at my limbs like claws.

"Not so long ago," he says, "Before the glitter field and the Misty Gallows, a man had the courage to defend his border village from the attack of a fae raiding party. The fae didn't give up. They attacked again, and each time, the man killed them. The King heard about this man and came to the village to ask the man to be his Champion. He offered him all the glory he could ever dream of."

Cyrian leans close to me, stroking his hand down my cheek, his fingertips burning across my skin so painfully that I squeeze my eyes shut, trying to breathe.

He continues. "The man said, 'Only if you guarantee the safety of my wife and newborn child.' The King agreed. He convinced the man to go to the castle, while the King left twenty soldiers to defend the village until the man's wife could come to the castle too."

Cyrian's fingers twine into my hair, tugging sharply. "The next day, a fae raiding party attacked the village and slaughtered everyone in it, including the man's family."

He exhales a slow breath, making a hum like a moan of pain. "The King wept tears for the man, but the man saw through them. Over time, he learned that the King didn't want a Champion. The King wanted a protector for his own newborn son. You see... the good witch Mathilda had fore-seen that Nathaniel's life would be filled with unbearable pain."

Cyrian grips each side of my face, forcing my eyes open. Released, tears leak down my cheeks.

"Nathaniel's father traded my family for his," Cyrian says. "Over time, my pain and anger festered until one day, I woke up with dark light glowing in the palms of my hands. Dark magic sprung from hatred itself."

He wrenches me around to face the arena, gripping my arms so tightly that dark light spills between us. "Nathaniel's existence is built on the blood and bones of others. If I take life, it is only because of him."

"Your choices are your own," I say, swallowing my groan of agony. "You're the one killing your people, not Nathaniel."

"My wife and son died first," he says. "It's time for Nathaniel to die too. Only *your* pain will distract him. You will scream for me, Aura. Even if I have to burn every thought from your mind."

Despite the pain seizing my insides, despite the sobs forcing their way into my throat, I manage to say, "I will not."

On the other side of the arena, Nathaniel and Hagan are locked together, muscles straining against each other.

Hagan's sword lies on the dirt beyond his reach—Nathaniel must have disarmed him—but Hagan's hands are clamped over Nathaniel's, both of them gripping the handle of Nathaniel's sword.

Nathaniel shoves their locked fists back at Hagan, who takes the knock across his cheek but refuses to let go, hooking his foot around Nathaniel's ankle and destroying Nathaniel's balance.

Nathaniel drops to the ground, releasing the weapon.

I stop breathing as Hagan drives the blade down at

Nathaniel's neck in a blow that has the speed and strength to cleave Nathaniel's head from his shoulders.

Nathaniel rolls to the side just in time, snatching up Hagan's sword from the ground.

Both men take a moment, pacing around each other, breathing hard. They're visibly tired. Sweat pours off their bodies, but their blows are no less violent—fists and swords. They're bloody and bruised, but neither has given ground.

Their fight has progressed beyond rational thought now. I know this from having trained long hours every day. There comes a tipping point past which nothing exists except the next move.

Every move is instinctive.

Distraction means death.

"Scream for me," Cyrian whispers as the pain levels inside my body reach breaking point.

I squeeze my eyes shut, trying to breathe through the agony, desperately allowing a small glow of starlight to ease across my chest. I'm alarmed at how little it protects me from the pain. He told me I should be more afraid of his power and now I wonder if he's right.

With an impatient scowl, he says, "If you won't break, then the chains must."

My eyes fly open.

On the other side of the arena, the female wolf strains at her restraints. Nathaniel and Hagan have fought around her, avoiding the radius within which she can attack.

Right now, Nathaniel stands with his back to her, close to the wall on that side, while she snarls at his heels and strains against her shackles.

I subdued her this morning, but her hatred of Nathaniel is irrepressible.

"You can't release the wolf." I gasp. "You can't interfere."

Cyrian smiles and it turns my blood cold. "I'm not inter-fering. The wolf will do whatever her natural instincts dictate."

He closes his fist and the wolf's chain breaks.

I barely have time to think, can't stop to care if I'm breaking rules. My power floods through my chest and arms, washing away the pain Cyrian's dark magic is causing me.

"Wolf!" I scream, my hands flying out and my power streaking across the distance.

My starlight explodes behind Nathaniel, just missing the leaping animal as Nathaniel spins to defend himself, his sword raised. At the same time, he turns his back to Hagan.

I gasp another scream as Hagan leaps forward, his sword swinging.

CHAPTER 40

*M*y eyes shoot wide when Hagan plants one big fist on Nathaniel's chest and shoves Nathaniel out of the wolf's path.

With a roar, Hagan drives his weapon into the leaping wolf's neck.

The force of the animal's jump throws Hagan back into the dirt. He lands with a heavy thud, the wolf's body sprawled across his chest.

Relief and shock flood through me because the wolf is dead, but Hagan pushed Nathaniel out of harm's way…

I seek Nathaniel where he stands very still beside the wall, his back to it.

He's still gripping his sword, but he seems stiff and frozen in a way that scares me. Even from this distance, I can see that something's wrong, but I don't know what it is.

Hagan shoves the wolf off himself, ripping his sword from her shoulder and throwing her body across the dirt as he rushes to get back to his feet, sword raised, preparing to defend himself.

Nathaniel takes a step forward, but it's labored and uneven.

When Hagan doesn't immediately strike, Nathaniel's focus shifts to me where I'm frozen with my hands still outstretched.

"Nathaniel." His name is a whisper on my lips. "What is it?"

As if he hears me, Nathaniel's lips press together in a soft line, his shoulders relaxing, but the sword clatters from his hand.

He drops to his knees, revealing a bloody spike behind him.

No. Please, no.

My body turns cold, my breath stops, the arena spins.

Cyrian tries to grab me, but my power floods the space around us, my hair flying around my face as I scramble to my feet and run.

Nathaniel slides to the ground and then I can't see him because Hagan's big body is blocking my line of sight.

Panic runs like a freezing river through me as I sprint, pushing my legs as fast as they can go, my boots racing through the sand, my white hair flying out behind me.

As I arc to the right, Nathaniel's sword comes into view where it lies in the dirt. His blood on the spike glitters in the torchlight.

My heart thuds, a cruel beat.

Hagan has frozen where he stands and doesn't try to get in my way as I slide through the bloody sand to reach Nathaniel's side.

Nathaniel's eyes are closed. He lies on his back now, but his chest still rises and falls.

He's breathing, but it's shallow. Blood pools across his

chest and beneath his back, spreading fast and gathering against my legs.

The point of origin is above his heart and the small tear in his shirt tells me the spike's tip extended through his front.

I press my hands against his face, his chest, needing to help him, trying to… trying… *Oh, please.*

He's losing too much blood. I need to cauterize the wound, but I can't use my magic to do that until the Three Chances releases him at dawn.

Dawn is still half an hour away. Maybe more. It's too long. He won't survive until then.

Whimpers form in my throat, releasing through my lips as I try to think.

Nathaniel's eyes remain closed and he doesn't seem aware that I'm kneeling beside him. I would give anything for him to see me.

He loved me for a fleeting moment and now I'm losing him.

My thoughts scatter, my logic unreachable, because all I feel is pain. Too much pain. More pain than the torture Cyrian inflicted on me. Nathaniel and I are bound in more ways than Law. More ways than battle and blood. We're bonded to each other in truth and courage. In loyalty and betrayal, compassion, and even in grief.

We're bound—terrifyingly and cruelly—in hope.

I can't stop my power flooding in my chest and spearing down my arms, lighting up my hands where I press them over his heart.

I prepare for the magic of the Three Chances to repel me, to hurt or even kill me, but all that happens is my magic glows, soft and comforting.

For a second, I'm sure Nathaniel's heart responds, an

answering light spreading beneath his shirt, the same as when he defended me against the hunters.

I tell myself the glow isn't caused by the tears swimming in my eyes or the reflection off the backs of my hands.

It isn't a trick of the light or a futile wish.

It has to be his heart—his bright heart coming back to me —even though his breathing slows so much that his chest barely moves.

Hagan suddenly looms over me, his weapon dangling from his fist. He's dripping sweat and his breathing is heavy. His shoulders slump as he stares down at us.

"There's nothing you can do." He drives his sword into the ground at his own feet. "I have to end this."

I try to evade Hagan as he grabs me, his big hands closing around my torso and dragging me up and away from Nathaniel.

Struggling and spinning, I smack his face. "No!"

He flinches, but if I bruised him, it simply mingles with the wounds he has already sustained.

My fists crash against his face and shoulders, but he lets them land, taking the blows. Until my final fist hits his heart so hard that he releases me, and I stumble back under the force of my own attack.

Landing in the dirt, I sprawl and inhale dust. Cruel dust.

Hagan steps around me to kneel at Nathaniel's side. "You know I have to end this," he says, his voice low and strained. I don't know if he's talking to me or Nathaniel, whether he's asking for forgiveness or warning me about what he's going to do.

I can't stop him.

Can't fight for Nathaniel.

As I kneel in the sand, I've never been so powerless, tears

streaming down my cheeks, unable to stop Hagan or beat back the pain.

"Please," I whisper. "Don't."

Hagan freezes, squeezing his eyes closed, his fists clenching and unclenching, before he opens his eyes again without looking at me.

He wraps his left hand around Nathaniel's neck, raises his right fist and smashes it across Nathaniel's cheek, knocking blood across the dirt.

Nathaniel stops breathing.

My scream echoes in my ears, a hollow sound as the world spins around me, faster and faster until my starlight wrenches out of me against my will, white light splitting the air, cascading around Hagan and Nathaniel without touching them.

My power rises and grows in a wave that hits the arena walls and vanishes. Fading into nothing.

The shouting up in the stands is beyond me. People are screaming and crying Nathaniel's name. The lords and ladies are clinking glasses and laughing.

Cyrian approaches from behind and I brace for his dark magic to take hold of me again.

Hagan straightens Nathaniel's arms and legs before he exhales quietly and staggers to his feet.

Blood trails across the sand between us—Nathaniel's blood connecting Hagan and me.

It drips from Hagan's hands as he hunches his shoulders and towers over me, dropping me into the coldest shadow I've ever felt.

Behind him, the sky begins to lighten. The first hint of sunlight taints the hazy air.

Dawn will be here soon.

The final day is about to begin.

Today I will fight for my life.

I will fight without fear because I have no heart left to break.

Find out how far Aura will go to save Nathaniel in Infernal Dark (Bright Wicked 3), the final book in the Bright Wicked series.

INFERNAL DARK (BRIGHT WICKED BOOK 3)

One death changed it all.

When Nathaniel Shield risked everything to protect me, I could not have predicted the truth and lies that my heartbreak would reveal.

Two broken hearts.

Faced with the knowledge of my power, I must fight for my life against the Bright Queen, the Fell King, the vengeful humans, and even my own people who want me dead. But there's far more at stake than my own life.

Three fates hang in the balance.

No matter how much they fear me, the fate of the humans and the fae rests in my hands.

When the lure of darkness becomes too much, only
Nathaniel can pull me from the shadows.

But how far will I go to save him?

I have three days to live. The final day has begun.

*Content information: Infernal Dark is a fantasy romance, the final
book in the Bright Wicked series, a trilogy told over three
consecutive days. Recommended reading age is 17+ for sex scenes
and language.*

4. A Soul Like Glass

MORTALITY - COMPLETE

(Science-Fantasy Romance)

Mortality Complete Set: Books 1 to 4

1. Beyond the Ever Reach
2. Beneath the Guarding Stars
3. By the Icy Wild
4. Before the Raging Lion

<u>Stand-alone fiction - dark romance</u>

Corrupt Me: Immortal Vices and Virtues

ALSO BY EVERLY FROST

BRIGHT WICKED - COMPLETE

(Fantasy Romance)

1. Bright Wicked

2. Radiant Fierce

3. Infernal Dark

STORM PRINCESS - COMPLETE

(Fantasy Romance)

1. Book 1

2. Book 2

3. Book 3

ASSASSIN'S MAGIC

(Dark Urban Fantasy Romance)

1. Assassin's Magic

2. Assassin's Mask

3. Assassin's Menace

4. Assassin's Maze

5. Rebels

6. Revenge

7. Rogue

8. Assassin's Match

SOUL BITTEN SHIFTER - COMPLETE

(Dark Urban Fantasy Romance)

1. This Dark Wolf

2. This Broken Wolf

3. This Caged Wolf

4. This Cruel Blood

DEMON PACK - COMPLETE

(Dark Paranormal Romance)

1. Demon Pack

2. Demon Pack: Elimination

3. Demon Pack: Eternal

SUPERNATURAL LEGACY - COMPLETE

(Angels and Dragon Shifters)

1. Hunt the Night

2. Chase the Shadows

3. Slay the Dawn

4. Claim the Light

DARK MAGIC SHIFTERS

(Dark Urban Fantasy Romance)

1. Wolf of Ashes

2. Bond of Flames

3. Crown of Fate

KINGDOM OF BETRAYAL

(Fantasy Romance)

1. A Sky Like Blood

2. A Sin Like Fire

3. A Storm Like Iron

ABOUT THE AUTHOR

Everly Frost is the USA Today Bestselling author of fantasy romance, urban fantasy and paranormal romance novels. She spent her childhood dreaming of other worlds and scribbling stories on the leftover blank pages at the back of school notebooks. She lives in Brisbane, Australia with her husband and two children.

a amazon.com/author/everlyfrost
f facebook.com/everlyfrost
o instagram.com/everlyfrost
BB bookbub.com/authors/everly-frost
g goodreads.com/everlyfrost

www.ingramcontent.com/pod-product-compliance
Lightning Source LLC
Chambersburg PA
CBHW030603120726
47904CB00006B/1749